THOMAS F

THE INVISIBLE WIFE

THE INVISIBLE WIFE

THE INVISIBLE WIFE

THOMAS FINCHAM

The Invisible Wife
Thomas Fincham

AUTHOR'S NOTE
This book is a work of fiction. Names, characters, places and incidents are products of the author's imagination or are used fictitiously. Any resemblance to actual events or locales or persons, living or dead, is entirely coincidental.

THOMAS FINCHAM

Visit the author's website:
www.finchambooks.com

Contact:
finchambooks@gmail.com

THE INVISIBLE WIFE

ONE

Detective Dana Fisher was in her Honda SUV. She had a clear view of the restaurant. Fisher had been sitting there for twenty minutes, but she could not muster the courage to get out.

She was a ten-year veteran of the Milton Police Department. She was five-foot-five, weighed close to one hundred and ten pounds, and she had dark, shoulder-length hair. Her thin nose pointed upwards, and it moved whenever she opened her mouth.

She anxiously tapped the steering wheel.

Maybe this is a mistake, she thought. *I should let Holt handle this.*

Detective Gregory Holt was her partner, and, over the years, he had also become a friend and confidant.

Holt would have relished making the arrest, but he knew Fisher had a history with the suspect, so he trusted her to do what was required. She was not going to disappoint him. She also did not need backup. The suspect was not a threat. But she never thought he would be a suspect either.

He was already inside the restaurant when she drove up. There were a few other places Fisher could have found him, but the restaurant seemed like the best place to start.

Fortunately—or in his case, unfortunately—she would not have to look for him anywhere else.

He was in his normal corner booth by the windows, sipping a cup of coffee, and having a meal. On a number of occasions, she had seen him munching on pancakes, waffles, or whatever he could afford. He would always offer to share his meal with her, but she would decline. She was not a breakfast person. A cup of coffee was all she needed to start her day.

She took a deep breath and gripped the steering wheel tight. She suddenly felt lightheaded. She was not ready for what she was about to do.

Maybe I should wait until he leaves, she thought. He was a frequent customer, and it would be wrong for her to embarrass him in front of the whole staff. But this was no time to be concerned about saving face, nor thinking of delaying making the arrest. She had to stay objective, no matter who the suspect was.

What he did was serious, and in many ways, unforgivable.

She shut her eyes.

It is better that I do this than Holt, she thought.

Holt would go in hard, and he would not hesitate one bit to use force if necessary.

She knew the situation required a delicate approach.

She counted to ten, opened her eyes, and got out of the SUV.

Her heart pounded inside her chest, her knees felt weak, and sweat broke out around her temples as she walked up to the restaurant.

She entered and made a beeline to the other side of the restaurant. The suspect's head was down as he cut into a piece of waffle.

He looked up and smiled. "Dana, what're you doing here?"

She gritted her teeth and said, "Lee Callaway, you are under arrest for the murder of…"

TWO

One Week Earlier

The house was an eyesore compared to the other houses on the street. The owner had bought three houses which stood next to each other, torn them down, and built one massive structure in their place. The owner's taste in architecture left something to be desired, however.

A marble water fountain shaped like a giant dolphin's mouth was in the front. The exterior of the house was painted in a variety of bright colors, ranging from yellow and green to even purple.

The middle structure was a dome with spiral chimneys on either side that made it look more like a cheap Taj Mahal than anything else. There were more dolphin statues near the house's front steps, and palm trees surrounded the property.

Holt had little or no opinion when it came to design, but even he saw how gaudy the property looked.

He parked next to a vintage Rolls Royce and got out.

Holt had thick arms, thick hands, and a thick neck which made his shirt collar tight. His head was shaved clean, exposing a wrinkled skull. His eyes were small and black, and they absorbed everything in his vicinity.

He was six-four and weighed close to two hundred and fifty pounds. He was an imposing man who did not hesitate to use his size to his advantage.

As was his ritual before each new investigation, he rubbed his wedding ring three times. The gesture was his way of reminding himself why he chose to be a detective.

His family meant the world to him, and he deeply believed he was making the world a better place for them.

He spotted an officer leaning against a police cruiser. The officer was tall, had deep blue eyes, a prominent chin, and blond hair that was hidden underneath his police cap. A woman who looked distraught was in the cruiser's backseat.

The officer straightened up the moment he spotted Holt.

"Officer McConnell," Holt said.

"Detective Holt," Lance McConnell replied.

"You were first on the scene?"

"Yes, sir."

"And is it secured?"

"It is, sir."

"Are you sure?"

"I am."

Holt's eyes narrowed. "Is Detective Fisher inside?"

"She is."

Holt looked around. "I don't see her SUV."

McConnell coughed and cleared his throat. "She came with me, sir."

Holt raised an eyebrow. "She did?"

"Um… yes. When the call came I was not too far from Dana's—I mean, Detective Fisher's place, and so I offered her a ride."

Holt's stare bore into him. If McConnell was sweating, he did not show it. Holt took a step closer. His nose was inches away from McConnell.

"I care a great deal about Fisher," Holt said.

"So do I," McConnell quickly replied.

"That's good to hear," Holt said. "Fisher is a wonderful person and a damn good detective. If you hurt her, I will make it my mission to hurt you worse. Understood?"

McConnell swallowed hard. "Understood."

Holt smiled, which made him even more threatening. "I'm glad we had this talk," he said, slapping McConnell on the shoulder.

Holt entered the house.

THREE

The twelve-foot-high ceilings made the space look twice as big. The pattern-tile floor was recently polished and glistened in the light. A spiral staircase was in the middle of the space with an overly large chandelier hanging just above it.

At the foot of the staircase, a woman was standing next to a body. Her arms were crossed over her chest, and she scowled at Holt as he approached.

"I saw you drilling Lance outside," Fisher said.

"Was I?" Holt replied with mock surprise.

"Yes, you were."

"Officer McConnell and I were having a polite chat."

"You were inches away from his face."

"I was making sure he understood me."

"I know what you're up to," she said.

"And what is that?"

"You don't want to see me get hurt."

Holt was genuinely surprised. "You heard our conversation?"

"I didn't have to. Your body language told me everything I needed to know."

"I was just reminding him how to treat a lady properly."

"I appreciate your concern, Greg, but you have to remember I grew up with three brothers. I know how to take care of myself."

Holt knew this was her way of saying, *Mind your own business.*

"Got it," he said.

Fisher finally broke into a smile. "Thanks, though."

He nodded.

"Are *you* okay?" she asked.

After his nephew's death, Holt was sent to a conference in Vegas. Upon his return, the department assigned him to desk duties. Holt refused a psychiatric evaluation, which did not help his case. He insisted he was fine and was ready to get back to work, but the department did not want to repeat what happened to Leo Calderon.

Leo was a beat cop who was called in to investigate a domestic disturbance. What he found inside the house was straight out of a horror novel. A father had butchered his wife and four children. The father had then taken a paint brush and painted the walls with their blood.

The father was arrested without incident, but he pleaded insanity during the trial. Leo knew the father was not crazy. When Leo had cuffed the father at his house, the father had quipped that he would not see the inside of a prison cell.

The father's lawyers brought in medical experts. They all believed the father had a psychotic episode where he heard voices in his head that told him his wife and children were evil. The father had a history of domestic violence, and a few days before the murders, his wife had gone to a divorce lawyer.

The first trial resulted in a hung jury. The second trial found the father not guilty by reason of insanity, resulting in him having to serve time in a mental institute rather than a prison.

In court, as the father was being led away, he turned and gave Leo a smile and a wink. He also mouthed, "I told you so."

Leo snapped. He drew his gun and fired at the father four times. The father took two bullets in the heart, dying instantly. One of the two stray bullets hit an officer of the court. Leo was immediately taken into custody and charged with first-degree murder.

Leo's twenty-four years of exemplary service had gone down in an instant. The department had failed to see the signs that Leo had been under a lot of stress. His wife was dying from cancer, and the insurance company had refused to pay for an experimental procedure that could potentially save her life. Also, a few months earlier, his six-year-old grandson was hit by a car as he was crossing the road. The driver drove off and had still not been found. The grandson spent months in the hospital, going through eight separate operations.

When Leo was interviewed after the shooting, he said the father's sentence was an insult to justice and he felt it was his responsibility to right a wrong.

It was understood that what Leo really wanted was justice for his wife for the way the insurance system was treating her, and for his grandson, because they had yet to locate the driver who had put him in the hospital.

Had the department taken steps to remove Leo from high pressure situations, this tragedy could have been avoided. Leo was now spending the remaining years of his life in prison instead of spending it with his family in retirement.

Holt took a deep breath. "I'm good."

"You sure?" Fisher asked.

"I'll let you know if I'm not."

She paused and then said, "You recognize the house?"

"It looks somewhat familiar."

"While it was being built, it was regularly on the news. The owner was constantly fighting his neighbors and the city."

Holt's brow furrowed. "Now I remember… it's the guy who won thirty million dollars in the State lottery."

"Yep. The house belongs to Big Bob."

"And is that him?" Holt asked, nodding in the direction of the body.

She turned to the victim. There was a pool of blood underneath the body, and blood trailed to another room in the house.

"Unfortunately, no amount of money could have saved him from what happened," Fisher said.

FOUR

Robert Burley stood six-feet, five inches, weighed two hundred and ninety pounds, and he had a belly large enough that he could use it to push someone aside. He got the name "Big Bob" because of his stature, but it was his occupation that elevated his name.

Prior to winning the lottery, Big Bob owned a successful car dealership in the city, aptly named *Big Bob's Auto*. He had become a local celebrity because of his dealership ads, which often could be found airing in the middle of the night on local TV stations.

The ads were made on the cheap and so the production values were subpar. In each ad, the camera would be aimed at the dealership's front door. Big Bob would emerge from behind the door as if he was making a big entrance on a grand stage. He would wave at the camera as if he was inviting a customer into his dealership. He would then proceed to walk the camera through the dealership and over to a particular vehicle. All the while, in his gravelly voice, he would be talking to the camera as if he was talking to one of his best friends. He would praise the vehicle's best features, and at the end of the ad, he would look directly into camera, point a big finger, and say, "Don't think too long. This car could be gone before you know it."

The story went that on the day he won the lottery, Big Bob gave all his employees a day off. He later gave each of them a vehicle of their choice as a gift. He even wrote a check for ten thousand dollars to the clerk who sold him the ticket. He called her his good luck charm.

That night he celebrated at a steak house with his family and friends, and the next morning, accompanied by his wife, son, and daughter, he drove up to the lottery office in a rented Bentley.

The photo of him holding a big check for thirty million dollars was on all the newspapers' front pages. When a TV reporter asked what he planned to do with all that money, Big Bob grinned and said, "I'll do whatever the hell I want."

Instead of taking the full amount in payments over twenty-five years, Big Bob opted for a single lump-sum payment for a reduced amount. After taxes he was left with a little over half the lottery prize.

He quickly sold the dealership and then began a life of indulgence and excess. That should have been the last time people heard of Big Bob, but over the ten years after he won, Big Bob's life had been filled with drama and even tragedy.

Fisher stared at his lifeless body. As a kid she had seen Big Bob's ads on TV. She thought he was a typical car salesman. He made big promises but delivered very little. He once boasted he had sold a refrigerator to an Eskimo. He would even claim he had proof of this sale: it was the middle of July, and even the Eskimos needed a place to cool their meat.

He may not have been the most honest guy around, but he was a lot of fun to watch.

Who could have overpowered such a big man? she thought.

FIVE

The little girl eyed him with malice. She was wearing a pink dress, pink slippers, and her hair was tied back in a ponytail with a pink ribbon.

Lee Callaway stood at the entrance of a store located inside a shopping mall. The store specialized in all things girls: dresses, shoes, jackets, make-up, hair accessories, and even dolls.

Callaway was tall, tanned, and he had silver around his temples. Crow's feet had started to emerge around his eyes, but even then, he looked youthful for his age.

He wore a light blue shirt with a black tie, dark blue pants with side pockets, and black work boots. A walkie-talkie was attached to his black belt, and he had a notepad and pen stashed in his pants pockets.

Callaway adjusted his shirt collar even though it was not tight around his neck. The girl's stare was making him squirm.

How can you be so intimidating when you are so tiny? he thought.

Callaway had recently been hired as a store security guard. It was not on top of his list of chosen occupations, but the store was the only one that was willing to hire him.

He was once a deputy sheriff for a small town. The job came with a steady income and lots of benefits, but he left it to become a private investigator, which came with little money and no benefits. But at the time, quitting the county sheriff's department was the best decision he had ever made. He was tired of patrolling the town's streets looking for drunks or dealing with minor spats between neighbors. He could not wait to leave the job and the town.

As a PI, though, he was always living from paycheck to paycheck. He never knew when he would get another case and how much it paid. In desperate times he would even take on cases that he would otherwise turn away.

One time, a client wanted to see if his fiancée would cheat on him. He hired Callaway to follow his fiancée and strike up a conversation with her. Callaway caught up with the fiancée at a coffee shop. After a short chat, Callaway asked if she wanted to go around the block and have a drink at a bar. She agreed. The client took this as a sign that she was unfaithful.

Callaway felt the fiancée loved the client. She had just got caught up in the moment. She believed she had gone to the same high school as Callaway (a lie made up by Callaway to break the ice). She also thought Callaway had a fiancée (another lie to ease her concerns so that she would take to him).

Callaway relayed his feelings to the client, but he did not believe Callaway. Instead, he ended his engagement soon after. Callaway hated himself for what he was hired to do. He had slept with married clients before, but only because their spouses were caught cheating on them. In Callaway's eyes, the fiancée had done no wrong. The client's assumption that his fiancée would sleep with Callaway after having a few drinks with him was ludicrous. Such a notion said more about the client than the fiancée.

"How much longer?" the girl asked him.

The store opened in half an hour and there was already a long line that snaked through the mall. The fifty or so customers consisted mostly of mothers and their precocious daughters.

The store had received a shipment of the hottest line of princess dolls. They were all the rage. Every girl between the age of six and eleven wanted one.

Callaway had already snagged a doll for his daughter. This was another reason he had wanted to work at this location. The pay was slightly above minimum wage. He was used to not having a dime in his pocket, so the wage was more than enough for him. On top of a regular paycheck, there was the employee discounts on store items. He could buy whatever he wanted for his little girl without having to pay full price for it.

As the clock ticked closer to 9 a.m., he saw the look on the mothers' faces. They were ready to rush into the store like stampeding bulls, ready to fight each other over the dolls. They did not care who got trampled, maimed, or gored in the process.

He swallowed and said a small prayer.

SIX

Holt and Fisher were examining the body up close. Big Bob's eyes were closed, and his skin was pale. He was wearing a white shirt that was now covered in red. The stain was darkest where he was stabbed. Without removing the shirt, Fisher guessed Big Bob was stabbed multiple times.

She squinted and said, "What do you think that is?"

She pointed to a raw gash on Big Bob's cheek which streaked down from the eye to the corner of his lip.

"Maybe it came from his assailant."

"We'll swab it for DNA." If Big Bob and his killer had gotten into a fight and during the altercation the attacker scratched his face, their fingernails would have left some evidence.

The blood on the cheek had dried, but Fisher saw a spot that was still wet. The Crime Scene Unit would be arriving soon. They would gather the necessary evidence. But Fisher did not want to lose the opportunity. She pulled out a small plastic container which held a cotton swab. She dabbed blood onto the swab and then sealed it back in the container. She made a note on the container's label about where she got the sample and then placed it in her coat pocket.

"Take a look at this," Holt said.

He held up Big Bob's right hand. A bloody stump was where his thumb should have been.

"Someone cut off his thumb?" Fisher said, surprised.

"Looks like it."

"But why?"

"Maybe the victim gave the killer a thumbs-down," Holt replied.

Fisher rolled her eyes. Holt was not good with jokes, and he rarely smiled to begin with, but Fisher knew he was trying his best to lighten the mood.

The Milton PD had invested heavily in the Officer Assistance Program. A full-time counselor was on staff to help officers navigate through the stresses they encountered on a daily basis. The counselor's main initiative was to get officers to smile, laugh, and joke more. Studies had shown that this released endorphins which helped with depression and anxiety. The department also held weekly laughter yoga sessions which involved exercises that included clapping, laughing for no reason, and deep breathing.

Holt had gone to one session. He was embarrassed to see officers laugh so hard and loud that some of them fell off their chairs.

Childish, he had thought at the time, and he vowed to never go again.

Fisher looked around. "Where do you suppose the thumb is?"

Holt looked around as well.

She stood up and followed the blood trail from the house's main entrance to the living room. There was a deep red stain on the carpet, located next to an armchair.

That's where Big Bob must have collapsed after getting stabbed, she thought.

Next to the large stain was another smaller stain.

The killer must have cut off his thumb at that very spot.

She surveyed the living room. When she did not find what she was looking for, she returned to the body. "Why didn't Big Bob crawl to the front door?" she said. "Why did he go to the stairs instead?"

"That's a good question," Holt said. "I wish I had an answer."

SEVEN

The house had five bedrooms and eight bathrooms, and it also had a gym, sauna, game room, a swimming pool in the backyard, and a theatre room. It had everything a person with money could want. The décor was tacky and unpleasing to the eye, however.

There were semi-nude paintings of large women in each room, the wallpaper was either too bright or too dark, and the furniture was neither modern nor classic. Sometimes the furniture looked like it had been picked up from someone's yard sale.

The house had so many themes going at once that Fisher was not sure if it was intentional or if Big Bob just did not bother to hire an interior decorator.

If Fisher had Big Bob's money, she would have opted for a regal décor, something she had seen in European palaces. Such décor was expensive, but the result would have been magnificent.

Fisher only played the lottery when the jackpot was astronomically high. She knew it was a bad time to play when everyone else was playing as well. The odds of getting hit by lightning twice was far more than winning a single jackpot, so she wanted to use her "luck" on a substantial prize that could change her life forever.

Winning a million was no longer enough to retire on. The government would take half in taxes, and after purchasing a modest home, she would still need to work.

But what if she did win the big one? Would she quit being a detective?

The simple answer would be no. She loved her job too much to give it up.

The more complex answer would likely be yes.

Spending eighteen-hour days chasing a lead, digging through filth for clues, and analyzing a case's every detail can take a toll on a person. This was on top of the emotional beating a detective took on a regular basis. Dealing with death and its aftermath was not easy.

The crimes were shocking and brutal. The impact on the grieving was even worse. Some never recovered from losing a loved one in such a horrific manner. It was Fisher's job to bring them closure. Each case left unsolved was a victory for the bad guy.

If money was no longer an object, Fisher would contemplate leaving the grind behind her.

But what would she do with her life then? She had no idea.

She shook her head. *I don't have millions in my bank account*, she thought. *So why am I wasting my energy thinking about it?*

She had already scoured the kitchen. She found no knife missing from the wooden block. This told her the assailant had brought his own weapon. On the off chance the killer picked up some other knife from the kitchen, he or she must have taken it with them.

She took the stairs up to the second floor and checked the bedrooms. The first room contained a collection of items, including an odd one. There were signed music records on the walls, vintage guitars, sports memorabilia, and even the skull of a dinosaur.

When you can afford to buy anything, you buy everything.

She moved to the master bedroom which had a king-sized bed, an armoire, a dresser, and a small writing table. She checked the closet and it was half empty.

Maybe Big Bob didn't have time to shop for clothes.

She knew that was not the case. Along with men's clothing, she also saw high heels, scarfs, and a purse.

There was a photo on the dresser. She walked over and picked the photo up. Big Bob was standing next to a woman. He was wearing a tuxedo while the woman was wearing a wedding dress. The woman looked much younger than him.

Why does she look familiar?

Fisher remembered. When she had arrived at the scene, there was a woman who had answered the door.

I guess it's time I had a word with Mrs. Big Bob.

She left the master bedroom and was about to head back downstairs when her eyes caught something across the hall.

She walked over to take a closer look. The door of the third room had two holes. The holes were the size of a dime, and when she squinted, she could see through them into the room.

She slowly pushed the door back. The room was being used as a guest room. There was a double bed in the corner with a closet and table across from it.

She spotted two additional holes in the wall next to the bed.

Fisher pulled out a pen and stuck it in one of the holes. She was fidgeting with the pen when something fell out of the hole and hit the carpet. She leaned down and picked the object up. It was a bullet.

Someone had fired at the door!

The bullets had gone straight through the door and had lodged in the wall. She placed the bullet in a plastic baggie. The CSU would be notified about the second bullet.

Several questions raced through her head. Who fired into the room? And more importantly, who was the intended target?

EIGHT

Fisher returned downstairs and found Holt in another room which, by the looks of it, Big Bob used as an office. The walls were made of dark wood panels. There was a coffee-colored desk in the middle with a leather chair next to it. A large shelf filled with books was behind the desk, and a large globe was near the window.

Fisher spotted a framed picture frame on the wall. The photo showed Big Bob holding the giant check for the winning prize. He was flanked on either side by his family.

"Look what I found," Holt said, waving her over.

She walked around the desk and saw what Holt was pointing at. An open safe was hidden underneath the desk. On the floor next to it was Big Bob's severed thumb.

"Now we know why the killer chose to cut it off," Holt said.

Big Bob was a big man. There was no way the killer could have dragged his body across the house without exerting a ton of energy. It was simpler to remove what was needed in order to access the safe.

Fisher leaned down and looked inside the safe. She found some documents for properties and investments Big Bob had purchased, his passport, a copy of a check for the very first car he had sold in his dealership, certificates for savings bonds, and some old photographs likely of Big Bob as a child. What she did not find was any cash.

This discovery begged a question: how did the killer know where Big Bob kept his safe?

As if reading her thoughts, Holt said, "Do you think this murder has something to do with a break and enter?"

"I think it just might."

Several years ago, Big Bob was robbed at gunpoint. Two masked men forced their way into the house. After roughing him up and tying him to a chair, they ran away with two hundred thousand in cash and almost fifty thousand in jewelry. After that, Big Bob had increased his security and he started carrying a gun with him at all times.

Fisher pulled out the baggie with the bullet. "I found this in one of the rooms upstairs," she said.

Holt frowned. "Who was doing the shooting?"

"I don't know, but it can't be the killer."

Holt nodded. If the killer had a gun, why did he or she not shoot Big Bob instead of stabbing him?

Fisher rubbed her chin. A thought occurred to her. She hurried out to the hall, crossed the entrance, and went into the living room. A leather armchair was in the corner, next to a wall. At the foot of the chair was a half empty bottle of whiskey and a glass.

Fisher had seen this during her initial survey of the house but paid little attention to it.

This time, though, she wanted to be thorough. She looked behind the chair but saw nothing. She was pulling the chair towards her when she spotted something on the floor, wedged between the wall and the chair. She reached down and retrieved a semi-automatic pistol. She held the gun up as Holt came up behind her.

His eyes were wide in disbelief. "How'd you know it would be there?"

"I didn't, but I have a theory forming in my head."

"Okay, let me have it."

Holt and Fisher had been partners long enough that they loved to bounce theories and scenarios off each other.

She said, "There is only one gun in the house and it was next to the chair likely used by Big Bob. A bottle of alcohol supports the theory that he may have been drinking prior to the attack. This means that there is a strong likelihood that the bullets found in the room upstairs belong to Big Bob's gun."

"But if he had a gun, then why did he not use it on his assailant?"

"Good question. The killer stabbed Big Bob, which means he came into the house only armed with a knife. He may have even surprised Big Bob, who could have been a little inebriated. He may have even inadvertently knocked the gun off the armrest and could not access it in time."

"Okay, sure, but who did he shoot in the room upstairs?"

"It wasn't his assailant, that's for sure. I found no blood in the room."

"Perhaps it was another person who was with the assailant."

24

Fisher frowned. If it was, then it did not fit the narrative. If two people came to rob Big Bob, then why would he shoot at one and not the other? And then why would he go downstairs and have a drink while they were still in the house? It just didn't make sense.

She then said, "I think I know why he crawled to the staircase and not the front door."

"And why is that?"

"He was trying to get to the safe."

"Why? He had far more money in his bank account than what he had in the safe."

"That is something only he and his killer know."

NINE

Callaway waited in line at a fast-food restaurant. It was lunchtime, and the mall's food court was packed with hungry shoppers. Callaway was famished and exhausted. The moment he had opened the store's doors, the mothers and their daughters rushed in. He tried to keep order, but they were like an angry mob.

He saw one mother snatch a doll from a girl's hand. He tried to intervene, but the look on the mother's face told him to back off. Her eyes were wide, and she was foaming at the mouth. He did not want to get his arm bitten off.

Another mother had grabbed four doll boxes and was racing to the cashier when another mother literally tackled her to the ground. Callaway had to admit it was a clean tackle. If she were playing football, there would be no penalty. The woman who did the tackle was close to two hundred pounds, and yet she had moved as fast as a gazelle. Callaway was deeply impressed, but he had to pull the women apart before they hurt each other. He warned them to behave, but his warning fell on deaf ears. After some expletives and pointed fingers, the mothers went their own way.

The chaos lasted thirty-five minutes. After all the princess dolls were sold, the store rapidly quieted. Callaway was left feeling like he had just been through a war zone.

I may have PTSD now, he thought.

The store's employees, however, were not the least bit jaded. They looked like they were used to this type of behavior.

His turn at the counter came and he ordered a combo that consisted of a chicken wrap, fries, and a drink. He grabbed his lunch and left the food court. He scanned his card and entered a door for mall employees only. He went through a tunnel, down two flights of stairs, and entered a room in the back with no windows.

The room was used as a cafeteria by the mall's employees. There was a vending machine, a small television, and several tables and chairs. Two cleaning staff were seated at one table. They were conversing with each other in a different language. They nodded and smiled at Callaway. He smiled back and took the table in the corner.

As he gorged his meal, he pulled out his cell phone. He smiled as he began to scroll through photos on his phone. They were mostly of his daughter, but some were of his ex-wife too. They were the reason he was wearing this awful uniform and arguing with deranged mothers.

He had vowed to get his life in order, starting with getting a steady job that came with benefits. He hoped this would allow him to spend more time with his little girl.

He was not like that before. He preferred having zero responsibility when it came to parental duties, but an encounter with his mentor, Jimmy Keith, changed all that. He learned that no man was an island, and that without someone to care for, there was no point to life. He could not spend his days looking for excitement and adventure with strangers when he could be having an exciting adventure with his family.

TEN

Andrea Wakefield's eyes darted over the victim's body as if she was recording and storing all relevant information for a later time. As a medical examiner, her opinion held a lot of weight.

Wakefield was petite with short, cropped hair and she wore round prescription glasses that constantly slid down her thin nose.

She pushed her glasses up and said to Fisher, "Did you know that seventy percent of lottery winners end up bankrupt within a few years of winning the lottery?"

"I had no idea," Fisher said.

"Do you want to know why?"

"Why?"

"They can't handle the responsibility of so much money."

"I don't understand," Fisher said.

"They never spent their lives building wealth, and so, when it's given to them, they don't realize that without restraint it will all go away. They splurge on extravagant items such as boats, or in some cases, planes. They buy houses that are too big for them. They invest in businesses they have no knowledge of, and then there is the matter of family, friends, and strangers constantly begging them for money. There was a lottery winner in Ohio who shot himself in the head because he could not deal with people asking him for money. Winners don't realize how complicated their life ends up becoming."

"I didn't know you were so interested in the lottery," Fisher said. She had worked with Wakefield for years, but she hardly knew much about the woman, apart from the fact that she was one of the most well-respected medical examiners in the state.

"Contrary to what most people think, I find human beings fascinating."

Fisher glanced over at Holt, who was standing two feet away from them. According to him, Wakefield preferred the dead over the living. His opinion had something to do with the fact that she spent more time at the morgue dissecting cadavers than interacting with people.

"Do you play the lottery?" Fisher asked.

Wakefield shook her head. "I wouldn't know what to do with all that money."

"Well, if I won," Fisher said, "I'd buy myself a house, make sure my family is taken care of, and the rest would go to charity." Like millions of Americans who played the lottery, Fisher had also spent a great deal of time thinking about what she would do if she won.

Holt coughed, signaling his impatience.

Wakefield turned to the body. "From my initial assessment, I would have to say death was caused by stabbing." She unbuttoned the victim's shirt. "As you can see, there are puncture wounds all along the chest. The amount of blood found at the scene further supports this conclusion. Naturally, I will provide an official cause of death after the post-mortem."

"Of course," Fisher said.

Holt asked, "Time of death?"

Wakefield looked at the body once more. "My educated guess would be ten to twelve hours."

Fisher turned to Holt. "That's last night."

"We will have to find out who may have been in contact with him around that time," he said.

Fisher turned to Wakefield. "The scratch on his face. What can you tell us?"

Wakefield squinted. "It doesn't appear to have been made by a fingernail, that's for sure."

Fisher's eyes frowned. There went their chance of procuring DNA evidence.

Wakefield said, "The scratch is too wide to have come from a fingernail, and from a cursory look, it is also quite deep. The assailant would have had to dig his or her fingernails deep into the skin and then move it across the cheek to get that mark."

"Is it possible that they did?" Fisher asked. She still held out hope for something.

Wakefield thought a moment. "Sure, I suppose, but why is there a single mark and not more?"

Fisher knew what she was getting at. If someone did forcefully scratch someone, there would be multiple marks from multiple fingers, not just one.

"What else can you tell us?" Holt asked.

"The victim's right thumb is missing," Wakefield replied.

"We can see that for ourselves," Holt said.

"Oh right. Of course," she said, realizing the obvious in her earlier comment. "That's all I can see for now, but I will have more once I complete the autopsy."

"Thank you," Fisher said.

ELEVEN

Fisher thought it was time to talk to the woman in the backseat of McConnell's cruiser. Fisher always preferred to examine the scene *before* she spoke to witnesses. She did not want their comments to contaminate her observations. She wanted an unadulterated view of the situation. This also helped her see if any witnesses were being untruthful or uncooperative.

She once had a case where the witness mentioned finding the door to a shed was locked when he had arrived at the scene. Fisher instantly knew that was a lie. From her initial inspection of the scene, she knew the door could only be locked from the outside. There was no way the victim could have shot herself in the head, disposed of the weapon, and then went outside and locked the door. Only her killer could have done this.

Suzanne Burley had dyed hair, smooth skin, perfect teeth, and full lips. She was twenty years younger than Big Bob, but with all the cosmetic procedures, she looked even younger.

Suzanne wiped her eyes with a tissue and asked, "Who would do something like that to my husband?"

"We don't know yet, but we are trying to find out," Fisher replied. "What can you tell us about this morning?"

She swallowed. "Before coming, I phoned Big Bob…"

"You call your husband Big Bob?" Fisher asked, curious.

"Yes, everyone did. He likes being called that."

"Okay, go ahead."

"When he didn't answer his phone, I drove over to the house."

"You don't live here?"

Suzanne looked away in embarrassment. "We are separated."

"Where do you live?"

"I'm renting a house five miles from here. It's under Big Bob's name."

"If you don't mind me asking, why did you guys separate?"

"I love Big Bob, but after five years together, we kind of started drifting apart."

"How did you two meet?"

"I was the makeup artist on his commercials," Mrs. Burley replied. "I could tell he was interested in me by the way he talked. He was married at the time, so we didn't hit it off right away. After he won the lottery, he called me up one day and asked if I wanted to go out to dinner with him. I agreed, and during dinner he told me he was thinking of leaving his wife. We dated for a couple of years, and then he proposed to me and we got married."

"Were you attracted to him before you found out he had won the jackpot?" Fisher was trying to gauge her motives. A spouse was usually the main suspect in a murder investigation, especially one where the victim had a lot of money.

Suzanne laughed. "I know people call me a gold digger, and I don't blame them. Big Bob was not my type. He was older, married, and he had kids. But what most people don't realize is that Big Bob had money before he even won the lottery. I know this for a fact because, for the commercials, we reminded customers that his dealership was number one in the state, which it was. And those commercials were really popular at that time."

They were, Fisher silently agreed. *Everyone in Milton was familiar with them.*

"So, money wasn't a factor in your decision to marry Big Bob?" Fisher prodded.

"It was," Suzanne replied, "I won't lie, but when I met Big Bob, I had come off a bad relationship which involved verbal and physical abuse. I was thirty-five with no kids and no job prospects. The makeup work was always on a contract basis. So yeah, I knew someone like Big Bob would take care of me."

"After you got married, I assume you quit your makeup work. So, what did you do?" Fisher asked.

"I thought about going back to school. I wanted to become an interior designer, but when Big Bob built the house, he asked me to decorate it."

That explains the gaudy décor.

"Did your husband have life insurance?" Fisher asked. It was a big motivator for spouse-related murders.

Suzanne shook her head. "Big Bob didn't believe in them. He had enough money that if something ever happened to him, it would be plenty to take care of his loved ones."

"Did he have a will?"

"Yes."

"And what do *you* get in the event of his death?"

"I don't know. Maybe the things he bought me."

Fisher blinked. "That's it?"

"I mean, we have a pre-nup that protected me if the marriage broke down."

Fisher pondered her next question.

"Okay, tell me what happened when you came to the house."

"After calling Big Bob, I came over."

"Is the Rolls Royce yours?"

"No, it's Big Bob's."

"I don't see your car parked outside."

"A friend drove me over."

"Okay, please continue."

"I still have a key, so I let myself in."

"The door was locked?" Fisher asked.

Suzanne's brow furrowed. "Actually, it was not. I was surprised Big Bob would be so careless. I mean, after what happened with the robbery, he had become extra vigilant with security."

"Where were you during the robbery?" Fisher asked.

"I was at my mother's home in Tampa. Big Bob was home alone. I flew home the moment I heard about it."

"Okay, so when you went inside the house, what did you do?"

Suzanne's eyes welled up and she put a hand over her mouth. "I saw Big Bob on the floor of the entrance. He was all bloody and… and…" She choked up. "I ran out and called nine-one-one."

"Why were you at the house?"

"I had to pick up some of my belongings I'd left behind."

That explains the half empty closet in the master bedroom, Fisher thought. "You said your husband took security seriously…"

"Yes, he did," Suzanne quickly replied.

"So, I'm assuming the house is equipped with an alarm system."

"It is."

"Do you know the code?"

"Of course I do."

"Do you think your husband changed it after you moved out?" Fisher asked.

Suzanne thought a moment. "He may have, but like I said, the door was unlocked."

"But what if he had changed the alarm code and the door was *not* unlocked? Then what would you have done?"

"I would have kept ringing the doorbell until Big Bob let me in."

"One last question. Do you know if anyone else knew the code for the alarm system?"

Suzanne shrugged. "I'm not sure."

TWELVE

Fisher walked over to McConnell, who was standing on the other side of the driveway. McConnell's smile widened when he saw her.

"What's the situation inside?" he asked.

"We still have a lot of evidence to gather."

"So, it's going to be a long morning," he said.

"What? You got someplace to be?" she teased.

He shrugged. "I was going to take a special lady out for breakfast. I know this place where they have all-you-can-eat waffles and pancakes."

She smiled. "There is always the next time."

McConnell beamed.

"Sorry about Holt," Fisher said. "He can be a little protective."

"Don't be. It's nice that he is concerned about you."

The first time Fisher saw McConnell was at the annual police games. He had won the hundred-metre track. The second time was at the crime scene of Holt's nephew. The third time she saw him, she knew she liked him. She found herself blushing whenever he was near her. She waited for him to make the move, but he never did.

She bumped into him at the station some time later. He was heading out to his cruiser. He smiled at her as he walked by. She did not want to lose the opportunity. She asked him out for coffee. He immediately said yes.

Later, she asked why he never made the move on her. She was certain the attraction was mutual. He told her he wanted to, but he was not sure how she felt about dating someone with a lower rank than him. He was a patrol officer, and she was a detective.

It was not a secret in the department that Fisher was ambitious. She moved up the ranks faster than most people on the force, and she had her sights set on becoming captain one day.

McConnell, however, was laid back. He was content in his position. He grew up on the West Coast, skateboarding and surfing. He had no major plans in life other than to fully experience whatever came his way. Fisher found this refreshing. In a way, their relationship balanced each other.

"See you tonight?" he asked.

"I don't know. It'll depend on how the day goes."

"No problem. You do what you have to," McConnell said. This was another reason why she felt comfortable with him. He understood the responsibility that came with the job.

She did not have a set schedule like a 9-to-5 job. On a new investigation she could work from early morning until late at night. Sometimes she would even sleep in the department's break room if she had work to catch up on.

This did not make for an ideal situation when it came to relationships. She was known to cancel dates at the last minute if something urgent came up—and in her job, everything was urgent. Then there was the job itself. Even though she was a professional and had learned to distance her feelings from a case, it still weighed on her mind, body, and soul. Death was not something one could easily ignore. Only when a case was solved could she expunge herself from the burden that came with being a homicide detective.

She was not sure how far her relationship with McConnell would go, but right now she did not care. She was just happy to have someone in her life.

She smiled at him once more. "I'll call you later, Officer McConnell," she said.

He smiled back. "Good luck, Detective Fisher."

THIRTEEN

Callaway stood by the store's main doors and watched as shoppers entered and exited. He had to make sure no one left without paying for their purchases.

The rare princess dolls were sold out. The empty shelves would soon be filled by another item. A few customers came in hoping to still buy the doll. He would give them a sad look that said, "If you snooze, you lose."

After the chaos came the boredom. A security guard's job was not particularly exciting—excluding what happened that morning, of course. Callaway would spend his shift's remaining hours pacing the store, making himself noticed. He was more of a deterrent to would-be shoplifters than anything else. He did not have a gun or a Taser. When he was hired, he was given a walkie-talkie and a flashlight. He could always bonk a thief on the head with the flashlight, but he was not sure what to do with the walkie-talkie. He was not really a mall cop. He was a store employee. His jurisdiction ended at the door. Whatever happened beyond that was not his responsibility.

The mall cop was a guy named Jerry—that's what it said on his name tag. He was a really prickly guy. Jerry looked down on people like Callaway. He felt he alone was enough to protect all the mall's businesses. He did not realize he could not be everywhere. There were over a hundred shops.

Callaway, on the other hand, could focus his attention solely on one location. So far in the past few days he had worked, Callaway had caught two people trying to shoplift items. The culprits were both eleven years old, and the items in question were a hairband and a bracelet. They cost less than ten dollars, but Callaway's intervention went beyond the price of the items. If he had not apprehended and scolded the would-be shoplifters, they would have grown up to become master thieves. Art galleries and museums around the world should be calling and thanking him for how he prevented young minds from going down the dark path.

Callaway was not sure about the last part but thinking so made him feel good about his job nonetheless.

He adjusted his shirt collar. The various spotlights all around the store were making him hot. The last time he wore a uniform was when he was a deputy sheriff. He could not believe his life had come full circle. He had now left his PI business to become a security guard.

A part of him wished he had never left the sheriff's office. He would likely still be married, and he would have likely spent more time with his daughter.

He overheard a mother talking to the salesperson behind the counter. "My sister was here this morning and she said it was mayhem," the mother said.

"We are having a bigger sale next week," the salesperson replied. "If your sister thought today was bad, wait until she sees what happens then."

Callaway inhaled deeply.

FOURTEEN

Fisher watched as Big Bob's body was loaded into the back of a van. Wakefield would accompany the body on its way to the morgue.

The CSU was conducting its final sweep of the scene. They too would be gone soon.

The property was sealed off from the public. An officer would be stationed in case Fisher and Holt needed to come back and gather more evidence.

Fisher saw a couple of news vans outside the yellow police tape. The media turnout was nothing compared to her last big case: the murder of Hollywood star Dillon Scott.

Big Bob's death was nothing more than a curiosity. Here was a man who had won thirty million dollars and now he would never live to enjoy his wealth.

She could see how some people would relish his death. Society wanted decent people to deserve the good fortune that came their way. Big Bob was not a decent person. He was a blustering salesman who said and did anything to get a sale, even if it meant fudging paperwork to get someone a car loan. Big Bob had been investigated and fined multiple times by the Better Business Bureau, but he continued to do business in a manner that made him the most money.

Holt came over and asked, "Did you learn anything from the victim's wife?"

"They were in the middle of a separation," Fisher replied.

"Divorce is rarely ever amicable," he said. "Is she a suspect?"

"I'm not sure. Mrs. Burley is half her husband's size."

"Nancy is half my size," he retorted.

"Okay, but do you think she is capable of murder?"

Holt paused.

Fisher said, "If you have to think about it, then the answer is yes."

"It's not a no either."

Fisher knew Nancy was the love of his life. Holt would do anything for her, even if it meant quitting the force. But Holt lived and breathed the profession. His two passions in life were his wife and his job.

"Listen, Nancy is the gentlest soul I know," Holt said, "but she is human. If I did something that deeply hurt her, who knows how she would react."

Fisher understood where he was going with this. "In Big Bob's case, you think it's a crime of passion?"

"The victim *was* stabbed multiple times."

"But again, Mrs. Burley is five foot four inches at best and Big Bob was a good foot taller than her. She would have had to stand on something in order to stab him in the chest."

Holt shook his head. "I don't agree. She could have easily reached up and stabbed him."

"Okay, but it would require a lot of strength to get the knife through his ribs."

"What if he was seated when she attacked him?" Holt suggested.

"If he was attacked while seated, there would have been blood on the armchair."

"He was drinking prior to the attack. The alcohol might have impaired his ability to defend himself."

"Sure," Fisher said, "but why would she stab him and then call nine-one-one?"

"Maybe she thought it made her look less suspicious."

Holt's eyes suddenly widened. "What if *she* was the one hiding in the room when the victim shot through the door? It's not uncommon for one spouse to use a weapon during domestic disputes."

Fisher considered Holt's theory. "Makes sense, but then why didn't she call the police when it happened? I mean, if he had a gun, then her life was in danger. She would know better than to try to defend herself with a knife while he had a gun."

Holt exhaled. "Alright, I'm out of ideas."

"I'm not saying she's not a suspect, but I still think we need to widen our scope."

"The CSU found the victim's cell phone. It was in his coat pocket. There were several outgoing calls last night but no outgoing calls this morning."

"We'll need to speak to the people he had called."

"One other thing," Holt said. He held up a clear plastic baggie. "It's a receipt from a casino. It was in the same coat pocket as the cell phone. The victim had bought alcohol at the bar. The date on the receipt was from last night."

"Let's go visit this casino," Fisher said.

FIFTEEN

Callaway was glad to be rid of the uniform. He was wearing a T-shirt, jeans, boots, and a leather jacket as he stood next to his beloved Dodge Charger outside the school. He saw other parents waiting to pick up their children as well.

A few of the mothers eyed him with interest. One even smiled in his direction.

Callaway looked like a cool dad who was devoted to his offspring. He did look younger than he actually was, but he was far from being a responsible parent. He had abandoned his wife and infant child because he could not take being a husband and father. His decision was a selfish act—one he should have been severely punished for—but, to his ex-wife's credit, she always kept the door open for him to see his daughter. She was far more mature than he was. She knew no good would come from cutting off their only child from her father.

Even after that, Callaway rarely saw his little girl. The first couple years of his so-called liberation was spent with women, alcohol, and seeking danger. He and his friend Jimmy Keith had no shortage of ladies vying for their attention. Most were clients—Callaway and Jimmy caught their cheating husbands, so the clients needed company—and they met others while partying and boozing. The danger came with the nature of the job. Husbands did not take too kindly to being followed, and to being photographed in compromising positions. They lashed out with threats of litigation and violence. Some even went so far as to point a weapon in their direction.

Fortunately, Callaway came out of those situations unscathed. The husbands were not violent to begin with. They were scared. They just wanted their problems to go away. They offered more money than their spouses did, but Jimmy had taught Callaway one important lesson about the profession which he held close to his heart: *you did not renege on an agreement.*

If clients could not trust him to hold his end of the bargain, then he had no business being a private eye. Clients trusted a private investigator would conduct his business with delicacy, understanding, and honesty. Families were broken, careers were tarnished, and lives were destroyed by what PIs dug up.

Callaway remembered a case where he caught the husband being unfaithful to his wife. The husband begged and pleaded with Callaway to not expose his infidelity. He vowed to end the affair. But Callaway could not go against his agreement.

The marriage ended, the wife took the children, and the man ended up jumping in front of an eighteen-wheeler.

Callaway did not regret what he did. The wife deserved to know the truth—why else would she procure his services? But he still wished the outcome would have been different.

Life was precious. Family was precious. Both were something he had recently learned when Jimmy Keith arrived at his doorstep unannounced.

The bell rang, and the children rushed out.

He smiled when he spotted his daughter.

SIXTEEN

Sabrina Callaway, or as they liked to call her, "Nina", was nine years old. She had long, dark hair that reached down all the way to her lower back. Her eyes were emerald green and she had a smile that could light up any dreary day.

She looked a lot like his ex-wife, Patti, and she also had her wit and intelligence. Callaway was not the least bit envious of that. Unlike most divorced parents, he felt no ill-will toward his ex-wife. In fact, he realized he still harbored feelings for her.

He was trying hard to be a changed man, and he now dreamed of the day they could be a family again.

Would Patti be up for it?

He had no idea.

But he was willing and eager to find out.

The moment Nina saw him, she smiled and rushed over.

"Hi, Daddy," she said.

"Hi, baby," he replied, giving her a hug.

He spotted a female teacher by the school's entrance. She was staring at them with a frown on her face. She likely knew what kind of a father Callaway was. He never showed up for his daughter's school events, and even when he did pick up Nina from school, too much time passed between the next time he did.

Patti had already informed the school that he would be coming, so they could not stop him from taking his daughter home.

The teacher can frown all she wants, he thought. *I'm here, aren't I?*

A boy walked by with a backpack slung over his shoulder. He waved at Nina, and she smiled and waved back.

Callaway eyed him suspiciously. "Who's he?"

"He's a friend."

He suddenly turned protective. "What's his name?"

"Jamie."

"What does Jamie do?"

"Huh?"

"Does he have a job?"

Nina laughed. "No, Dad. He's only a kid."

44

"Right," Callaway replied. *I don't trust him.*

They got in the Charger. Nina said, "Daddy?"

"Yes, honey."

"Can I get a cell phone?"

"Sure, why not? I get paid next week, and then we'll go and get you a fancy one that you can take pictures with."

"You can take pictures with all of them now," she replied. "But maybe you should ask Mom first."

"Oh, right." Patti made all the decisions when it came to their daughter. Callaway explicitly trusted her in that regard. He had no choice anyway. He had wanted zero responsibility as a parent, which gave him zero rights to her upbringing. "Why don't you ask your mom yourself?" he asked.

"She'll say no."

Callaway thought a moment. "So, you want me to convince her?"

"Yes, please."

He shrugged. "Okay, I'll try, but I can't make any promises."

She kissed him on the cheek. "Thank you, Daddy."

He beamed, and then he reached over and retrieved a bag from the backseat.

"What's this?" she asked, eagerly looking inside.

"It's a one of a kind princess doll. All the girls want one."

She gave him a weak smile. "I'm not really into dolls."

He felt sheepish. "I can take it back," he said.

Nina's smile widened. She hugged him. "No, I'm going to keep it next to my bed. It's the thought that counts."

He smiled. *She is wiser than I will ever be.*

SEVENTEEN

The casino manager was a short, stocky man with a gray handlebar moustache and a buzz haircut. Suspenders held up his loose pants.

Holt and Fisher were in a windowless room located in the casino's basement. The manager's desk was covered in telephones, and in a wall cabinet were several TV monitors that displayed footage of the casino floor.

Gus Colburn caught Fisher staring at a red telephone. "It's for when we have emergencies in the casino," he said with a smile. "It usually has to do with security."

Fisher nodded. "I see you have a lot of telephones. Wouldn't it be easier to have *one* cell phone instead?"

"It would," he agreed. "And I do have one, but I keep losing the darn thing. I've been a manager here for almost thirty years, so I have a system—which some might think is outdated—but it works for me."

Holt said, "Robert Burley is a member of your casino."

"Big Bob," Holburn replied with a grin. "He's a regular. He usually comes in a couple of times a week. If I'm not mistaken, he should be here later today."

"He's dead," Holt said.

Colburn's mouth dropped. "Oh dear..."

Holt placed a receipt on Colburn's desk. "We found this on him. It shows he was here last night."

Colburn did not touch the receipt, as if it might burn him. "I remember he came in and spent two hours at the slots. He was always a good customer. He was never rowdy, drunk, or belligerent to the staff. He tipped well, and from what I've heard he was a lot of fun." Colburn's eyes moistened, and he wiped them clear.

"Did you know him? I mean, on a personal level?" Fisher asked.

"I bought two cars from him. For a brief time, my son worked at his dealership when he was still in school. I didn't go to his house for dinners or anything like that, but I did have drinks with him. Big Bob was kind and generous. He bragged a lot about how successful he was, but he only did it to get attention. It was good for business, he would always say."

"That was before he won, right?"

"Oh, yeah."

"And after?"

"He was insufferable." Colburn laughed but then stopped. "No, in reality, he was far more subdued after winning all that money. I figured he would be even happier than usual, but he wasn't. I mean, at first, he was, you know. He came down and bought every customer in the casino a drink. But after a while, I guess, the excitement wore off and he seemed solemn."

Fisher had read a study about happiness which compared two sets of people: one who had won the lottery, and one who became quadriplegic after a horrible car accident. After six months, for the people in the car accident, their happiness level went back to what it was prior to the accident. The same thing happened for the lottery winners, albeit their happiness was slightly *less* than what it was the day before they had won. Psychologists believed that with all that money, the winners were no longer happy with the little things in life. This was one of the reasons why they made big purchases to give them the same rush they felt when they had won the money in the first place.

"Did you speak to Big Bob last night?" Fisher asked.

"Only briefly. Like I said, he was playing slots, and I only said hi to him."

"Was he depressed or maybe under stress?" Fisher asked.

"I don't know, but later, as I was doing my rounds, I saw him having a drink with a couple of guys at the bar."

That's where he got the receipt! Fisher thought.

"Do you know where we can find these guys?"

Colburn pointed to a TV screen behind Holt and Fisher. "As a matter of fact, they are at the bar right now."

EIGHTEEN

The sun was still up. Callaway was not in the mood to head home, so he decided to drop by his office.

The Callaway Private Investigation Office was located above a soup and noodle restaurant. In order to get to his office, you had to go to the back of the restaurant and up a flight of metal stairs.

There was no sign anywhere to indicate his office's existence, but there was a telephone number taped to the black metal door.

There were several reasons for the telephone number. In his line of work, client's ex-spouses were known to seek him out, and it was not for a polite chat. Then there was his problem with money. He was not a saver, nor was he a savvy investor. He loved to be part of get-rich-quick schemes. Naturally, they never panned out as promised.

Instead of learning from his past mistakes, he always hoped the next investment would pay off. Whenever he would lose money—sometimes all of it—he would have to borrow from unsavory characters to pay his bills. And these people did not take kindly to not being paid on time. In fact, they took that as an insult and would go out of their way to make an example of him. So far, he had been lucky to avoid any serious injuries. He had gotten a black eye, a broken nose, and a bruised rib, but nothing a few painkillers and some rest could not cure.

He unlocked the door to his office and entered. The room was small and windowless. There was no air conditioning and the heating was spotty. Callaway could not complain because the rent was the cheapest in the city.

Now that he was employed as a security guard, it was time to close the PI business. The rent was paid for until the end of the month. He figured he would keep using the premises until then.

Shutting down his business was a hard decision, but it was one he did not regret. He was looking forward to having money at the end of the month to meet all his obligations.

He shut the door and pulled up a chair behind a desk. There was a sofa in the corner of the room. Across from the sofa was a flat-screen TV a client had generously bequeathed to him. He grabbed the remote off the desk and turned on the TV. The set was tuned to a 24-hour news channel so that he was always aware of what was going on in the city. This also allowed him to search out potential clients.

Unfortunately, he would not be looking for new business anymore.

He turned on his ten-year-old laptop. He shut his eyes and waited for the laptop to boot up, which took fifteen to twenty minutes. He always considered purchasing a new one, but for some reason he kept pushing it off. He knew the moment the laptop stopped working—which could be at the most inopportune time—he would be forced to find a replacement.

He had a website for his business and it was his main source of acquiring new clients, apart from the word of mouth.

The website would be another thing he would have to shut down.

Once the laptop was up and running, he checked his emails. To his surprise and dismay, there were several messages from people looking to hire him. Normally, he would pore through each message and sift out those who were only curious about what he did from those who were ready to hire a private investigator.

Today, however, he just deleted the messages without even looking at them.

NINETEEN

The two men were seated at a table in the middle of the casino lounge. The first one, Beck, had a goatee and curly hair. He was holding a beer bottle. The second, Jesse, was clean-shaven and bald. He had a glass of whiskey in front of him.

Holt and Fisher sat across from them.

Beck shook his head. "I can't believe Big Bob is gone. May he rest in peace."

"Amen," his friend said.

"How long did you know him?" Holt asked.

"Not long."

"Did you know him well?"

Beck frowned. "I mean, we met up whenever he was at the casino, but we never hung outside."

"What do you guys do?" Fisher asked. She was curious as to why both of them spent so much time at the casino.

"We're retired," Jesse said. "I used to work at a plant that built bumpers for cars, and Beck worked as an engineer for a railroad."

Beck nodded and took a sip from his bottle.

Holt said, "The casino manager said he saw Robert Burley speaking to you guys yesterday."

"Sure, we had a drink," Beck said.

"What did you talk about?" Holt asked.

"Nothing in particular. We usually shoot the breeze."

Fisher asked, "Was Big Bob worried? Stressed? Upset?"

Jesse replied, "Lately, he was kind of stressed…"

"About what?"

"I'm not sure, but he was going through a separation from his second wife."

"We know this. Did he talk about his relationship with his wife?"

Jesse nodded. "He did, whenever he felt up to it. Guys don't really like to share their feelings or what's going on with them. He still loved his wife—I mean, she was much younger than him, so I could see why he did it—but I guess the relationship wasn't meant to last forever."

Beck said, "I always thought it was a mistake for him to marry her, and I let Big Bob know this."

"Why would you say that?" Fisher asked.

"Big Bob wasn't the most refined guy you'd meet. He was generous, don't get me wrong. He always picked up the tab whenever we were having drinks. But Big Bob could be loud and abrasive. I've heard him have arguments with his wife where he'd call her terrible names. She was always doing something to piss him off."

"Like what?"

"She'd go out shopping and buy all her friends expensive gifts without telling him. She even pushed him to buy her mother a house in Houston. I could tell she was using him for his money."

"Do you think his wife is capable of murder?" Holt asked.

Beck put his hands up. "I never met her, so I can't say anything. My opinions are based on what Big Bob told us and what I overheard in their conversations."

Holt and Fisher pondered their next questions.

Fisher asked, "Do you know if Big Bob kept money in his safe at his home?"

Jesse replied, "I'm sure he did. He liked having cash around. He didn't really trust the banks. If he could, he would keep all his money under his mattress."

"Did he tell you how much money he kept in his safe?"

Jesse pondered the question. "If I had to take a guess, I would say a couple of hundred thousand."

Fisher's eyes widened. "That much?"

"Yeah, sure. He won millions, you know," Jesse said.

Holt asked, "Was there anything different about him last night?"

Beck jumped in. "He was quiet throughout the time he was here. We asked him if he was okay, but he said nothing. He then got a call and left right after hanging up."

"Do you know who called him?" Fisher asked.

Beck shook his head. "Don't know."

No worries, Fisher thought. *We can check his phone records.*

Holt and Fisher were getting up to leave when Jesse said, "I'm not sure if this will help…"

"Tell us," Holt replied.

"A couple of months back, Big Bob got into a fight with someone. I remember seeing them arguing in the casino parking lot."

"Do you know this person's name?"

"Sure."

"Give it to us."

TWENTY

Callaway was at his office when he had received the call. He recognized the number and he seriously debated not answering. But he knew if he did not answer, the caller would end up paying him a visit, which would not be a good idea.

He took the call.

He was now standing outside a steel door that was behind a strip club. He banged on the door and waited. A few minutes later, a small window slid open, revealing two eyes.

"Can I help you?" the man asked.

"Baxter, open the door."

"Your name?"

Callaway rolled his eyes. "It's Lawrence of Arabia."

"I thought your name was Lee Callaway."

"You already know what my name is. Now, let me in."

Callaway heard a bolt turning, a chain being removed, and then the door opened. Baxter was six-foot-four. He was two hundred and fifty pounds of pure muscle. He sported a buzz cut and he always wore tight T-shirts that made his arms look even bigger.

Today, he was wearing a T-shirt that read: *My Brain Is Bigger Than Yours.* *I doubt that very much*, Callaway thought, but he would never express his opinion to Baxter. He was not known for his sense of humor or common sense.

"Who's Lawrence of Arabia?" Baxter asked.

"He was my uncle," Callaway dryly replied.

"Why did he have the word *of* in his name?"

"Because that's where he came from," Callaway said, wanting to move past him and up the stairs. But Baxter's massive body was in the way.

"He was from Arabia?" Baxter asked.

"Yes."

"Can I have the word *of* in my name?"

"Sure you can. From now on, you will be known as Baxter of Glenwood."

"Why Glenwood?" he asked, confused.

"That's the street we are on right now."

A second passed before Baxter's face brightened up. "I get it."

Moron.

He turned around and moved up the narrow stairs. Callaway followed behind. They were met with another door. Baxter waited a second before he knocked and said, "Boss, Lee Callaway is here to see you. Can I let him in?"

Callaway hated coming down here. He felt like he was in a bad sketch comedy.

"Yeah," came the voice from behind the door.

Baxter smiled and held the door for Callaway.

The office was small and narrow. A wide desk took up most of the room. Callaway could never understand how anyone could move around in such a tight space.

Mason was seated in a leather chair behind the desk. He was short, rail thin, and every inch of his arms were covered in tattoos. He sported a small goatee, and he wore wire-rimmed prescription glasses.

Callaway spotted a tattoo on the side of Mason's neck he had not seen before.

"It's a dragon reading a book," Mason said with a smile. "According to the Chinese calendar, I was born in the year of the dragon."

"And why is it reading a book?" Callaway asked.

"Because I like to read, of course."

Right.

"Have a seat, Lee," Mason said, gesturing to a chair in front of the desk.

Callaway crossed his arms over his chest. "I'm fine where I am."

Mason was not offended. He steepled his fingers together and said, "There are rumors out there that you've quit the PI business."

"Where did you hear that?"

"I have my sources."

"Well, they are right. I'm done."

Mason was surprised. "Why? I thought you had a great thing going."

Callaway could not help but laugh. "You know better than anyone my business is struggling. How many times have I come to your office asking for money?"

"Too many times," Mason replied with glee.

Mason was a loan shark and a very good one at that. His rates were high, but he always extended loans, even to people with the worst credit rating in the city. He loaned money knowing he would find a way to collect his money, including interest. Baxter was a big reason for that. He was not the sharpest tool in the shed, but he was a lethal one. He took immense pleasure in inflicting pain. Callaway came close to being at the end of his fist, but he always managed to talk his way out of a beating.

"Well, today is your lucky day," Mason said.

"How so?"

"I've got a job for you."

Callaway shook his head. "I'm not going to help you look for some guy who couldn't pay his loans."

"An agreement is an agreement."

"Regardless. If the guy had money, I guarantee he would pay you first. But he doesn't, and I'm not going to be the one to see him get hurt."

"This is a cruel business."

"Yeah, well, get someone else to do your dirty work. I already got a job."

"Yeah, I know: as a security guard watching teenyboppers shop for dolls."

Callaway's face hardened. "You following me, Mason?"

"Not me personally, but, like I said, I've got sources."

Callaway pointed a finger at Mason. "Don't. Follow. Me," he sternly said.

Baxter bristled next to him, but Callaway was not scared. Baxter would never hurt him unless Mason said so, and Mason was a businessman first. It was bad business to hurt clients or associates without a genuine reason.

Mason shrugged. "Okay, sure, suit yourself. But mark my words. You are made to be a private investigator. You can fool yourself and everyone else, but you cannot fool me."

Callaway wanted to tell Mason he was wrong. Instead, he turned around and left.

TWENTY-ONE

Holt and Fisher tracked Joseph Olsson to an office building in Milton's west end. According to Big Bob's drinking buddies, Olsson was the man Big Bob had a spat with outside the casino.

The building had three levels with no elevators. Holt and Fisher took the stairs. They knocked on the door with a sign that read: Olsson Consulting.

A man answered the door. He looked dishevelled and fatigued. "We are closed for business," he said, sounding weary.

"Mr. Joseph Olsson?" Holt asked.

"Yes."

Holt and Fisher flashed their badges.

"What's this about?" he asked, suddenly alarmed.

"Robert Burley," Holt replied.

Olsson's eyes widened. "Hey, listen, I promise I'll pay him back."

"Can we come inside?" Fisher asked.

Olsson reluctantly held the door open for them. The interior looked more like a loft. There were exposed pipes, a brick wall, and concrete flooring. They spotted a bed to one side, a kitchen in the corner, and a sofa by the window.

"You live here?" Fisher asked.

"Yeah," Olsson sheepishly replied. "It was supposed to have been my office, but I kind of ran out of money and had to move in."

Holt got to the point. "What were you and Mr. Burley fighting about?"

Olsson hesitated.

Holt said, "Mr. Burley's dead, so it would be in your best interest to be truthful with us."

The color drained from Olsson's face. "When... did he die?"

"Last night. He was found stabbed to death in his home."

Olsson reached over, pulled a chair close, and sat down. He covered his face with his hands. After a brief moment, he looked up. "I had nothing to do with his death. I swear."

"Where were you last night?" Holt asked.

"I was here the entire night."

"Do you have anyone to verify this?"

"I… I was by myself."

"What did you do?" Fisher asked.

"I watched a movie."

Holt waited a moment before he said, "You didn't answer my question. Why were you and Mr. Burley fighting?"

"I used to be a programmer for a software company, but I got in trouble for doing something I shouldn't have done, and I was fired. After a year of no work, I was running out of money. One day, I went to the casino to blow off some steam when I saw Big Bob— he told me to call him by that name. I knew he had won a lot of money, but it was the first time I had seen him in person. I asked around the casino and they told me he came by often. I then came up with a plan." He stopped and looked at the floor, as if he was drifting away in his thoughts.

"What was this plan?" Holt asked.

Olsson sighed. "I wanted Big Bob to invest in my company."

"Olsson Consulting?" Fisher asked.

Olsson looked at her and nodded. "But the thing was, there was no company. I got the building's landlord to agree to give me a lease without any upfront money. I borrowed furniture from people I knew and set up this place to look like an office. I then approached Big Bob. I told him I had created an app that helped people control their gambling addiction. I knew this would appeal to Big Bob, because from what I was told, he loved to spend time at the casino."

"Did you create this app?" Fisher asked, curious.

Olsson shrugged. "Well, I wrote the code for it and I setup a dummy interface. It was only to show Big Bob that such an app existed. And you know what? It worked. The moment he heard me talk, he agreed to become an investor."

"How much?" Holt asked.

"Fifty thousand."

"Let me guess," Holt said. "When he found out it was a sham, he wanted his money back?"

Olsson sighed. "I had planned to use that money to create a legitimate company, but I had no idea how to go about doing this. I'm a programmer, not a businessman. I officially leased this place and made it the headquarters for Olsson Consulting, and I even hired an employee, but the money ran out faster than I could do something with it. The lease is paid for until next year, and that's why I'm still living here."

"Why did you go to the casino when you knew Big Bob was looking for his money?" Fisher asked.

"I received a letter from his lawyer threatening legal action. I went to speak to Big Bob about it. I hoped we could come up with a resolution."

"Like what?"

"I don't know. Honestly, I never thought this whole thing out. I figured, for a guy who won millions of dollars, fifty thousand dollars would be nothing. In fact, from what I've heard, he burned through far more than that at the casino."

"No one likes to be scammed," Holt sternly said.

Olsson lowered his head. "I know, and I'm sorry."

Holt said, "You still don't have an alibi for the time of Mr. Burley's death."

"I conned him, I'll agree to that," Olsson said. "But I did *not* kill him, whether you believe me or not."

Holt stared at him. At the moment they did not have enough evidence to detain him. He was a person of interest only.

Holt leaned down until his face was close to Olsson's. "Don't leave the city. If you do, and I have to come find you, I promise it will be something you'll come to regret. Do you understand?"

Olsson swallowed. "Yes, sir."

TWENTY-TWO

After his visit to Mason and his guard dog, Baxter, Callaway was spent. He decided to grab something to eat before he headed home.

He entered the restaurant and made a bee-line for a booth in the corner. Whenever he came to the restaurant, and if that table was empty, it was his. He liked how the booth faced the windows and was more private.

The waitress soon appeared. Joely Paterson had blonde hair which she always kept in a ponytail. She wore a fitted T-shirt which had an apron over it.

Joely was aware Callaway had decided to quit being a private eye. She had always admired him for following his true calling. She had always wanted to be a singer, but those dreams evaporated when she got married and then pregnant. Her then-husband worked for a rock band as their equipment manager. He was on the road a lot while she stayed home and took care of their son. One day he called and told her he did not want to be a husband or father. She then moved back in with her mother, and with her help she was raising her son, Joshua, who was now six years old.

Callaway and Joely had briefly dated. When she found out he too had abandoned his wife and daughter, she was repulsed. But once she got to know him a little better thanks to his regular visits to the restaurant, she became a trusted friend.

When he told her he wanted to get a steady job, so he could spend more time with his little girl, she wholeheartedly approved.

"How was work today?" she asked with a smile.

"I didn't know such evil existed until this morning," he replied. "The look in some of those mothers' eyes scared the daylights out of me."

"It couldn't have been that bad," she said.

"Even their daughters were terrified of them. And it was all for some doll."

"Did you get one for Nina?" Joely asked.

"I did, but I don't think she's into them."

"It's not the gift but the thought that counts."

"That's what she said," Callaway replied. "Anyway, I don't know if I have it in me to spend another day as a security guard." He had to admit that deep down he still wanted to be a PI.

"Just remember why you're doing it," she said.

He gave her a noncommittal shrug.

"Do you think I want to stand all day serving customers?" Joely asked.

"I thought you loved your job," Callaway replied with a laugh.

She put a hand on her hip. "Not funny," she said. A second later, she smiled. "I do enjoy my customers, just as long as they pay for their meals."

Callaway knew she was taking a jab at how he was always asking for freebies. Her boss, Bill, had specifically given her instructions not to serve Callaway unless he paid for his meal first. Callaway could not blame him. He rarely had money in his pocket. Today was not one of those days, however. He pulled out a twenty and dropped it on the table. "I'll have your special," he said.

Joely snatched up the twenty as if Callaway might want to take it back. "I thought you didn't get paid until the end of the week?"

Callaway smiled. "I don't, but when I was cleaning up my office—for the time when I do move out—I found the bill tucked beneath the sofa cushions."

"Alright then," she said with a smile. "One special coming right up."

TWENTY-THREE

When Holt and Fisher returned to Milton PD, the officer at the front desk said, "There's a woman here to see you."

"Did she say who she was?" Holt asked.

"No, but she said it had something to do with Robert Burley."

Holt looked over at Fisher, who was just as eager as him to find out what this woman knew.

"Where is she?" Holt asked.

The officer pointed to the waiting area on the other side of the lobby. "She's the one in the red dress," he said.

She was seated on a hard, plastic chair. She had long curly hair that flowed to her shoulders. She wore bright red lipstick, purple mascara, and she had pointy fake nails.

She got up when she saw them approach. She smiled, revealing a gap in her teeth.

Holt said, "I'm Detective Holt and this is Detective Fisher. It is my understanding that you have information on Mr. Robert Burley?"

"Yes, I do," she replied.

"Okay."

She looked around. "Can we go somewhere private?"

"Sure."

They escorted her to a room down the hall. Once seated, she said, "I was so sad when I heard Robert was dead."

"You mean Big Bob?" Fisher asked. "Everyone who knew him called him that."

She smiled again. "I know that, but *he* wanted me to call him Robbie."

"Alright."

"Robbie and I were lovers," she said. "And our love produced a child."

"Oh, okay," Fisher said, surprised.

"Yes, well, not a lot of people knew."

"Was Mr. Burley aware of this?" Holt asked.

"Of course, he was the father, so why wouldn't he know?" She looked down at her fingernails. "Robbie didn't want the child. He wanted me to get an abortion, but I didn't. And he refused to take responsibility for him, even though it's his, you know." She suddenly put her hands over her face and began to cry. "Now that he is gone, I have no one to take care of me and my child."

Holt shifted in his chair, looking clearly uncomfortable. "I'm not sure how we can help you, Ms.—?"

"Vanessa."

"Um… Vanessa, like I said, it's not our jurisdiction to get involved in these kinds of matters."

Fisher glared at him. She leaned over and soothingly said to Vanessa, "Maybe you should go get a lawyer."

She looked up. "I did," she replied.

"And?"

"It still didn't help."

"What do you mean?"

"I got a judge to get a paternity test."

"What did it reveal?"

"It came out negative."

"So, doesn't that prove he is not the father?" Fisher asked.

"No, it doesn't. I know Robert…"

"You mean, Robbie…"

"Yes. I know Robbie paid them off."

"Paid who off?"

"Everyone. The lawyers, the judges, the people who did the test. They are all against me."

Fisher suddenly realized what this was about. With Big Bob's death, everyone was out to get a piece of his estate, even if it meant fabricating lies.

"Where were you last night?" Holt asked.

"What?" Vanessa replied.

"Last night. Where were you?"

"Why?"

"That's when Mr. Burley was murdered."

Vanessa blinked. "I… I was at home with our child."

"Do you have any witnesses?"

"I… I…" Vanessa stammered. "I don't…"

Holt leaned closer. "This is how I see it. You blame Mr. Burley for not taking responsibility for fathering a child—"

"I do," Vanessa interjected.

"—and because of that you went to his house and stabbed him five times." Holt turned to Fisher. "I told you it was a crime of passion."

Fisher smiled. "I think you are right."

Vanessa bolted up. "I don't know anything about that. Maybe the judge was right. Maybe Robert…"

"Robbie," Fisher corrected her for fun.

"Yes, maybe Robbie was not the father, you know. And… and I should be home right now with my child."

Vanessa moved to the door. Holt said to her, "Please make sure you leave your full name and address with the officer at the front desk. We might have to ask you some more questions later regarding Mr. Burley's death."

Vanessa looked like she was about to faint. "Okay, sure," she said.

She raced out of the room.

Fisher doubted very much that Vanessa would leave her information with the officer. She was probably looking forward to getting as far away from the police station as possible.

Fisher turned to Holt. "I had no idea you had a sense of humor."

"I don't know what you found so humorous. I was just trying to find a way to remove her from the premises."

Fisher almost fell off her chair laughing.

TWENTY-FOUR

They had settled behind their desks when Fisher said, "We may have to go back to our original motive for Big Bob's murder."

"And what's that?" Holt asked.

"Robbery."

Holt's eyes narrowed as he considered the possibility.

"Someone stabbed Big Bob multiple times," Fisher continued, "and then they proceeded to remove his thumb in order to gain access to his safe—which, by the way, his buddies at the casino claim he kept a lot of cash in.'"

"Mrs. Burley may have wanted the cash because she knew at the time of their divorce she would get nothing as per their pre-nuptial agreement," Holt suggested. "Then there was Joseph Olsson, the conman, who scammed Mr. Burley out of fifty thousand. He could kill two birds with one stone by killing him. Get the cash in order to alleviate his financial difficulties and have the case against him thrown out."

"Yes, but there was someone else who may have wanted Big Bob dead."

"Who?"

Fisher faced her computer and, after a few keystrokes, turned the monitor around so that Holt got a clear view. On the screen was the photo of a man with a scar across his face, deep set eyes, and a busted boxer's nose. "Corliss Looms," she said. "He broke into Big Bob's house, tied him to a chair, knocked him out, and then stole two hundred thousand from his safe."

Holt shook his head. "Looms is serving twenty years in prison for armed robbery and assault. There's no way he could have done this while still locked up."

"Yes, but the prosecutors always believed Looms did not act alone. Even Big Bob confirmed in his state of semi-consciousness that he heard Looms talking to someone. He didn't see who this person was or even get a name, though."

"If I remember the case correctly," Holt said, "wasn't Looms the only one arrested and charged for the crime?"

"Yes, because he refused to give up his accomplice's name."

They both mulled this possibility over.

"So, are you saying Looms's partner may have killed Mr. Burley out of revenge?" Holt asked.

"Maybe."

"But the robbery was years ago, so why now?"

"Why don't we find out?"

Holt blinked. "What? You mean go to the Milton Penitentiary right now?"

"Yes."

"But it's late."

"When has that ever stopped you before?"

Holt was quiet.

"Unless you've got something planned with Nancy," Fisher said.

He shrugged.

She laughed. "Alright, we'll go there first thing in the morning. You go see Nancy."

"And you can go see Officer McConnell."

Fisher gave him a coy smile. "Who said I plan to see him tonight?"

"It was just a thought, Detective Fisher," Holt replied. "It's none of my business what you do in your free time."

There was a glint in his eyes.

TWENTY-FIVE

Callaway's dinner included a cheesesteak sandwich, hand cut fries, and a glass of cold ice tea. Joely even snuck in a piece of lemon pie for him. Callaway was already full by the time he got to dessert, but seeing that it was free, he ate it nonetheless.

He now regretted his decision as he huffed and puffed his way up the flight of stairs. Callaway's room was on the third floor of a hotel. The place was neither a five-star nor a four-star; it was more like a two and a half star, but it was cheaper than renting an apartment. Management did not ask for first and last month's rent and they asked for no references. Just as long as he paid for the entire month upfront, there were no questions asked.

He preferred such an arrangement. He could up and leave whenever he wanted. He only had a single suitcase and a hand carry to take with him. He could also change rooms if he wanted to, which he had not had to do yet.

There were benefits and drawbacks to living in a hotel. There was a revolving door of neighbors. He had gotten friendly with a retired naval officer. He and Callaway would go down to the bar and have drinks, but after two weeks, he left. Then there were two college students who had rented the room next to his. They were loud, obnoxious, and there was a party every night.

Callaway would have tolerated the noise if they had invited him over once to their parties. They did not, so he complained, and they were thrown out. Callaway had a feeling the action taken against them was not because of his complaint but because management found out the students were also using the room to sell drugs.

Similar to his office, the room was small and cramped. But unlike his office, his place had a window the length of the room. The sun streamed through each morning, forcing him to wake up. There was a bed on the right, and a futon was next to it. A TV was across from the futon. The room had running water, proper plumbing, and the heating worked during the cold winter months.

Most people took those things for granted, but with little money in his pockets, Callaway had been forced to live in far worse conditions. He could tolerate a lot, but not rodents. He had a phobia that they would crawl up his pants legs and bite his nether regions.

He shivered at the thought.

His room had a bathroom with a shower stall barely big enough for him to squeeze in for a quick shower. There was no kitchen, but the room did come with a microwave. Callaway had managed to lug a mini-fridge up the flight of stairs. He had found the fridge on the sidewalk, and to his surprise, it still worked. He kept cold drinks and frozen dinners inside the fridge.

Right now, food was the last thing on his mind.

He took off his coat and threw it on the futon. He went inside the bathroom and washed his face. He came out, flopped onto the bed, and turned on the TV.

It was set to a 24-hour news channel, which he was in no mood to watch.

I'm no longer a PI, he thought. *I don't need to know what's going on in the city.*

Instead, he watched a classic Western, one he had seen over a dozen times but never got tired of.

TWENTY-SIX

Corliss Looms was a heavyset man. His head was shaved smooth, revealing a wrinkled skull. He had a teardrop tattoo under one eye.

Even wearing the orange prison uniform, he still looked intimidating. But his hands were cuffed to the table.

Corliss had gone to prison for assault with a deadly weapon and for breaking and entering, but during his stay, he had stabbed another inmate with a homemade shank. His sentence was upgraded to attempted murder.

After robbing Big Bob in his home, he was caught a week later while trying to buy a brand-new Hummer with the stolen cash.

Holt started the conversation. "Robert Burley is dead."

Corliss smiled. "I saw that on the news. We got TVs in our cells, you know."

"What did you think about his death?"

He shrugged. "I dunno."

"Were you happy someone got him?"

"Why would I?"

"At your sentencing, you looked at him and you told him you were going to make him pay for what he did."

Corliss shrugged again. "I was going to prison for a long time, so yeah, I said some stuff." He straightened up in his chair. "What? You think I had something to do with him getting killed? I've been locked up like an animal for the last ten years, man."

"Maybe you know someone who killed him."

He scowled. "How would I? And even if I did, why would I tell *you*?"

"We could work out a deal," Holt offered. "I can't do much about the robbery and assault, but I can see what I can do about the attempted murder. The inmate was threatening your life, so you had to protect yourself, right?"

Corliss stared at him. He turned to Fisher. "Is he for real?" he asked.

"That's why we are here," she replied.

He curled his lip and then nodded. "I can ask around and find out if anyone knows something."

"No," Holt said. "We know you were not alone when you went to Robert Burley's house. Tell us who this person is."

Corliss's eyes instantly filled with fire, but the next second they were back to normal. "I got nothing to say to you."

Holt leaned closer. "Why are you protecting this person? You are rotting in a cell while they are not. They are free to live their life however they choose, while you have to live by the rules of this prison. Take this deal. This is your only chance. Give us his name. And maybe one day down the road, you too can live your life as a free man."

Holt was trying to appeal to Corliss's better judgement. The man was a hardened criminal and he would not easily rat on someone, but even then, Holt knew he would prefer to be outside a prison than inside.

To seal the deal, Holt said, "We just want to talk to this person. No charges related to the robbery will be laid against him. You are already serving time for it."

"Yeah, but then you would want to charge this guy with Burley's death, right?" Corliss said.

Holt fell silent.

Corliss stared at him and then shook his head. "It would not do you any good talking to him anyway."

"Why is that?"

"He's dead."

Holt and Fisher looked at each other.

Corliss said, "He was shot and killed last year in a drive-by shooting."

"Who was he?" Holt asked.

Corliss's eyes welled up. "He was my baby brother."

"Is that why you didn't give him up?"

He nodded. "He was family, you know. They didn't even let me go to his funeral."

Holt realized their visit to the prison was a waste of time. Corliss had nothing to do with Burley's death.

Before they got up to leave, Fisher asked, "Do you know anyone who'd want to hurt Big Bob?"

Corliss smiled. "Yeah, everyone."

"What do you mean?"

"The guy won a shitload of money. He had a bullseye on his back. Why do you think I chose to rob him in the first place?"

TWENTY-SEVEN

Callaway opened his eyes and blinked. The sun was blinding him. He squinted and checked the time. It was a little before eight a.m. He shut his eyes and tried to get back to sleep. When he could not, he got up and went to the bathroom. Afterwards, he turned on the TV, sat on the futon, and watched the news. There was a three-vehicle crash on the highway which caused a traffic jam that lasted for several hours. A man was caught trying to lure a minor on the internet. He was a coach for his children's soccer team. A woman was wanted for fraud. She had embezzled thousands of dollars from unsuspecting new immigrants.

If aliens came down to earth and watched the news, they'd think our world was falling apart, he thought.

There were positive news items as well. A family's pet dog returned home after disappearing for several weeks. The family was not sure how the dog survived, but they were happy to have it back. Money was raised for a single mother whose purse had been stolen. She was unable to pay her rent until strangers stepped up to help her out. For the first time ever, a Milton resident had won the city's marathon. The female runner who did it won in record time.

Callaway understood that even with all the feel-good stories, it was the bad ones that people remembered the most. This was why the news channels were more devoted to covering matters involving fear. Fear brought the highest ratings.

Fear was good for his business too, he knew. Fear made people hire him to follow their spouses. Fear made his clients want to know what their competitors were up to. Fear made ordinary people want to know what their neighbors were doing. Fear paid his bills. There was no other way to look at it.

He was glad that was all behind him now. He could focus on the positives rather than the negatives. As a security guard, his duty was to keep order and provide security. In return the position provided him financial security via a steady paycheck and gave his life the order and structure it was missing as a private eye.

He checked his watch. It was still early, but he decided to get ready nonetheless. He showered, shaved, and changed into his uniform.

He walked down the block to a convenience store. He still had change left from his meal at Joely's restaurant. He bought coffee from a vending machine and he picked up a granola bar.

Breakfast of champions, he thought as he took a bite.

The mall did not open until ten a.m. so he still had some time to kill beforehand. He decided to go for a walk to get some fresh air. Once he was at work, he would be inside the mall for the duration of his shift.

He finished the granola bar and tossed the wrapper in the garbage. He sipped coffee and was walking down the block when he felt movement behind him. He turned and saw nothing out of the ordinary.

He kept moving. After another block, he had the same feeling.

He glanced over his shoulder.

A black limousine he had seen the first time he had looked back was pulling into the lane closest to the sidewalk. And then, as if on cue, the limousine accelerated and pulled up on the curb next to him. A man got out of the driver's side. He was wearing a black suit and black sunglasses.

"Lee Callaway?" he said.

Callaway's back arched and he suddenly wished he had his gun on him, but it was locked up in his office desk.

"Who wants to know?" Callaway asked in a serious tone.

The man walked around and opened the back door. Callaway leaned down and saw a woman inside.

"If you would please get in," the man said. "My employer would like to speak to you."

Callaway looked around. The street was empty.

A part of him wanted to tell the man to go to hell. But then he saw the woman was smiling at him.

He got in.

TWENTY-EIGHT

Like most government buildings, the structure had not been renovated in years due to lack of funds. The place was made of concrete and cement, which meant it would last a long time, but it did not mean it was no less cold and ominous to look at.

The interior was far worse. The walls were painted a dark shade and the floor tiles that were once white had now turned an ugly yellow. The fluorescent light bulbs flickered in the hallways, making the place look like a scene from a horror movie.

Fisher was not bothered by her surroundings as she and Holt made their way to the morgue. She was used to death. Her job gave her a front row seat to some of the most brutal crimes imaginable. Having said that, she still could not see herself working in a place filled with dead bodies. Maybe that was why she could never be a medical examiner.

They found the ME standing before a gurney. A body was covered in a green sheet.

"I was waiting for your arrival," Wakefield said.

"Sorry, we got stuck in traffic," Fisher replied, knowing Wakefield was a stickler for being on time.

Wakefield nodded and then pulled down the sheet. Big Bob's lifeless face stared back at them.

"Unfortunately, I did not find anything we did not already know," she said.

"Meaning?" Holt asked.

"The victim died from injuries to his internal organs." She pulled the sheet back further, revealing dark wounds on the chest and abdomen. "I counted five areas where the knife penetrated the body."

She rolled the body onto its side. Big Bob weighed close to three hundred pounds, and he weighed even more as a corpse. Wakefield was tiny in comparison, but Fisher was impressed by how effortlessly she pushed. "There are two additional wounds in the back." She pointed to the dark spots in the upper shoulder and lower back. "These wounds are consistent with the others."

"Was Big Bob stabbed in the back or the front first?" Fisher asked.

While Wakefield pondered this, Holt asked, "Why is that important?"

Fisher replied, "What if—and I'm only hypothesizing here—Big Bob was asleep in the armchair when he heard a noise in the house, and when he went to check, he saw his attacker in the hallway. Big Bob realized his gun was still by his armchair, so when he turned to retrieve it, the attacker struck him in the back." Fisher turned to Wakefield. "Were there any defensive wounds on the arms and hands?"

Wakefield shook her head.

Fisher said, "This would explain how someone with his size would not defend himself from a knife attack, because he was already hurt. The killer then struck him in the chest repeatedly as he lay on the ground. The blood on the carpet would further support this theory. Also, once he was dead, his thumb was severed from his hand."

"But he wasn't dead," Holt said.

"What do you mean?" Fisher asked.

"He may have been attacked in the living room, but his body was found in the entrance by the stairs because that's where he crawled to and eventually died. So how could the killer not have known he was not dead when he cut his thumb off? I mean the victim should have made some noise to indicate he was still alive."

"I can explain that," Wakefield said. "When the body suffers extreme trauma—like being viciously stabbed—it can go into a shock. The victim may have been numb to what's happening around him. It's like the soldiers who are badly injured in battle: if you ask if they were feeling pain at that moment, a lot of them will say they felt nothing or that they blacked out. It is only when they wake up in a hospital bed do they realize they have lost limbs."

Holt and Fisher soaked in this information.

"Plus," Wakefield added, "there was alcohol in the victim's bloodstream at the time of death."

"We found a half empty bottle of whiskey next to the armchair," Fisher said.

Wakefield nodded. "Excess alcohol can impair judgement or reaction time. The victim may have had a fighting chance if he wasn't drinking."

They were silent a moment before Holt said, "Anything else you can tell us?"

"Like I said before, I didn't find anything that you didn't already know."

Another dead end, Fisher thought.

TWENTY-NINE

"Mr. Callaway, I have heard great things about you," the woman said with a smile. She was seated across from him in the limousine. She wore an oversized black coat, dark sunglasses, and she had long silver hair.

"I don't like being followed," he said.

"I apologize for that. I went to your office and I called the number on the door. I even left a voicemail, but when I didn't hear back, I decided to seek you out."

"How did you know where I'd be?" Callaway asked.

"I asked your landlady…"

"Oh, right." Anyone could easily ask her. But then again, she did not know where he was currently residing. He kept that bit of personal information to himself. "How long have you been following me?" he asked.

Even with the dark glasses, he could tell she was staring at him. "For a couple of days," she slowly replied.

"Okay, goodbye."

He reached for the door. She put out her hand to stop him but then quickly pulled it back.

"I'm sorry, but I'm desperate," she said.

"First, tell me how you knew where I'd be?" If she could find him, then his creditors and irate clients could find him as well. The whole point of not having a sign outside his office was for his protection. If he chose to ignore their telephone calls, then that was his prerogative.

"Okay, your landlady didn't know where you would be. So, I began asking around. I went to a bar that you are known to frequent and someone said they had seen you in this neighborhood. I assumed you lived nearby, so I had my driver bring me here every day, hoping I'd see you. It was only when you left the convenience store that I knew I was right." A smile spread across her face. "I must admit, at first I didn't recognize you, even though I've seen your photos in the papers."

"You have?" he said, surprised.

"Sure. I followed the Julia Seaborn and the Paul Gardener cases with great interest." Julia Seaborn's body was found underneath a bridge, and Paul Gardener was charged for the murder of his daughter. In both cases, Callaway was hired to find out the truth.

The woman pointed at his attire. "Why are you wearing that?"

Callaway looked down at his security guard uniform. He was not sure how to explain his current situation.

"I feel like I'm at a disadvantage," he said. "You know my name, but I don't know yours."

"I'm sorry, I should have introduced myself at the beginning. It's Isabel Gilford," she said.

"What do you want from me, Ms. Gilford?"

"It's Missus, but you can call me Isabel."

"Okay."

"Mr. Callaway…"

"Call me Lee."

"Lee, I believe my husband is cheating on me and I want you to confirm this for me."

Callaway laughed. "Let me give you some free advice. In my experience, if you feel your husband is being unfaithful, then the odds are that he is."

"How can you be so sure?" she asked.

"Spouses get suspicious *after* they start noticing a pattern they hadn't seen before. For instance, the other spouse is always leaving the room to take a call. Or the other spouse is taking longer and more frequent business trips. Or the other spouse is more distant or reserved than before. These are signs spouses pick up on very fast." He paused and then said, "Now, don't get me wrong. I'm not saying that if your husband is away for work longer than usual, that means he's definitely cheating. What I'm saying is that it could be a red flag that there is something going on with him, or that you and he need to sit down and talk about your relationship."

"I want proof," she said.

He stared at her and then at his watch. *I'm running late for work*, he thought. "I'm sorry, but I'm not taking on new clients."

"I am willing to pay twenty-five thousand dollars."

Callaway's heart nearly stopped. After lifting his chin from the floor, he said, "How much did you say?"

"Twenty-five thousand. All cash. All upfront."

He licked his lips and swallowed. A range of emotions suddenly raced through him. He knew that kind of money could make a significant impact on his life. But then he remembered why he had chosen to leave the PI life behind.

I'm doing this for Nina, he thought. *She needs a dad who will always be there for her. Not someone who doesn't know where the next paycheck will come from.*

He said, "I'm sure you can find other private investigators who will be willing to take on your case, but I'm closed for business."

She looked undeterred. She smiled and held out a piece of paper. "I am only interested in hiring *you*. My telephone number is on there. If you change your mind, give me a call."

He took the paper and exited the limousine.

THIRTY

Caroline Leary was sobbing uncontrollably. Fisher was seated next to her. They were in a room at the Milton PD. Holt had excused himself, leaving Fisher to console her on her own.

Caroline was Big Bob's daughter from his first marriage. She had shown up at the station unannounced, which was not uncommon in Fisher's line of work. Caroline was on the heavier side, with highlights in her hair, manicured fingernails, and dark eyeliner.

"I didn't know my dad was dead until I saw it on the news," she said.

"Your mother didn't tell you?" Fisher asked. Big Bob's ex-wife still lived in Milton.

She shook her head. "I spoke to her and even she didn't know. Suzanne should have told us—we are his family, after all—but she's nothing more than a gold digger."

Fisher took this as her opportunity and jumped in. "Do you think your stepmother might have had something to do with your father's death?"

Caroline looked at her. Her eyes were red and puffy. "I don't know, but I warned my dad to be careful."

"You two spoke regularly?"

"Sure, almost every other day. My dad and I were very close, but then I got married and moved to Connecticut because my husband is stationed there."

"He's in the military?"

"Yes."

"So, did your dad tell you he was going through a separation?"

"He did. And it wasn't amicable. He still loved her, but she didn't love him back. I don't think she ever did, but he was lonely, and he needed companionship, so she took advantage of him."

"I'm assuming you and your stepmother didn't get along?" Fisher asked.

Caroline's face hardened. "Like I said, I don't think she cared about my dad. She was in it for the money. She was much younger than him and, you know, she was attractive, and she knew it. She would try to make my dad jealous by talking to other guys so he would buy her whatever she wanted. He didn't want her to leave him."

"It's my understanding that they had an ironclad pre-nup."

"Thankfully, my dad listened to me and got *our* lawyer to draft one up. I told my dad if she didn't sign it and he still went ahead with the wedding, I'd never talk to him. My dad's stubborn, but I convinced him by showing him newspaper clippings of all the people who were killed by their spouses for their money."

"Is that why he never got life insurance?"

She nodded. "He refused it outright even when Suzanne pushed for it. She cried day and night about who would take care of her if something were to happen to him. But he held his ground. She eventually signed the pre-nup because she realized she would get nothing if she did not. I mean, her career wasn't going anywhere. She wasn't getting any younger, and she figured this was her chance. There aren't that many millionaire lottery winners in Milton, you know."

"So, she had nothing to gain financially from his death?" Fisher asked.

Caroline thought a moment. "I guess not."

After a brief pause, Fisher asked, "Did your dad have enemies?"

"Sure, lots," Caroline replied. "I mean, everyone was after him for his money."

"What about you? Did you ask him for money?"

Caroline fell silent. Her head fell to her chest. "I can't lie and say my dad didn't shower me with gifts. He paid for my wedding, he paid for my honeymoon, and he even helped us to buy a house. But I would *never* hurt my father for money." Her eyes welled up and Fisher saw genuine pain in them. "We were a happy family before he won the lottery. The money should have made our family stronger, but instead it broke us apart. Don't get me wrong, it did do a lot of good, but it also did a lot of harm, too. I would give it all up to have my dad back."

Caroline covered her face and began to sob again.

THIRTY-ONE

Callaway stood at the store's entrance. The place was relatively quiet. A few customers came in, browsed, and then left.

He suddenly found himself getting antsy. This happened whenever he was bored, and it was exactly how he felt when he left the sheriff's office. His current job was not ideal, but at least it paid enough to cover his expenses.

He had knocked on dozens of doors before an agency got him his current position, and it came at the right time. He was struggling to come up with the money to pay his hotel bill, and if he failed, he would have been out on the street.

I need this job until I can get my life in order, he thought.

He strolled around the store with his hands locked behind his back. An employee was folding clothes on a display table. She smiled at him. He smiled back.

He still did not know her name, and he doubted she knew his. She was a student who worked at the store during her days off from college. He noticed her staring at him, and on a few occasions, she even blushed when he stared back. She was cute. She had flawless skin, perfect teeth and there was an eagerness in her eyes.

Callaway had dated girls far younger than him, but he drew the line at college age. They were still in the process of finding themselves, and he did not want to be *that* older guy who took advantage of them.

He liked the attention, for sure. He still had a few good years left in him before no woman batted an eye in his direction. But right now, he was in no mood to chat with the girl.

His mind was preoccupied with the woman in the limousine. *Isabel Gilford.*

She had gone out of her way to speak to him. While he did not like her methods—even though *he* followed other people in his line of work—he was still impressed that she wanted to hire him.

Then there was the matter of the money. Twenty-five thousand dollars was a lot for a job that involved catching a cheating husband. He had done similar jobs for far less, sometimes for even a couple hundred dollars.

The woman had money she was willing to spend to satisfy her suspicions.

She was also willing to pay the entire fee up front. He would be stupid not to take the job.

But do I want to get sucked back into that life? he thought.

His situation reminded him of what recovering alcoholics went through trying to stay sober. They did not take a drink for days, weeks, or months, but when they saw their poison of choice, all sorts of questions would go through their minds.

How bad could one drink be?

What if I only took a sip?

Who would even know?

It was delusional to think such thoughts would not lead to more drinks or even going back to becoming a full-time alcoholic.

He shook his head.

He had finally taken a step in the right direction and he was not about to turn back.

THIRTY-TWO

Holt and Fisher were seated inside a poorly ventilated office. The space was small, and it felt even smaller with a desk and several chairs.

The man seated behind the desk was Ed Wallis, owner of Big Lot Autos, formerly Big Bob's Autos. The name was changed after Wallis purchased the place from Big Bob. It did not make sense to keep Big Bob's name on the sign when he was no longer involved in the business.

"I liked the location, so I bought it," Wallis said. "And the lot is big too. So, the new name fits perfectly, in my opinion."

Fisher asked, "Did Big Bob want to sell the dealership? I mean, the dealership had made him very popular around the city."

"I don't think he did," Wallis replied. "He loved the business and he loved cars. But after he won, he suddenly had other interests in life. From what I heard, he ended up investing in so many other businesses he had no experience with before."

Some of them were scams, Fisher thought.

Wallis said, "I think the real reason he sold it was so that his ex-wife, Joan, didn't get it during the divorce."

"She was also involved in the dealership?"

Wallis nodded. "What most people didn't see was that she was a big part of why the business was a success. Big Bob was the face of the dealership, but she was the heart of it. When customers came in, she made them feel like they were a part of her family. They trusted her, and they brought their friends, colleagues, and even strangers to purchase a car. She always joked that one day she'd change the name to 'Lady Joan's Lot.'"

"How did you end up buying it?" Fisher asked.

"I owned a dealership down the block. I'll confess, mine wasn't as successful as theirs, but I did okay. Big Bob would show up in my dealership and gloat about the number of cars he had sold that day or week. But a lot of the time, though, he came in just to talk. He wasn't the loudmouth he portrayed himself as in commercials. He actually cared about car business. He would give me a heads-up on people I should be wary of doing business with, or if there were other dealerships who were playing loose with the rules. Big Bob and I weren't friends, but he was friendly, you know. So, when I heard he was thinking of selling his dealership, I jumped at the opportunity. The price was right, and like I said, I thought his location was better than my old one."

"When was the last time you spoke to him?" Fisher asked.

"It was actually a couple of days ago. He sounded depressed, to be honest with you. He kind of wished he'd torn up that lottery ticket."

Fisher's eyes widened. "He said that?"

"Numerous times. I got the feeling he wanted things to go back to how they were before. He missed his life prior to winning all that money. After winning, Big Bob would drop by the dealership every so often to pick up a new vehicle. He always paid cash. He would tell the staff all these stories about his time owning the place. Before leaving, he'd always say that one day he'd buy the dealership back from me, and I'd always say it wasn't for sale. He'd grumble and say he'd open one across the street from me, but I knew he was joking. He just missed the place."

"You know anyone who'd want to hurt him?" Holt asked.

"No one at this dealership, I can tell you that," Wallis replied. "Big Bob made it cool to buy a used vehicle. I owe him a lot for what he did for the business."

THIRTY-THREE

Callaway was on his fifteen-minute break when he walked to a café in the mall. He bought a coffee and a donut. He found a bench and munched on the donut.

The morning had been uneventful. The store saw very few visitors. It was the middle of the week and business was slow as most people were still at work. Stay-at-home moms were their regular customers at this time of the day.

Even with the quiet, Callaway was battling a war inside his head. He could not stop thinking about the woman in the limousine and the twenty-five thousand.

He could do a lot with that much money.

It was odd that the moment he decided to walk away from his PI business, everyone wanted to hire him. He had received emails and voicemails from people inquiring about his services. Even Mason had summoned him to his office with an offer for a job. Callaway would think twice before agreeing to work for a man like him. Mason was a businessman, but Baxter was crazy and dangerous. There was no telling what he would do to Callaway if he got the chance.

Then there was Mrs. Gilford.

How long will she wait for my reply? he thought.

He knew she wanted *him* for the job, but he also knew people with money were not known for their patience. They were used to getting whatever they wanted, and fast. If he took his time, she would surely look elsewhere.

He pulled out the piece of paper she had given him. The telephone number was scribbled in blue ink.

A part of him wanted to dial the number and tell her he was taking the job. But then he looked down at his watch. His fifteen minutes were up. He finished the donut, downed the coffee, and returned to the store.

He spent the next hour strolling the aisles. He was still trying to talk himself out of taking the job when he saw a woman down the aisle. The woman was in her mid-forties, with streaks of gray in her hair, and a large handbag swung over one shoulder. She was constantly looking around to see if the coast was clear. She had not seen him yet, so he watched her from a distance.

She removed a price tag from one item and placed it on another. He could not make his move just yet. He wanted to see what she did next.

She headed for the cashier.

Callaway approached her.

"Ma'am," he said as professionally as possible. "Are you purchasing that item?"

She nodded. "I am."

"Then you must know it is fraudulent to switch price tags." He was not sure if this was true, but he was certain it was wrong.

"I did no such thing," she huffed.

"I saw you. I was down the aisle when you did it."

Meanwhile, the cashier stared at them in horror. She was hoping the situation did not escalate.

The woman put her hand on her hip. "Are you accusing me of something?"

"No, I'm just saying..."

She pointed a finger at him. "You got no proof."

"We have cameras in the store. They'll show that you switched the tags."

The woman's face turned red. She turned to the cashier, who looked like a deer caught in the headlights. "I want to speak to the manager," the woman demanded.

The cashier instantly picked up the phone and spoke a few words. A moment later, the manager emerged from a door in the back of the store.

"How can I help you?" she asked with a smile.

The woman pointed to Callaway and said, "This man is accusing me of a crime."

Callaway put his hands up in defense. "All I said was that I saw her switch price tags from one item to another."

"And I told him I didn't do it," the woman shot back.

The manager's smile never wavered. "That's alright, ma'am. Why don't we checkout your purchases?"

Callaway could not believe it. The cashier entered the price on the tag, and the manager gave her an additional ten percent off for her troubles.

The woman then turned to him. "You should stop harassing honest people and get a real job."

Callaway was seething. He had to grit his teeth from saying something he might regret.

After the woman left the store, the manager said to him, "Next time you see someone switch tags, don't confront them."

"But you just lost money on that item," he said, baffled. "She switched it with a lower price tag."

"They do that all the time."

"And you don't do anything about it?"

"What can we do?" she replied. "The customer is always right."

Callaway's head was spinning. "If I see something improper, I'm not supposed to take any remedial action?"

"That's right."

"Then what am I doing here?" he asked.

"You're supposed to stand in the corner and keep your mouth shut," the manager replied.

That's it, Callaway thought.

He shoved his hand in his pocket and pulled out a card. He held the card out for her.

She was confused, but she still took the card. "Lee Callaway Private Investigations?" she read aloud.

"That's right," he proudly said. "When you are ready, give me a call. I'll give you a discount."

"Why would I need a private investigator?"

"Last week I saw your husband waiting for you in the parking lot. Right before you arrived, he was on the phone with someone. It wasn't hard to tell he was talking to a woman."

The manager's face hardened. "You can't accuse my husband…"

"I think I heard him call her Shelley," Callaway interjected.

The blood drained from the manager's face. "That's his ex-girlfriend's name."

Callaway headed for the door.

"Where are you going?" she said.

"I quit," he replied, and left.

THIRTY-FOUR

Big Bob's ex wife lived in an affluent neighborhood where all the houses were gated, had French windows, and a manicured lawn. Unlike her ex-husband's gaudy mansion, hers was elegant and sophisticated.

After introducing themselves, Holt and Fisher were lead to a room with a brown sectional sofa, a fireplace, and a coffee table made of marble.

Joan Burley looked like she had just returned from the salon. Her hair was permed, her eyebrows were waxed, and her face was shiny and smooth.

"Can I get you guys anything to drink?" she asked as a good host.

Holt and Fisher declined.

"We have to ask you some questions regarding your ex-husband," Fisher said.

"You can ask whatever you want about Robert," she replied.

"You don't call him Big Bob?" Fisher asked.

"Everyone did except for me. I knew him before he became Big Bob. We saw each other in high school, but we never dated. While I was in college, we met up through a mutual friend. Robert never pursued a higher education. After finishing high school, he started working for his uncle's dealership. He had a knack for salesmanship. If you came to the dealership only *thinking* about buying a car, by the time you left, you had already bought one. He made you feel like he was doing you a favor by selling you a car. The customers always went away happy."

"We found out you were also involved in the business," Fisher said.

Joan nodded. "Once we got married, Robert planned to open his own dealership, but we didn't have the money. But Robert was undeterred. He waited for his time, which was almost two years later. His uncle was considering selling his dealership when Robert worked out a deal with him. He would take out a loan from his uncle and buy the dealership. He would then spend the next ten years paying back the loan plus interest. But with Robert's enthusiasm, we paid the loan back in half that time. Once the dealership was ours, the sky was the limit."

"I heard you wanted to take over the dealership?" Fisher asked.

"I did," Joan replied. "I loved that place as much as Robert did. I actually loved the people who worked there even more. Our receptionist had been with us since the time we took over. Some of the salespeople were with us for years. When I say it was like a family, I mean it."

Fisher said, "Why didn't your husband let you have it? I mean, he was already looking to sell it?"

Holt knew where Fisher was going with this. She wanted a motive. Did Joan Burley kill her husband out of spite? The murder had hints of a crime of passion.

Joan looked down at her hands. "We were a team, he and I. We weren't struggling or living paycheck to paycheck. We were successful. But the moment he got his hands on *all* that money, he suddenly became a different man. It was like all his demons came out. He bought things he didn't need. He started building that eyesore of a house." Joan shook her head. "I even caught him going to strip clubs."

"But that still doesn't explain why he wouldn't let you have the dealership," Fisher prodded.

Joan said, "A year after we won, someone took a photo of Robert passed out drunk in front of a bar. It ended up in the newspapers. When a reporter came to our house, I told him how I wished we never won that money. Robert read what I said, and he was furious. We had a big fight. By then we were going at each other. I didn't like what he was turning into. I told him we should give the money away as it was bringing us nothing but bad luck, like the universe was punishing us for something we did. I remember he quieted down, and then the next day he sold the dealership to Ed. It was soon after that we separated."

"After your divorce, you received half the winnings. Why didn't *you* give it away?" Holt asked.

"I did, almost all of it," Joan replied. "This house and my living expenses are paid for from the money I received when we sold the dealership, from the sales of our old house, and from any joint assets we had during our marriage. I wanted nothing to do with that God-forsaken lottery money. I knew it would destroy us as a family, and I guess in the end it destroyed Robert."

Holt glanced over at Fisher. He knew she was thinking what he was.

Money was one of the biggest motivators for murder. Jealousy was second. The third was revenge. Prior to coming here, they hoped to fit Joan into at least one of those categories.

Money was not a factor in this case. Joan had given most of it away. And also, as per the law, she did receive half of her husband's winnings during the divorce, which was enough to take care of her.

Maybe she was jealous that her husband had found a younger wife. But why kill him after all these years, especially when he was separating from his second wife? It did not make sense.

But what about revenge?

Holt asked, "Didn't it make you angry that instead of selling the dealership to you, your ex-husband sold it to someone else?"

"I was very upset about it. I hated Robert for what he did. It was another reason why I sold everything from my previous life that would remind me of my time with Robert. And also…"

Her voice trailed off.

Holt sat up straight. "Also, what?"

"I'm not sure if Ed told you this, but he and I are in a relationship," she replied, sounding a little embarrassed. "He's a good man. He's honest and hardworking. Sometimes I'll go to the dealership. Ed's retained some of our old staff, so it's nice to see them again. But I don't go there often. I prefer to keep our relationship private." She paused to collect her thoughts. "Even though Robert hurt me badly, no one deserves to die like he did."

Holt and Fisher thanked Joan for her time and left.

THIRTY-FIVE

The first thing Callaway did after leaving the mall was go straight to a bar. He needed a drink to steady his nerves. He had made a lot of effort to get the security guard position. He had to interview at an employment agency, pass some standardized competency tests, wait for a position to become available, and then apply. And now he had thrown all that away in an instant. He did not have a degree he could fall back on, and his skills as a private eye did not transfer from one job to another.

He pulled a stool up to the bar and ordered a drink. He downed his drink and ordered another. Halfway through the second glass, he started to feel better.

This is the right decision, he thought. *I wasn't going to last long at the store anyway.*

Sooner or later something would have pushed him to quit. The woman who changed the price tags was just a catalyst. He was waiting for someone like her to give him a reason to go back to what he loved.

I'm a private investigator, dammit!

He looked at the time. It was still too early to get drunk. He had work to do.

He dialed the number on the piece of paper, and after saying a few words, he hung up.

He was slowly sipping the remainder of his drink when his phone buzzed. He answered, and then he left the bar.

The familiar limousine was parked across the road. He walked over and got in the back seat.

Isabel Gilford had a smile on her face. "I'm so glad you changed your mind."

He shrugged. "Yeah, well, you made an offer I couldn't refuse."

Isabel placed her hand in her purse and pulled out a thick envelope. "So, how does this work?" she asked.

"First, you tell me something about your husband," Callaway replied.

"What would you like to know?"

"His name would be nice."

"Of course. It's Cary Gilford."

"What does your husband do?"

"He is president and C.E.O. of Gilford Investments."

Callaway searched his memory. He never heard of that company.

Isabel said, "It's a private equity firm. They have a portfolio of two hundred and fifty million dollars. It's relatively small compared to some other firms. They specialize in natural resources such as oil, crude gas, and shale."

"How long have you and your husband been married?" Callaway asked.

She stared at him. "Why is that important?"

"It's not, I suppose, but it gives me a better idea of who I'm dealing with."

"We've been married over twenty years."

"Children?"

"Two."

"Ages."

She paused again. "Nineteen and seventeen. But please don't ask me their names. It's no one's business."

Callaway nodded. "That's fair. Do you know who your husband is having an affair with?"

"His assistant."

"Okay. Have you seen them together?"

"Of course."

"You have?" He suddenly wondered why she was even hiring him.

"As his assistant, she has to work closely with my husband and this has caused major arguments in our relationship."

"What do you mean?"

"As a wife, I can sense when my husband is not being honest with me. I have confronted him to find out if he is sleeping with her. He has denied it. He always says she is an invaluable employee of the firm. I've asked him to fire her."

"Why?"

"She's young and attractive."

"What did she do prior to becoming your husband's assistant?"

Isabel paused a moment. "She used to be an actress," she replied.

"Have I heard of her?"

"Likely not. She starred in a few movies."

"What's her name?"

She hesitated.

"I need to know all the parties involved," Callaway said.

"Jackie Wolfe."

He frowned. "Jackie Wolfe?"

"It might be her stage name, I'm not sure. But that's what I've heard my husband call her."

"Okay. Where can I find your husband?"

Mrs. Gilford smiled. She handed him the money. "The address is on the envelope."

THIRTY-SIX

Chad Fenwick was a large man with a heavy beard and long hair that fell down the back of his neck. He was wearing a dark-colored sweatshirt, jeans, and army-style boots. He looked every bit like a private security specialist.

He stood next to his black Hummer with his arms crossed over his wide chest. He had still not taken off his sunglasses, which annoyed Holt, but not Fisher.

She knew people like Chad tried to exude authority by *looking* intimidating. This was something they were taught in some class run by an ex-Navy SEAL or ex-Marine. They had already found out Chad was neither a former SEAL nor Marine. In his previous life, he was a door-to-door insurance salesman. But then one day he had an epiphany that the world was a dangerous place and that he—Chad Fenwick—had to do something to protect its citizens. And so Chadcore Security Specialists was born.

Fisher was not sure why Big Bob had hired someone like Chad to protect his home. Maybe Big Bob liked Chad's salesmanship—something he had picked up selling insurance, or maybe he liked Chad and saw something of himself in him. Regardless, when Holt and Fisher contacted the security company listed on the sign on the property, Chad showed up at the Milton PD in his Hummer.

"When did Mr. Burley hire your company?" Holt asked.

"Right after he was robbed," Chad replied. "I heard about it on the radio when it happened. I knew *I* could help protect Big Bob."

"What kind of a client was he?" Fisher asked.

Chad looked confused.

Fisher said, "Was he careless or reckless when it came to security?"

"At first he was careful. He was pretty shaken up about what happened. It's not every day normal folks have a gun pulled on them."

"Have you?" Holt asked.

"Have I what?" Chad asked back.

"Had a gun pulled on you?"

Chad straightened up. "Yeah, of course I've had a gun pulled on me."

"In training or in real life?"

Fisher could tell Holt was waiting for the chance to test Chad.

"In training, but if it happened in real life, I know how to handle myself," Chad said.

"Right," Holt said, not believing him. Chad was a wannabe tough-guy, whereas Holt was tougher-than-nails.

Fisher decided to jump in. She did not want this to turn into a pissing contest. "You said at first Big Bob took security seriously, but then what happened?"

"After a year or two, he became relaxed. There were many times I could see that he was not at home and the security system had not been activated."

"What would you do during those times?"

"I would contact Big Bob, and if I couldn't get him, I would drive by the house to make sure everything was okay."

Fisher was surprised. "You do that for all your clients?"

"Most of my clients live in—let's say—more affluent neighborhoods. So, once a day I drive through the neighborhood to make sure the clients are following security protocols."

Fisher raised an eyebrow. "Security protocols?"

Chad nodded. "Locking all doors and gates. Keeping the shades down on all the windows when they are not home. Making sure someone is picking up their mail while they are on vacation. Stuff like that."

"Doesn't your security stop criminals?" Holt asked.

Chad shrugged. "It's more of a deterrent. For instance, if a burglar knows exactly what they are looking for in the house, then it becomes sort of like a smash and grab. By the time the police arrive, they are already gone."

"So, you also drive by Big Bob's property?"

"I do. But unfortunately, he built his house in a neighborhood I would have advised against."

She understood what he was saying. The neighborhood had a higher crime rate.

Chad said, "But there is no way for someone to break into a property and disable the system from the inside. It's not possible."

Fisher mulled this over. "The alarm system was off at the time of Big Bob's attack, is that correct?" she asked.

"Yes. He turned it off once he returned home."

"So, if the alarm was off and he was home, do you think Big Bob let his attacker inside the house?"

"I would have to say, yes," Chad replied.

THIRTY-SEVEN

Callaway returned to his office feeling like he was on some psychedelic drug. Everything looked vivid, almost colorful. His senses were heightened. He could almost smell and taste the air.

He knew why he was feeling this way. He was a private investigator again.

He had not broken the news to Nina and Patti yet. He would do so the moment he got the chance. They were taken aback when he had first told them about the security guard position. Patti was skeptical at first, but she quickly came around to his new job when she saw how serious he was. Nina was elated that she would get to see him more often. Now she and her mom would be disappointed he had quit. Patti would even say, "I knew it wouldn't last long." But the moment he would tell them about the twenty-five thousand dollars, everything would be okay—at least he hoped it would.

He shut the office door and locked it. He moved the laptop off his desk and pulled out the envelope from his pocket. He then proceeded to slowly and carefully count the cash. When he was done, there were two hundred and fifty $100 bills

He suddenly felt light-headed. He could not believe this was happening to him. One moment he was arguing with shoppers for minimum wage and the next moment he had on him as much as a year's worth of salary for the average person.

Contrary to what most people thought, the movies got it right when they portrayed private eyes as down-on-their-luck shmucks. The work was unglamorous and often dull. The pay was peanuts when compared to the hours spent on a case. And sometimes being a PI was even dangerous.

What the movies got wrong was that every client was a femme fatale who needed a knight in shining armor to get her out of her predicament.

Callaway had bedded a dozen clients, but most of them were older and in control, not the damsels in distress the movies made them out to be.

He heard a noise that sounded like feet hitting metal.

He jumped out of his chair.

Someone's coming up the stairs!

He looked at the stack of bills on the desk.

Did someone see me with the money? That's not possible. I kept it in my coat pocket the entire time.

He pulled the desk drawer open and removed his gun. He had a licence for concealed weapons, but he preferred not to carry the gun with him. He did not often need the weapon for protection.

Right now, was a different case.

He heard a key being inserted into the lock and then the door handle being turned. He jumped up and grabbed the handle. When the door opened, he was right there to block anyone from entering.

"Ms. Chen," he said, relieved. "What are you doing here?"

Ms. Chen was his landlady. She was short, slim, and Asian. She wore a pastel-colored dress, flat shoes, and her hair was pulled back in a ponytail.

"What are *you* doing here?" she asked.

"Where would I be? I'm in my office."

"I thought you got another job," she said. "Don't you work during the day?"

"I do."

Her eyes widened. "Why do you have a gun?"

He realized he was aiming the pistol at her. He quickly hid the firearm behind his back.

He then noticed an Indian man standing next to her.

"Who's he?" he asked.

"This is Mr. Sharma," Ms. Chen replied with a smile. "He wants to open a bookkeeping and accounting office."

Callaway remembered. He had already given notice to his landlady. He remembered her being elated at the prospect of him leaving. He could not blame her. He was never a good tenant to begin with.

"I'm not leaving," he said.

The smile fell from her face. Her voice became hard. "Why? What happened?"

He shrugged. "Nothing happened. I'm back in business."

She was clearly disappointed. Mr. Sharma looked like a nice, hardworking man who would not only use her property for what it was intended for—as an office—he would also pay his rent on time.

Whenever Callaway was kicked out of his home for one reason or another, he would always crash at the office. The place did not have a shower, which meant after a few days of him living there, the place would reek of body odors. He always used the toilet at the 24-hour gas station across the street when the need occurred, though.

Whenever he was short on money, he would make himself scarce, which annoyed his landlady when she came to pick up rent.

"Mr. Sharma wants to move in next month," Ms. Chen said.

"I haven't decided," Mr. Sharma quickly said. "I haven't even seen it."

Ms. Chen turned to him. "Can we come inside?"

He thought about the stack of money on the desk. "Give me one minute."

He shut the door and put the gun back in the drawer. He then counted a few hundred-dollar bills and returned to the door. He held the money out to her.

"What's this?" she asked, staring at the money.

"It's next month's rent, and for the month after as well."

Her jaw nearly hit the floor. She quickly recovered and then snatched the money from his hand. She then turned to Mr. Sharma. "I'm sorry, but the office is no longer available for rent."

Mr. Sharma did not look too heartbroken. He probably figured if the old tenant carried a gun, this place must not be safe.

Callaway shut the door, locked it, and then sat back at his desk. He then smiled and began counting the money once again.

THIRTY-EIGHT

Holt and Fisher were on their way to the station when they received the call. Fisher turned the SUV around and drove in the opposite direction.

The house was made of brown stone. The home had a courtyard in front, a white picket fence, and a triangular roof. Holt and Fisher parked next to a Porsche Cayenne and approached the front door. Before they could even ring the doorbell, the door swung open.

Suzanne Burley was wearing a white gown. Her blonde hair was pulled back into a bun and she had on little or no makeup.

"Please, come in," she said.

They followed her down the hall and to the living room. Like her previous house, the décor was all over the place. The furniture did not match the paint on the wall, and the artwork on the wall did not match the theme of the room.

"What's the emergency?" Fisher asked. On the phone Suzanne sounded exasperated and angry. She wanted Fisher and Holt to come over right away.

Suzanne took a deep breath to compose herself. "I had my lawyer look into the pre-nup again. I wanted to make sure we didn't miss anything in it."

"Like what?"

"Prior to signing the pre-nup, I had Big Bob put in clauses that if the marriage lasted ten years, I would get something additional, fifteen years, then something more, and so on. It was a way to protect me further. I mean, I was not going to invest so much into this marriage and after twenty years not have enough to last me into my old age, you know."

"And?" Holt impatiently asked.

"There was also a clause that if Big Bob was the one to end the marriage, then I would receive a bigger share of his assets. With Big Bob dead, *he* ended the marriage, you see."

"But he was murdered," Fisher said.

"I know, but like I said, I now have to look out for myself," Suzanne said.

100

When it came to money, love or death was no longer a priority. The only thing that mattered was: "*I get what's mine.*" Even though Suzanne Burley and Big Bob were separated at the time of his demise, it was not legally formalized, which meant she was looking at all angles to see if she could get an even bigger payout than what she already got being married to a millionaire lottery winner.

"I don't know how this helps our investigation," Holt said with a scowl.

"Oh, right," she said, suddenly realizing her error. "While my lawyer was going through the legal documents, he discovered that Big Bob had amended his personal will."

Now, this is interesting, Fisher thought. "And why did he do that?" she asked.

"His original will named his law firm as the executors of his estate with the beneficiaries being his son and daughter."

Fisher glanced over at Holt. *We still have to speak to his son*, she thought. Holt caught her drift.

"I knew I was not named in it," Suzanne continued. "I was hoping I was, but neither was Big Bob's first wife, Joan. So, I didn't feel too bad, but then in the amended will I found another name added."

"Who is it?" Holt asked.

"I don't recognize the name, but I think I have an idea. I had caught Big Bob cozying up to a waitress who worked at a restaurant he went to regularly. I even spotted her in his car one time, and when I confronted him about it, he said he was giving her a ride to her house."

Fisher's brow furrowed. "You think your husband was having an affair with this waitress?"

"I think so, yes."

"Was this the reason for your separation?"

She shrugged. "There were other issues too."

"Do you know the waitress's name?" Holt asked.

She shook her head.

"Then give us the name on the amended will."

THIRTY-NINE

Gilford Investments was located on the twenty-first floor of a glass and steel tower. Callaway was parked across the street with an unobstructed view of the building. He had located the place via a quick internet search. The photo of Cary Gilford showed him wearing a light blue blazer, white shirt, and no tie. A handkerchief neatly folded in his front jacket pocket completed the ensemble. His hair was slicked back, he was clean shaven, and his smile revealed pearly white teeth.

Gilford exuded the aura of a confidant and trustworthy investor, but Callaway had no faith when it came to bank managers, investment advisors, stockbrokers, or even insurance salespeople. They were all out to get *his* money, plain and simple. He barely had any savings, so he had no money to invest, but he knew people who lost everything from bad advice, high commissions, and unnecessary fees.

The financial market was a complex beast, one he was not qualified to put his foot in. Unfortunately, people who professed to know what they were doing were not qualified either. If they did, then *every* investment would be a home run. Some stocks went up from little market pressures, while other stocks went down for no apparent reason.

If you asked Callaway, investing was a crapshoot. That was why he preferred to keep his money in cash. True, he risked losing his money via robbery or disaster, and his funds never grew while they sat in his coat pocket, but he did not care. He liked to keep his money close to him. Plus, there was the matter of taxes. Callaway had not filed a tax return in years. If the IRS ever audited him, they would find no bank accounts and thus no deposits. If they chose to seek him out, he had moved so many times that it would be a difficult task. And even if they did end up finding him, once they saw the condition of his office and his rental accommodations, they would surely close his file without an assessment.

Callaway lived on the fringes of society. He was a man with no fixed address and no social ties. But he did have family.

What if the feds came knocking on Patti's door? he thought. *What if they go after Patti for my unpaid taxes?*

He shook his head. He was being paranoid. He and Patti had been divorced for many years now and his problems were his only. She was constantly getting him out all sorts of predicaments, however. The very first time he was evicted from his home, she let him store all his belongings in her garage. When he owed money to a nasty loan shark (not named Mason), she let him hide at her house. But in hindsight, hiding at her place was a dumb and dangerous move. There was no telling what the loan shark would have done had he tracked Callaway down at her house.

He checked his watch. So far, Gilford had not come out of the building. Fortunately, the employee parking was next to the steel tower, clearly visible from his vantage point.

Callaway hoped to catch a glimpse of Gilford soon.

FORTY

The restaurant was on the corner of a busy intersection. It had a large glowing sign on the roof with the word DINER on it.

Fisher had been to quite a few diners in her life, and according to her they all looked the same. It was as if the same designer designed all of them. They had the red leather seats, narrow tables and booths, red stools and counters, and black-and-white checkered floors.

Some diners had swapped the red for pastel blue, but even then, the interior did not deviate too far from other diners.

Holt and Fisher spoke to the owner, a wrinkled man who looked to be in his sixties and were informed that Sasha Turbin had not come into work.

Sasha Turbin was the new name in Big Bob's will. Suzanne Burley was correct when she said she believed Sasha Turbin was the same woman she had seen Big Bob cozying up to.

The owner then gave them Turbin's address. A twenty-five-minute drive led them to a tan brick apartment building. They took the elevator to the eighth floor. They knocked on a door to an apartment and waited.

A few minutes later, a woman answered. She had a light brown complexion, curly jet-black hair, and full lips. Her emerald green eyes were raw, and her eyelids were puffy.

"Can I help you?" she said.

"Sasha Turbin?" Fisher asked.

She nodded.

Holt and Fisher flashed their badges as Fisher said, "We would like to ask you a few questions about Robert Burley."

Sasha's eyes welled up at the sound of Big Bob's name.

"Can we come inside?" Fisher asked.

Sasha held the door for them, and they entered. The apartment was sparsely furnished. There was a single couch in the living room with a TV on a stand across from it. A small table was in the corner with two chairs. A couple of photos were hung on the wall. They were all of a young Sasha with an African-American woman.

"That's my mom," Sasha said as Fisher stared at it.

"She's beautiful," Fisher said.

"Yeah, she was."

"Was?"

"She died of a brain aneurysm two years ago. It was sudden. She was working at the diner when…"

"The same diner you now work at?" Fisher asked.

"Yeah, she got me the job. She had a severe headache all morning, but she never complained to anyone. It wasn't like her to make a big fuss. She was a proud woman who worked hard. She kept spilling coffee whenever she was trying to fill a customer's cup, so George…

"Who?"

"The owner of the diner."

"Okay."

"George realized something was not right. He drove her to the emergency room, where they found the blood vessels that went to the brain had swelled. They cut out a piece of her skull to reduce the pressure. Then they placed her in an induced coma for a month. Her condition stabilized, and I thought she would make it through, but then one day she just…"

Her words trailed off.

Fisher let the silence hang for a minute. She could see that even after all these years, it was painful for Sasha to talk about what happened to her mom.

Sasha said, "We didn't even have health insurance."

Fisher knew the answer, but she still had to ask. "Who paid for her care?"

"Big Bob."

"Why would he do that?"

"He had been coming to the diner for years, even before I started working there. When he found out what happened to my mom, he wanted to help. He was a wonderful man."

"Is that why you were crying?"

Fisher pointed to a pile of crumpled tissues on the couch.

Sasha nodded. "I can't believe someone would want to kill him."

"Mrs. Burley said she saw you in Big Bob's car. Were you and he…?"

Sasha was horrified. "Oh no. Nothing like that ever happened between us. I mean, he was old enough to be my father."

"So, what was your relationship?" Fisher asked.

"We were friends," Sasha replied. "He would come to the restaurant and ask for me. He tipped well, and he was generous. He gave me five-thousand dollars, so I could pursue my degree in social services."

"Did he give you anything else?"

"He tried to buy me a car, and furniture, but I thought the five-thousand was more than enough. I didn't want him to think we were friends because he bought me stuff, you know."

"Were you aware that Big Bob had included your name in his will?" Fisher asked.

Sasha's eyes widened. "Why would he do that?"

"That's what we wanted to ask you."

"I have no idea. I really don't. I mean, I was nobody to him."

Fisher had a strong feeling that was not true.

FORTY-ONE

At lunch time, Callaway watched a stream of people leave the office tower. He hoped he did not miss seeing Gilford, but even if he did, he could always come back.

There was still so much he did not know about his target. What was his daily routine? Who were his friends? What were his hobbies?

All this was useful information in his investigation. The daily routine would allow him to track his target more easily. He would know where his target would be at a given time. By knowing more about his social circle, Callaway would know who he hung around with. What if they were helping the target hide the affair from his spouse? If that was the case, then Callaway's job would become trickier. The hobbies would let Callaway know about the target's interests. Did he play tennis? Did he go to the gym? Did he like to gamble? He could use this to find out if he met his mistress at any of those locations.

He watched as more people came out of the building. He did not want to lose the opportunity, so he got out of the Charger and approached the main entrance. He found a lamppost adjacent to the doors and casually leaned against it as if he was waiting for someone.   Ten minutes later, he spotted him—no, *them*!

Cary Gilford was wearing a dark suit and polished shoes. He looked just like the photo on his website. Next to him was a woman. She was wearing heels, a skirt, and a blouse. Her blonde hair was short, almost resembling a boyish cut. She wore bright red lipstick, and she was smiling.

Is that the assistant Mrs. Gilford was referring to? he thought. *The woman whom she believes her husband is having an affair with?*

Callaway had to be sure. He diverted his attention to someone else in case they looked his way.

Fortunately, they turned right and headed for the parking lot. Callaway followed them until he saw them reach a white Audi parked a short distance away. They entered the vehicle together.

Callaway's brow furrowed. They were not trying to be discreet with their affair.

He raced back to his Charger and got behind the wheel. He waited until the Audi pulled out of the parking lot before he followed. He trailed behind them for a good five blocks until they entered a plaza. They parked in front of a Thai restaurant. They got out and went inside. A few minutes later, they appeared at a table by the windows.

Callaway parked the Charger and pulled out his camera. He zoomed in and began snapping photos of Gilford and his assistant.

He smiled as a thought occurred to him.

This is the easiest twenty-five thousand I'll ever make.

FORTY-TWO

Holt and Fisher were back at the Milton PD.

Fisher said, "You won't believe this."

"What?" Holt asked.

Fisher was staring at her laptop. "Guess who worked for Big Bob over twenty years ago?"

Holt frowned. "Who?"

"Sasha Turbin's mother, Gloria Cole."

"How did you find that out?"

"I did an online search for her name and scanned through the images that popped up. I noticed one that resembled her from the photo I'd seen at Sasha's apartment. When I clicked on it, it took me to an article from the Milton *Inquirer* regarding the grand opening of Big Bob's Autos. Gloria was apparently one of the dealership's original employees."

Fisher turned the laptop around so that Holt could get a better look. In the photo, Big Bob was standing next to his then-wife, Joan, and next to them were three men dressed in suits and one woman who was clearly Gloria Cole. All six individuals were smiling for the camera.

Fisher said, "I think Big Bob is Sasha's father."

Holt did not look convinced.

"Listen," she said. "Sasha is a child of an interracial couple…"

"How can you be certain?"

"You saw the photos of Sasha with her mother. Sasha's complexion is lighter compared to her mother's. Also, there were no photos of her father anywhere. I bet Big Bob had an affair with Gloria Cole and it produced a child. I don't think Sasha is aware of this, and with her mother gone there is no one to confirm it. On top of that, why would Big Bob pay for Sasha's school? Because he knows the truth. And don't forget, he also paid for Gloria Cole's medical bills while she was in the hospital."

Holt scratched his chin. "Okay, but what does this have to do with our investigation?"

"I'm not sure, but what if someone found out Big Bob had another child and they confronted him with this information."

"Why would they do that?"

"For money, of course. Maybe they tried to blackmail him, and if he didn't pay up, they threatened to expose him."

Holt was still not convinced. "The affair was years ago. Robert Burley was divorced from his first wife and was in the process of divorcing his second. The revelation he had a child out of wedlock would have done him no harm in my opinion."

Fisher was silent. She then grabbed the phone on her desk and dialed a number.

"Who are you calling?"

"You'll see." Fisher put the call on speaker and waited as the phone rang.

"Hello?" a voice said.

"Joan Burley?" Fisher asked.

"Yes."

"This is Detective Fisher from the Milton Police Department. Do you mind if I asked you a few questions?"

"Um, I guess so."

"Did a woman by the name of Gloria Cole work at the dealership when you owned it?"

"She was our receptionist. She was with us for less than two years, I think."

"Do you know why she left?"

There was silence on the other end.

"Mrs. Burley?"

"Messner."

"Sorry."

"It's Messner now. My maiden name."

"Ms. Messner," Fisher said, "why did Gloria Cole leave your dealership?"

There was an audible sigh on the other end. "I caught Robert having an affair with her." Fisher gave Holt an *I-told-you-so* look.

"We had just opened the dealership and things were tough. The business didn't take off right away, so Robert was under intense pressure. He apologized for the affair and took full responsibility. I was angry, like any wife would be, but I had two young children at the time and the dealership was everything to us. I loved Robert, and I made him pay Gloria to make her go away. After that I never saw her again."

"Did you know she was still living in Milton?"

"I did, but like I said, I never saw her again."

Fisher paused. She then said, "Were you aware Gloria Cole had a child with your ex-husband?"

Fisher expected a gasp or an angry outburst, but instead, Joan calmly said, "I was aware of this."

"And you were still okay with this during your marriage?" Fisher asked.

"I wasn't okay with it," Joan replied. "How can you be, knowing your husband fathered a child with another woman? But you can choose to live with it, which is what I did."

"Did anyone else know about this?"

"It was a secret only Robert, myself, and Gloria knew."

Two out of the three were dead, and if Joan Burley did not take any action against her husband when the affair had occurred, why would she do it now?

They had hit another dead end.

FORTY-THREE

Once Gilford and his assistant had returned to the office tower, Callaway decided to end his stakeout. He had enough photos of them together to prove to his client that they were indeed in a relationship.

In one photo Callaway had caught them leaning close, as if they were sharing an intimate moment. In another, he captured them in mid-laugh, as if Gilford had said something which his assistant had found amusing. And in yet another, Gilford had his arm out, as if he was holding his assistant's hand.

As far as Callaway was concerned, his job was done.

He decided to stopover at a cell phone shop. He spoke to the sales rep, who showed him a half a dozen smartphones and their wireless plans. He was so overwhelmed that he chose whatever model the sales rep recommended, and he signed up for the best data plan money could buy. He paid cash and headed straight for Patti's house.

He was excited when he rang the doorbell.

Patricia "Patti" Callaway opened the door. She had short dark hair, brown eyes, and her lips were always curled in a smile. Patti could spot a lie from a mile away. Callaway could bullshit many people, but not Patti. He had learned early on to be straight with her. It was not easy. There were many things he could not tell her while they were married. So instead of outright lying to her, he would avoid answering her questions, which, in essence, was the same as being untruthful. But this was the only option he had if he wanted to keep some form of relationship with her.

Every time Callaway saw her, his heart skipped a beat. She still had that power over him. He could not believe he had walked away from her. All throughout their marriage, he kept thinking he did not deserve her. He did not, but that still did not mean he should not have tried harder to be a good husband. She was the best thing that ever happened to him.

"Nina's at her friend's house," Patti said, leaning on the door with her arms crossed over her chest.

"Oh," he replied, feeling disappointed.

"How's the new job?" she asked.

Did she hear about the Gilford case? he thought. *But how?*

"Nina told me you got her a doll," Patti said. "You picked it up from the store you work as a security guard at. Isn't that right?"

"The store I *used* to work as a security guard."

"So, you quit?"

"I wasn't cut out for it."

"You got a new case instead?"

His mouth nearly dropped. "How did you know?"

"I didn't, but I know *you*. How much does this one pay?"

He hesitated.

"Don't worry," she said. "I'm not going to ask you for child support."

He paused and then asked, "Does the house need repairs?"

There was always something wrong at the house. If it was not the plumbing, then it was electrical, or the shingles needed to be replaced after the last thunderstorm. He may be a nonexistent father, but he did help occasionally.

"No, everything is fine. I'm just worried you'll throw all your money at some—" she made air quotes with her fingers— "investment opportunity."

"I'm going to be extra careful." He then changed the subject. "Do you know when Nina will be back?"

"In an hour."

He frowned. He then held up a plastic bag for her. "I got this for Nina."

"What is it?"

"It's a cell phone. She told me she wanted one."

Patti said, "Nina had already asked me, and I told her no."

"Why?"

"She's only nine, Lee."

"Won't it be safe for her to have one? In case she needs to get in touch with you in an emergency?"

"When we were growing up, we didn't have cell phones, and we managed to stay safe."

He scratched his head. "I don't know why you are being so rigid about this."

"I'm not being rigid. I'm being a mother. Nina's too young to take on this responsibility."

"It's only a cell phone."

"It's also dangerous."

"Dangerous?"

"Haven't you heard of sexting?"

Callaway turned pale. "Um… I don't think she's into that stuff yet."

"She may not be, but some boys might be. There was a girl in her school who was blackmailed by a boy into sending him photos of her naked. That girl had to change schools because she couldn't take the embarrassment."

Callaway's mouth went dry. He could not imagine anything like that happening to his little girl.

"It's a dangerous world out there," Patti said. "You wouldn't believe how many girls have come into the hospital after they tried to take their own life because of all the pressure from the bullies at school."

Patti worked as a nurse at the Milton General Hospital. She had more life experience than the average person. Birth and deaths were a daily occurrence, along with finding a cure for all sorts of other ailments. A hospital was a hub for people from all walks of life. A CEO could be lying on a bed next to a homeless person. The hospital did not discriminate. This gave Patti a front row seat of what was going on in the city.

"Take it back," she said, referring to the cell phone.

"Okay," Callaway said. As a single mother, Patti had done a great job with Nina, so he trusted her judgement.

"What are you doing later tonight?" he asked.

"My feet are killing me after a long shift. I'm going to shower, make dinner for Nina, and then head to bed. Why do you ask?"

He shrugged. "No reason. Tell Nina I dropped by."

He walked away.

FORTY-FOUR

Fisher took a sip of her black coffee. Holt drank his green tea.

They were seated in the back of a café. Fisher could tell Holt was uncomfortable. "Relax, Greg," she said. "We deserve a break once in a while."

"Not when we have a killer loose on the street," he grumbled.

While working on a case, Holt was known to become obsessive. He thought of nothing else but capturing the perpetrator. This made him a very good detective. No detail was too small for him. He liked to check out every lead, interview every witness, and examine each piece of evidence twice.

Right now, though, they had hit a brick wall. There were many characters in Big Bob's case, but so far, they could not point to any of them as the main suspect.

Big Bob's current wife, Suzanne Burley, had an iron-clad pre-nup that would prevent her from benefiting further from Big Bob's death. Big Bob's ex-wife, Joan Burley, received half his winnings at the time of their divorce, so she had little reason to want him dead. Sasha Turbin, Big Bob's child from another woman, was not even aware that Big Bob was her father, which meant she had nothing to gain from his demise. Also, Big Bob was already generous toward her. He paid for her college. On top of that, she had refused his help when he offered to buy her furniture and a car.

Then there was the scam artist, Joseph Olsson. Big Bob had threatened him with legal action. But Olsson was clearly shaken up when they told him Big Bob was murdered. He could have been acting, but Fisher had been around enough killers to know who was faking and who was genuine. Then there was Corliss Looms, who had robbed Big Bob. He was currently serving twenty years for the crime and was locked up at the time of Big Bob's murder, so he obviously could not have done the deed either.

Holt's voice broke her from her reverie. "We have to go back to the facts," he said.

"And that is?" she asked.

"The victim was robbed of his possessions. The safe inside the house was opened using his severed thumb. So, whoever robbed the victim also killed him."

"But none of the people who knew Big Bob had a motive to rob him," she said.

"Then we have to believe that it could be a stranger who was aware the victim had money and he or she forced their way into the house, murdered the victim, and then took whatever was inside the safe."

Fisher realized they would have to widen their investigation.

Holt finished his tea and said, "I'm going back to the station."

He got up and left Fisher sitting in the café by herself.

Instead of running after him, she leisurely drank her coffee. *If he doesn't want a break*, she thought, *fine. Well, I do.*

FORTY-FIVE

Fisher returned to the station and made her way to her desk. Holt came over, "I just received the victim's phone logs." He handed her a sheet of paper.

She scanned the calls. "Do we know who these numbers belong to?"

"I ran them through the online phone directory," he replied. "He called his wife several times throughout the day. But two calls stick out to me. One is from an unknown number; likely a prepaid phone. Another is registered to someone named Manuela Herrera."

"Do you have her address?" she asked.

He held up another piece of paper.

She smiled. "Let's go and see what she knows."

The drive took them to a predominately Latino neighborhood on Milton's west side. The houses were painted in bright colors. Some of the buildings were covered in graffiti depicting a Mariachi band or Spanish dancers. Most of the houses had large religious crosses on the front door.

Holt and Fisher pulled into a cream-colored bungalow. Wooden boxes and other debris were scattered on the lawn.

They got out of the car and walked to the front door.

They knocked and waited.

A group of young men strolled by on the sidewalk, giving Holt and Fisher suspicious glances. Holt gave them a hard look. The young men increased their pace, not wanting any trouble.

A moment later, a curtain was pulled aside, and they could see a woman behind the window.

They flashed their badges. The curtain fell back.

The lock was turned, and the door slid open slightly. "Yes?" a woman said.

"Manuela Herrera?" Fisher asked.

"Yes," came her reply.

"Can we talk to you?"

She hesitated.

"It's important you come outside and speak to us, ma'am."

Manuela came out. Her jet-black hair was silky smooth, and her olive skin was without a blemish. She wore a long dress which had a colorful pattern on it.

Fisher held up a photo of Big Bob. "Do you know this man? He goes by the name of Big Bob."

Manuela nodded.

"How?" Fisher asked.

"I work for him," she replied.

"Doing what?"

"I clean his house."

"Did you call him two days ago?"

"Yes."

"Why?"

"I wanted to pick up my money."

"So, you called Big Bob. What did he say?"

"He did not sound happy."

"Why?"

"I don't know, but I asked him if I can come to get my money."

"And what did he say?"

"He says he is at the casino, but he will be home later that night."

"Okay, then what happened?"

Manuela bit her bottom lip. She avoided looking at them straight in the eye. Fisher sensed she was afraid of something.

Manuela looked back into the house.

"Is someone else at home?" Fisher asked.

"No," Manuela quickly replied.

Fisher pulled out her weapon. "Please stay here, ma'am."

Holt had his weapon out too. He gave her a nod, silently telling her: *You go. I'll keep an eye on her.*

Fisher moved into the house with her gun at the ready. The house was poorly lit, and her eyes took a second to adjust. The living room was on the right with a sofa and coffee table. A kitchen was up ahead. Dishes were piled up in the sink. She moved down the hall. The door on the right led to a small room with a mattress on the floor. She checked the closet and then moved to the next room. Unlike the first one, this one had a bed, dresser, and a computer table stuffed inside. She stuck her head into the bathroom and saw no one was there. She then moved to the back of the house and peered through a window. The backyard was also filled with garbage and debris. She waited a second to see if there was any movement. When she did not, she holstered her weapon and went back to the front of the house.

She shook her head at Holt, silently telling him: *It's all clear*.

Manuela had her arms wrapped around herself. She was staring at her feet.

Fisher said in a soothing voice, "Manuela, everything will be okay. You can talk to us. What happened when you went to Big Bob's house?"

She took a deep breath and said, "I was walking up to the house when I heard a loud noise."

"What kind of noise?"

"Like people are fighting."

"Who was fighting, do you know?"

"At first I didn't, but then the door opened, and he came out."

"Who?"

She hesitated.

"Who came out, Manuela?"

"Chase."

Fisher's brow furrowed. "Who?"

"Chase Burley. Big Bob's son."

Fisher glanced at Holt. He was staring intently at Manuela.

"Keep going," Fisher said.

"Chase saw me. He looked angry, but he walked past me and got in his car and drove away."

"Where was Big Bob?"

"He was inside the house."

"Was he… *hurt*?"

Manuela shook her head. "He was okay, but he looked like he was a little drunk."

That explains the bottle of whisky next to the armchair, Fisher thought.

"What did he do next?"

She paused and then said, "Big Bob gave me the money and I went home."

Fisher turned to Holt. She could tell he was thinking the same thing.

They had to find Chase Burley.

FORTY-SIX

Callaway stood by the curb with a manila envelope in his hand. Inside the envelope were 8x10 prints of photographs he had taken of Carey Gilford with his assistant.

Callaway preferred using film cameras, but when companies stopped manufacturing them, he had to go digital. But he could not load the digital images onto a disc and wait for the sales clerk to print them for him. His photographs were confidential material, and his clients would not be pleased if those photos got into the wrong hands.

Callaway took no chances. He went to a department store, loaded his SD card into an instant-print machine, and printed out high quality copies of all the relevant photos. All he had to do now was hand them over to his client.

He was checking his watch for the umpteenth time when the black limousine turned the corner and pulled up next to him.

Callaway got in the backseat.

Isabel Gilford was wearing a long coat, black boots, and large sunglasses.

"I apologize for the delay," she said. "I was across town when you called."

"No worries," he said. "I would have gladly dropped them off if you had told me where." For twenty-five thousand dollars, he would have driven to Canada to make the delivery.

"It is better that *I* come to you and not the other way around," Isabel said. "I would hate for my husband to see us together. He would be incensed if he found out I had hired a private investigator."

"I completely understand," Callaway said.

He placed the envelope on the seat next to her.

She took the envelope with a gloved hand. She removed the photos. She then pressed a button on the side panel and the window closest to her slid down. She held the photo to the sunlight. She went through each photo carefully, as if she was searching for something in particular. She then dropped them on the seat and frowned.

"I need more," she said.

Callaway blinked. "I'm sorry?"

"I need more proof. These won't do."

"But… but…" he stammered. "They clearly show your husband out with his assistant."

"They do, yes, but they don't show he is having an affair with her."

Callaway blinked some more. "They show they are having a meal *together*."

Isabel paused and then said, "Let me ask you this. Did my husband and his assistant leave the office separately?"

"No. They left together."

"Which meant they were not trying to hide anything," she said. "If I confronted my husband about this, you know what he'll say? It was a professional lunch and that there was nothing between him and his assistant." She looked away, paused, and then looked back at him. "Do you know how many people my husband takes out for lunch or dinner on a regular basis? Dozens. It's how he procures investors for his firm."

Callaway ran his hand through his hair. He then reached over and grabbed the photos. He held one up. "In this one, your husband is leaning very close to his assistant like he is whispering something to her."

"He could be whispering something related to his work. He controls millions of dollars of investments and a lot of it is privileged information. He would be wise to be careful what he says out loud."

"Okay, then what about this one?" He held up another photo. "They are laughing like they are sharing something intimate or personal."

She scoffed. "My husband can be funny when he chooses to be. He could be telling her a joke."

Callaway was beside himself. He held up one last photo. "If you look at your husband's arm, it looks like he is holding her hand."

"I wish the photo showed this, but I can't see that. His hand could be resting next to hers, which could mean something or nothing." She exhaled. "Like I said, I need more proof." Her voice suddenly turned steely. "I need you to catch them in the *act*."

In all his years as a private investigator, Callaway never had a client ask him to catch their spouses in compromising positions. They did not want to see the hard truth. They preferred he catch them holding hands, out on a romantic dinner, or even kissing— which was as painful as catching them in bed.

Isabel said, "My husband is in discussions to merge with another, much larger brokerage. Together, they would control funds worth half a billion dollars. He will do anything for this merger not to fall apart, which means I can use this opportunity for a very hefty settlement. Does that explain my urgency and desire for indisputable proof?"

"Yes, it does," Callaway replied.

FORTY-SEVEN

Fisher could not believe they had not focused on Chase Burley earlier. There were several reasons for that. His address on file was for Westport, which was a good six-hour drive from Milton. And, by all accounts, Chase and Big Bob had a great relationship.

At least, that's what Fisher thought while reading the articles on the family. But things had suddenly changed.

Chase had become a person of interest.

They were still unsure if he was the killer, though. The maid, Manuela Herrera, confirmed Big Bob was still alive *after* Chase was seen leaving the house. But that did not mean he could not have returned later and murdered his father.

Holt and Fisher got in Fisher's Lexus SUV and made the trek down to Westport. Fisher had gone on long trips with Holt before, but she much preferred to fly than drive. Holt was not a big talker, so he spent most of the time staring out the window. Also, if he was not driving, he was sleeping. It was not uncommon for him to be snoring for two-thirds of the ride.

Which is what he did now.

Fisher had no choice but to sing along with all the songs on the radio, count all the towns they passed, or listen to an audio book.

When they were an hour away from their destination, Holt groaned, and then his eyes snapped open. He looked around in confusion, and then he wiped drool off his chin and sat up straight.

"Sleep well?" Fisher asked.

"Ah… yes. I needed a short nap."

"We are almost there," she said.

"Oh, is that right?" Holt said, blinking. "I must have been really tired."

A short time later, they pulled up to a large house.

Fisher squinted. There was a strand of yellow police tape across the front of the house. The windows were cracked and shattered, and bullet holes peppered the front door.

Fisher and Holt parked and got out.

They walked up, stopping at the police tape.

"What do you suppose happened here?" Holt asked.

"Let's find out," Fisher replied.

She walked over to the neighbor's property and rang the doorbell.

An old man opened the door. He had thick glasses, and he was wearing a robe. "Can I help you?" he said.

Fisher held up her badge.

The man squinted and got closer to take a better look at the badge. "You're from Milton, huh?"

"Yes, we are."

He glanced over at Holt, who was standing behind Fisher. The man said, "I've been to Milton once. It was years ago, when I was younger. Nice place, if I remember correctly."

Fisher worried the man might tell her the story of his visit, so she quickly said, "What happened to the house next door?"

The man frowned. "Scared the daylights out of me. I was on the sofa, watching TV. It had gotten dark when I heard a noise. It sounded like tires screeching to a halt. I then heard the car door open, which was followed by loud bangs.'"

"Bangs?"

"Gunshots."

"Okay."

"The shots came one after the other. I counted like six shots. I quickly dropped to the floor and cowered behind the sofa. Growing up, my parents didn't have much money, so we lived in some rough neighborhoods. I know a gunshot when I hear it. I was lucky a friend's dad got me a job working in construction. I later ended up opening my own company, and when I sold it for a nice profit, I moved here. So, what I'm trying to get at is that this is a quiet neighborhood. We don't see stuff like this here."

"After you heard the gunshots and took cover, what did you do next?" Fisher prodded.

"I heard a car door slam shut and then the car roared away. I stayed in the same spot for a minute or two before I went to check. The guy was out on the front porch of his house and he looked like he'd seen a ghost."

"Who was on the front porch?"

"My neighbor."

"Chase Burley?"

The man nodded. "He told me he was sitting on the porch having a beer when he spotted the car turning the corner at the end of the street. I guess he kind of knew what was going to happen next, because he raced inside the house in the nick of time. The bullets would have torn him to shreds, you know."

"Why did someone try to kill him?" Fisher asked.

"Beats me."

"Did you get to know your neighbor well?"

"Not really. He kept mostly to himself. I heard his old man had won a lot of money. I guess he bought him the house next door, because I doubt the guy had a job or anything."

"Did you notice anything else unusual about him?"

The man's face scrunched up in disgust. "When he moved in he was pretty much quiet, but later he started hosting parties. I used to see a lot of girls come in and out of his house. I think some of them were even hookers. On the weekends the noise would be too much. A group of us from the neighborhood got together and complained to the police. He wasn't pleased with that, I'm sure, but after a while, things quieted down again."

Fisher thanked the old man, and she and Holt left.

FORTY-EIGHT

Callaway was parked across from the office tower once again. He thought his job was done, but he should have known better. For the amount of money his client gave him, she could ask him to do whatever she wanted.

Client satisfaction was number one on his list, even if his discoveries broke a lot of hearts and marriages. He would be more than happy to go back to a client and show him or her proof that their spouse was not cheating on them. That would be a pleasant outcome for both parties. The marriage would still be intact, and he would feel better about his fee.

If people were always faithful to their spouses, Callaway would be out of a job. And yet, the PI business had changed from the time Callaway had started, which was not that long ago. The advent of cell phones and social networking sites had taken a big bite out of his work. Spouses could go through their partner's phones to see who they were speaking to and could keep track of who they were hanging out with via the posts on their social media pages. That, coupled with other advances in technology, meant that one day there would be no need for people like Callaway.

Until that time, Callaway intended to make the most of every opportunity that came his way.

He glanced again at the front of the office tower. So far, Carey Gilford had not once left the building, not even during lunch time.

Is he aware he's being followed? Callaway thought.

He shook his head. Callaway was many things—a lousy husband, father, tenant—but he was a damn good private investigator. His instincts would tell him when the target was on to him, because a good PI could sense when a target did something out of character. People tended to follow a daily routine. They rarely deviated from their pattern unless something provoked them to do so.

Callaway checked his watch and then grabbed a newspaper. He flipped to the classified section. He had been considering moving out of the hotel for some time. The hotel was not a long-term option. Sooner or later, he would have to find a place to put down his roots. He was waiting until he secured a permanent job before he did that, but now he had significant cash in his pockets.

Callaway had learned the hard way that with good times came bad times. Right now, the sun was shining on him, but it could very well turn cloudy. Thankfully, Isabel Gilford's fee could see him through until his next case.

FORTY-NINE

Mike Sprewell had an army-style haircut, steely eyes, and a handlebar moustache. He was the detective who had investigated the shooting at Chase Burley's house.

Holt and Fisher were seated with Sprewell on a patio outside a coffee shop. Sprewell took a sip from a steaming hot cup.

"You sure you guys don't want anything?" he said. "It's my treat."

Sprewell was across town when they had called him. He quickly dropped everything to meet them.

"We're good, thanks," Holt replied.

"What can you tell us about Chase Burley?" Fisher said.

"Where do I start?" he asked.

"Anywhere would be fine," Fisher replied.

"He moved down here a couple of years ago. From what I heard, he wanted to open his own recording studio. He—or should I say, his father—bought an old studio down on Pearl Street. A big shot record producer used to own that studio, but when people started moving to digital music, the equipment became outdated, and the producer closed the doors and walked away. Chase got a good deal on the place. He then invested half a million dollars to upgrade the equipment. But like most creative endeavors, you have to be really talented or hardworking to get a break. I don't think Chase was either."

"I'm assuming you spoke to him a few times?" Holt said.

"I did. The first time was when there was a fire at the studio. The fire investigator had determined that it was arson, but my investigation could not find who was behind it. I interviewed Chase several times. He said he was in Milton visiting his parents at the time of the fire, but that did not mean he couldn't have paid someone to light the place up."

"Why did you think he had something to do with it?" Fisher asked.

"The studio was losing lots of money," Sprewell replied. "Chase had hired top sound editors, recording engineers, equipment managers, and so on. There were rumours he was looking for a buyer, but when that didn't happen, he joked that he wished the place would burn down so he could claim on the insurance policy. And it did, and he got his money."

"But you couldn't point to him as the culprit," Fisher asked.

"I couldn't."

Holt frowned. "So how does this link up to what happened at his house?"

"After he got the money, he started hanging around with people who were involved in the drug trade."

This is interesting, Fisher thought.

"Chase began dealing cocaine out of his house. We didn't know this at the time, but it put him in the crosshairs of some very dangerous people. We once found him badly beaten up by the side of the road. He never told us who was behind it, but I had an idea. It was the gang whose turf he was dealing on. I wouldn't be surprised if they were the ones who tried to gun him down in front of his house, but Chase believes it's better to adhere to some arcane street code about not being a snitch. If someone is trying to kill you, you get the authorities involved, but they don't see it like that." Sprewell paused to collect himself. "Whenever I interviewed him, he didn't come across as dumb, but he didn't come across as bright either. I mean, his father set him up nicely, but the kid took it for granted."

"What was his relationship with his father? Did you know?" Holt asked.

"Not sure. He didn't talk about him much. But whenever I mentioned his father's name, he would get angry. I think he resented the fact that his father was always coming to bail him out of whatever trouble he found himself in."

Is that what they fought about on the night Big Bob was murdered? Fisher thought. *Chase wanted Big Bob to get him out of the mess that nearly got him killed, and this time Big Bob refused?*

FIFTY

Cary Gilford emerged from the office tower. He was carrying his suit jacket in one hand and a briefcase in the other.

Callaway watched as Gilford turned right and headed toward the parking lot. The assistant was nowhere in sight.

Maybe she's still at work? Callaway thought.

But he could not wait to find out. His mission was to follow Gilford and see what he was up to.

Gilford got behind the wheel of the Audi.

A moment later, he pulled out of the parking lot.

Callaway followed behind.

The Audi weaved through traffic until it stopped in front of a flower shop. Gilford got out and went inside. Ten minutes later, he returned to the Audi carrying a box of chocolates and a bouquet of roses.

Callaway's eyes narrowed. *Is that for your mistress?*

That explained why she was not with Gilford when he left work. She was likely already waiting for him at some other destination.

Callaway smiled. This could be what he was looking for. To catch them in the act. That was exactly what his client wanted from him, was it not?

The Audi was back on the road. Callaway kept a fair distance between it and the Charger. He did not want to spook Gilford and have him change his plans.

Callaway had the element of surprise in his favor. Gilford would think he was spending time with his mistress without any prying eyes. What he did not know was that Callaway would capture the rendezvous on his camera.

This was a feat far more complicated than it looked. He had to know where to be and when. People did not get intimate in front of an uncovered window. They preferred privacy. Callaway would have to get creative if he wanted to get the right shot.

Previously, he had hid inside a closet. He had peeked through windows with an opening of just inches between the drapes. He had even gone so far as to plant hidden cameras in a room. The last was illegal, for sure, but sometimes desperate times required desperate measures.

He was not proud of using hidden cameras, though. There was no sleuthing involved, because the hidden cameras did all the work. However, knowing where to stick a tiny camera came with its own set of challenges.

He once stuck a wireless camera inside an air vent. The day was hot, and the occupant decided to turn on the air conditioner at full blast. Callaway had not properly secured the camera. Needless to say, the pressure from the AC blew the camera down the vent. He did not get another opportunity for a shot for three weeks. The error cost him time and money. While he could have been working on a new case, he was still trying to wrap up the old one.

The Audi got off the main road and took side streets for five minutes until it pulled into a gated property. Callaway parked the Charger across from the home and watched as the Audi disappeared behind the high walls.

He debated whether to get out and take a look around the property, but he knew it was not necessary. The house belonged to Cary and Isabel Gilford.

It was highly unlikely Gilford was meeting his mistress in there. The chocolates and flowers were for his wife.

Callaway spotted a black sedan in his rearview mirror. The car was parked half a block away from the Charger. He looked back and he could make out a silhouette behind the wheel.

He squinted.

I've seen that car before, he thought. *But where?*

Before he could find out, the sedan did a U-turn and sped away.

Callaway did not know what to make of this new development, but he suddenly had a bad feeling in the pit of his stomach.

FIFTY-ONE

After returning to Milton, Holt and Fisher contacted Joan Burley. She had no idea there had been an incident at Chase's house. They did not go into any details. They wanted to know where Chase was. Joan Burley had last seen her son two weeks ago. She did not even know he had recently been in Milton. He always visited her when he was in town.

They then spoke to Caroline Leary, who was staying with her mother until her father's funeral. Caroline was aware of her brother's problems with drugs. She was certain he was not a user and that he only got into dealing because their father had cut him off financially. She too was not aware of the shooting in Westport.

Holt and Fisher told her it was important that they speak to Chase. She told them she had not spoken to him in months. She last saw him in Connecticut when he surprised her for her son's birthday. They pressed her for any scrap of information she could give, and she gave them a woman's name.

They found her working as a bartender in a small lounge in Kesseltown, a town an hour away from Milton. Tara St. Patrick was Chase's on-again, off-again girlfriend. Her hair was dyed bright pink, she had a large tattoo covering the entire length of her right arm, and she wore oversized glasses which looked like they were more for show rather than short-sightedness.

She was serving a customer when she came over to Holt and Fisher. "What can I get you?" she asked, revealing a stud in her tongue.

They flashed their badges. "We're looking for Chase," Fisher said.

"I don't know where he is," Tara said with a shrug.

"He's in trouble and we need to find him."

"Like I said, I don't know where he is."

Fisher decided to use a different tack. "Did you know that someone tried to kill Chase?"

Tara blinked. "What?"

"Yes. We just returned from Westport and it looks like someone sprayed bullets across the front of his house. We spoke to one of his neighbors and he said Chase barely escaped with his life. We also spoke to the detective at the scene and he believes a local gang is behind it. Apparently, sometime back Chase was roughed up badly—perhaps by the same gang, as a warning. If I was a betting woman, I'd say these people are still looking for him, and when they find him…"

She let her words trail off.

Tara's shoulders sank. "I was the one who got him into drugs," she confessed. "I was a recreational user. Cocaine was my choice of poison. The guy I was dating wanted to be a rapper and Chase had just opened his recording studio. I went to the studio a few times and saw Chase there. A short while later, I broke up with the rapper and I hooked up with Chase. When the recording studio was in financial trouble, Chase asked his father for money. I didn't know this at the time, but Chase had drained his trust fund to set up the studio. His father refused to help him out. I think he was against the studio from the beginning, but it was Chase's trust fund, so he could do whatever he wanted with the money."

"Was Chase angry at his father?" Fisher asked.

"Yeah, a lot."

"Did he ever threaten to kill him?"

Tara fell silent. She then said, "Chase said a lot of things about his father, but they were out of frustration. He felt betrayed."

"Betrayed, why?"

"He thought his father had turned his back on him."

"But he setup a trust fund in his name."

"Yeah, but he gave Caroline double what he gave Chase."

"Why would he do that?"

"I think because she had a family of her own and I think he knew if he gave Chase more money, he would only blow it."

Fisher paused. She then said, "You mentioned that you got him involved in drugs. How?"

Tara looked away. "After closing the recording studio, Chase owed money to a lot of people. He didn't know how to pay them back, so I introduced him to some people who were involved in the illegal drug business. He cut a deal with them and became a distributor. But there was a catch: they wanted him to open shop in his neighborhood."

Fisher understood why. "They knew it was someone else's turf?"

Tara nodded. "From then on Chase had a target on his back." She covered her face with her hands. "I just never thought they'd try to kill him," she said.

"That's why we have to get to Chase before they do," Fisher said.

Tara thought a moment. "I really don't know where he is, but sometimes he likes to hang out at this one place."

"Give us the name."

FIFTY-TWO

"So, what do you think?" Callaway said.

Nina walked around the empty space with a smile on her face. Patti stood in the corner and observed the interior.

The two-bedroom unit was on the fourteenth floor of an apartment building. The place was recently painted—the smell of fresh paint still hung in the air—and the parquet floor had been polished. The building was well-maintained, the elevators seemed to be in working order, and when Callaway checked, there was hot water as well as cold. Hot water was a luxury he had lived without in his previous rental accommodations.

"I love it, Daddy," Nina said, turning to him.

"How much is the rent?" Patti asked.

"Thirteen hundred," Callaway replied.

"Isn't that kind of steep for you?"

"I'm working on a case that will cover it and then some."

"Why two bedrooms?"

"I was hoping that once I'm settled in, Nina can visit me and maybe even sleep over, you know."

Nina jumped up. "Yay!" she yelled.

Patti frowned. "We'll see how the visits go first before we discuss sleepovers. Okay?"

Callaway nodded. "I haven't signed any papers yet," he said. "I wanted your approval before I did that."

Patti stared at him and then she relaxed. "It's nice and clean."

He smiled. "Once I hand over the first and last month's rent, I can move in in two weeks."

"Can I see the balcony?" Nina asked.

Callaway turned to Patti.

"Sure," Patti replied.

Nina scurried away.

When they were alone, Patti said, "I need to ask you a favor."

"Okay, what is it?" he eagerly asked. Patti rarely asked him for anything.

"My neighbor is away, so I need you to babysit Nina," Patti replied.

Callaway had met this neighbor and he did not like her. In fact, the neighbor liked Callaway even less. She knew what kind of parent and husband Callaway was, so her opinion of him was not entirely unjustified. Even so, Callaway would rather have his daughter spend time with him than her.

"Sure, I'll watch Nina," he said. "You have a long shift?"

"No. Actually, I have a date."

Callaway felt his chest tighten. He tried to hide the pain on his face. "Who is it?" he asked.

"It's none of your business who I go out with," she shot back.

She was right. They were no longer married, so she could do whatever she wanted.

"Can I rely on you to watch Nina or not?" Patti asked. "You've made promises before and not shown up."

"No, I'll be there," he replied.

Callaway felt momentarily dizzy.

FIFTY-THREE

Holt and Fisher drove to a seedy part of the city. The place used to be a strip club—there were still neon signs across the front—but it had now been turned into a dance club.

The interior was dark, and it smelled of cigarettes and marijuana. In the middle of the space was a stage with a pole—a remnant from the strip club—with tables all around. There was a bar in the corner.

Holt and Fisher approached the bartender. He was a gruff looking man with a tattoo of an American eagle on one side of his shaved skull.

Holt flashed his badge and asked a question. The bartender nodded at a table in the far corner. Two men nursing their drinks were seated at the table.

Holt and Fisher walked over to them. Holt said, "We're looking for Chase Burley."

The first man, who was wearing baggy clothes and a bandana, said, "I don't know any Chase Burley."

The second man, who was wearing a hoodie and a baseball cap, said, "Never heard that name before."

They started laughing.

Holt flashed his badge and then opened his jacket to reveal his holster. "I didn't find that very funny," he said. He turned to Fisher. "Did you think that was funny?"

"I don't find murder funny," she replied.

The smiles dropped from the men's faces. "Murder?" the first one said. "What are you talking about?"

"Chase's father, Robert Burley, was found murdered in his home," Holt said. "You are aware of this, are you not?"

There was a strong pungent stench emanating from both men. *They must have just finished a joint*, Fisher thought.

"We don't watch the news," the second man said.

"You should," Holt scolded them. "That's how you'll know what's happening around you."

Fisher said, "Have you seen Chase?"

The first man shrugged. "We saw him two days ago."

That's the day Big Bob was murdered, Fisher thought.

"Did you talk to him?" Fisher asked.

"Yeah, but only for a bit," the second man replied.

"What did you talk about?" Holt asked.

"Nothing much."

"Why was he here?"

"He wanted to blow off some steam."

"Why?"

"He was angry."

"At who?"

"His old man, of course," the second man said.

"Okay."

"He was always pissed at him," the second added. "It always had to do with money."

"Did he ever threaten his father?" Holt asked.

Both men clammed up.

"Was he ever violent toward Big Bob?" Fisher pushed.

The first man sighed. "Chase always said he wished someone would teach his old man a lesson, but I don't think he meant it, you know."

"How did you meet Chase?" Fisher asked.

"The three of us were planning to start our own record label. Chase said he would take care of the upfront costs. I was part of a rap group and—" he nodded to the second man "—he used to manage our group. But when Chase's studio biz fell apart, he bailed on the plan."

"And do you think he was bitter at his father for not helping him out?"

"Yeah, sure he was. You would be too if you knew your old man got millions sitting in the bank and he won't give you any of it."

"Do you know where we can find him?" Holt asked.

"He's got a place in Westport."

"We've been there. He's not there."

"You talk to his girl in Kesseltown?"

"He's not there either."

"Then you're out of luck, man."

Fisher said, "How do *you* contact him?"

His face contorted. "What?"

"If you need to speak to him, what do you do?"

"I call him."

"Give us his number," Holt sternly demanded.

FIFTY-FOUR

Callaway was surprised when he received the call from Isabel Gilford. She wanted to see him. Her voice sounded strained on the phone. He told her he would meet her at a place of her choosing. She told him she would pick him up.

As he stood waiting for her on the sidewalk, he had a feeling she would ask him about his investigation. But not enough time had passed since he last saw her. He did not have the concrete proof she was looking for.

Just then the black limousine turned the corner and pulled up next to him. He got in and sat across from her. She was wearing a black coat, a scarf covered her head, and she had her usual sunglasses on.

The limousine moved. Callaway asked, "Where're we going?"

"Someplace… private."

She stared out the tinted windows as they drove to their destination. Callaway studied her. Even in the low light he could see something was different about her.

After ten minutes, she turned to him and said, "Before you ask, it might be better if I showed you."

She pulled off her sunglasses.

There was a purple bruise under her right eye.

He clenched his teeth. "Who did that to you?"

"Who do you think?"

He knew. "Your husband."

She nodded and put the sunglasses back on.

"Why?"

"Yesterday was our wedding anniversary. My husband bought me chocolates and flowers. He had also reserved a table for us at one of the most exclusive restaurants in the city. I told him I was not going. I could not muster the energy to sit across from him when I know what he's been doing behind my back. Naturally, he was not pleased. He reminded me it was our anniversary and that I should go upstairs and get ready. I am aware that very important people go to this restaurant. So, my husband wanted to put on a show that our marriage was as strong as his investment firm. I was not in the mood to play his games. We got into an argument, and then he…"

"He hit you," Callaway finished for her.

Isabel said nothing. She turned and faced the window again.

He waited a moment before he asked, "Has your husband hit you before?"

"Once before, but he regretted it immediately. To show how remorseful he was, he bought me a five-hundred-thousand-dollar diamond brooch."

Callaway was horrified. "And you accepted it?"

She smiled. "Throughout history, women have endured far worse abuse and received far less for it. I sold that brooch and bought myself a nice property by the lake. I go there whenever I need to get away."

"Is that where we are going?"

She shook her head. "No."

There was a moment of silence.

Callaway said, "You need to report this to the police."

"I have taken photos of my injuries and I intend to use them during our divorce."

"Okay, sure, but I don't think it's safe for you to go back to your house."

She smiled again. "Don't worry about me. I can take care of myself."

The limousine came to a halt.

Isabel got out. Callaway followed her.

He suddenly realized they were parked at the curb on a busy bridge.

"What are we doing here?" he asked.

"I told you we were going someplace private."

He was confused.

Over the roar of the traffic, she said, "I think someone is following me."

"Who?" he asked, raising his voice.

"I don't know, but I've seen a car parked outside our house."

Callaway's eyes widened. He now realized why she chose this very spot to speak to him. If anyone was following them, they could not park their vehicle without getting spotted. "I've seen the same car as well," he said.

She frowned. "I believe my husband has hired someone to watch me, which means he may know I've hired a private investigator."

Callaway looked over the bridge at the water below. The water was still and calm, but the sight did not match what Callaway was feeling.

This is not good, he thought. *If Cary Gilford knows I'm following him, then my job just got a lot harder.*

"I need those photos, Lee," she said. There was desperation in her voice. "And I need them as soon as possible."

"Are you sure what I gave you is not sufficient?" he asked.

"I should have told you this earlier. I don't plan to just divorce Cary. I plan to use those lurid photos to blackmail him," she replied.

"*Blackmail* him?" Callaway repeated.

"Yes!" Isabel said, raising her voice. "I want to destroy him for what he has done to me, physically and emotionally. And I know exactly how to do that: by taking control of his firm. When he sees what I have on him, he will have no choice but to succumb to my demands. If he doesn't, then those photos will make their way onto the internet and the world will see what he has been up to. Then no one will ever want to do business with him."

Callaway was reminded of the saying: *Hell hath no fury like a woman scorned.* Isabel Gilford had been wronged and she would do everything in her power to get justice.

Callaway felt a shiver go up his spine.

FIFTY-FIVE

Holt rang Chase Burley's number and found it was no longer in service. They tried to trace the number, but even that was not possible.

Then they received a call from Suzanne Burley. She wanted to know when she could return to the house to gather her belongings. The house was still sealed off.

Mrs. Burley's interest in the property, Fisher knew, did not have something to do with anything she left behind. She had already moved out and taken most of her possessions. Mrs. Burley wanted to see what else she could take *before* the trustees took control of Big Bob's assets. The family—more specifically, Big Bob's heirs—would want their piece of the estate. If there was any cash, jewelry, artwork, or anything else of value left behind, Mrs. Burley wanted to get her hands on it without anyone knowing.

The crime scene had already been combed, so there was no reason to stop her from gaining access to the home, but Fisher decided to take one last look.

She and Holt drove up to the house and parked next to a police cruiser. An officer was stationed at the door to prevent anyone from entering and contaminating the scene.

They pulled on latex gloves and went inside. Nothing had changed from the last time they were there save for a chalk mark of Big Bob's body near the stairs.

Holt moved toward the office where the safe was. Fisher moved up the stairs to the second floor. She was interested in the room with the bullet holes. She examined the door closely. She put her eye to the hole and peeked through. The bullet had gone completely through the wooden door and then struck the concrete wall, where it had remained until the CSU removed it as evidence.

The ballistic report had not come back, but Fisher was confident the bullets would match the gun registered to Big Bob, making him the shooter.

She checked the other rooms before checking the bathroom. She was not sure what she would expect to find here. She noticed that someone had used the toilet but had failed to flush. It was a pet peeve of hers when people did not flush the toilet or put down the seat.

She flushed the toilet and was about to leave when she stopped and listened. She waited and then flushed again. There was an odd sound coming from the toilet. With gloved hands she removed the lid from the water tank. Submerged in the water was a black object. She placed her hand inside and pulled the object out. It was heavy, and the size of a clay brick.

She knew exactly what it was.

She went downstairs and found Holt in the living room. She held the object up for him. "I found it in the bathroom."

He took the item and frowned. "Do you suppose there are more in the house?"

"I bet there are."

They spent the next two hours checking every nook and cranny, and when they were done, they had five more bricks. One was found taped under the kitchen sink, another was found behind the refrigerator, a third in the toilet of the guest bathroom, and the last was in the air vent.

Just to be certain, Holt pulled out a Swiss Army knife and made a small cut across one of the bricks. He stuck the knife into the cut and when he removed it, there was a white powder.

The bricks contained cocaine.

If they had to guess, the bricks belonged to Chase Burley.

They now knew why Chase had come to the house. He had hidden the drugs in his father's property, and in the process of trying to retrieve them, he had a fight with Big Bob.

But that raised another question.

If Chase had killed his father, why did he leave the drugs behind?

FIFTY-SIX

Callaway rang the doorbell and waited. A moment later, the door swung open and he nearly lost his breath.

Patti was wearing a blue dress that flowed down to her knees. She had on matching blue heels. She wore a pearl necklace and pearl earrings. She had on eye shadow and red lipstick.

"You okay, Lee?" she asked with a raised eyebrow.

His palms were clammy, and his throat was dry. "I'm... I'm fine," he said, swallowing whatever spit he could summon up.

"Nina's had dinner, so don't give her anything else."

"Okay," he said.

"No, I mean it," she firmly said. "Whenever she eats late, her stomach is upset all night."

"Right. Gotcha."

"I should be back in a couple of hours. She can watch TV, but make sure she goes to bed on time."

He felt like a teenage babysitter who was given a list of precise instructions to follow.

"Okay, no problem," he said.

A car roared down the street and stopped at the curb. To Callaway's dismay it was a red Ferrari. A man stepped out and walked up to them. He wore a blue blazer, white dress shirt, and blue jeans. He had on brown dress shoes, and on his wrist was an expensive watch.

He walked past Callaway as if he was not even there and kissed Patti on the cheek. "You look absolutely stunning," he said.

Patti beamed like a little schoolgirl.

She turned to Callaway and said, "Lee, this is Dr. Michael Hayward."

He smiled and extended his hand. "How do you do?"

Callaway noticed he had perfect hair and perfect teeth. He seethed with envy.

Patti said, "Michael is a surgeon."

"Yeah, so don't squeeze my hand too tight," Hayward quipped. "I need it to save lives."

I would rather squeeze your neck, Callaway thought.

He smiled and gently shook Hayward's hand.

"Patti told me you're a private detective. Is that right?" Hayward asked.

"I am."

"I thought they only existed in comic books."

Callaway gritted his teeth. "You mean detective novels."

"Right, sure. I don't have time to read fiction. I prefer spending my time engrossed in medical journals."

If I punched him in the face, Callaway wondered, how *long would it take for him to stitch himself up?*

"I better go and say goodbye to Nina," Patti said.

She went into the house.

Callaway said, "It's a nice ride you got there."

Hayward smiled at the Ferrari. "Thanks."

"I prefer a manly car." He pointed to his Charger. "That's mine. It's all power and testosterone."

Hayward grimaced at the pot shot.

Patti returned. Hayward held her hand and escorted her to the car. He held the door for her like a gentleman. When she was inside, he turned to Callaway, grinned and winked, and then got in the driver's seat.

As they drove off, Callaway had the urge to get in his Charger and follow them. He then heard a voice ask, "Dad, you okay?"

Nina was standing by the door with a curious look on her face.

He blinked. "Yeah, I'm fine. Why wouldn't I be?"

"You don't look fine."

He smiled. "Let's go inside, honey."

FIFTY-SEVEN

Holt would rather be working on the case, but after the brutal murder of his nephew, Isaiah, Holt had vowed to spend more time with his sister, brother-in-law, and niece. They were the only family he had left.

Holt's parents died when he was young, so it was up to Marjorie, who was several years older than him, to raise him. She guided and protected him at a time when he needed it most. Their mother had a mental breakdown after her second child, a boy born before Holt, died of cerebral palsy. His father was a proud man who mourned the loss in his own quiet way: by drinking himself to death.

Holt had suffered his own loss. When Nancy found she could not bear any children, they decided to adopt a boy from the Ukraine. His adopted son did not live to see his first birthday, dying from a rare form of cancer.

Holt spent months trying to locate the boy's real parents. They knew the child was suffering when they gave him up for adoption. Even the adoption agency never mentioned this to Holt and his wife when they went to see the boy.

Would Holt have refused the child because of his illness? *Absolutely not.* He would have gotten the child immediate medical attention. He would have done everything to save him, just like he tried to do in the end, but by then it was too late.

Nancy wanted him to pick up a bottle of wine. His sister was not a big drinker, nor was his brother-in-law, Dennis, but if they had to choose, they would go with red over white.

He selected the finest bottle he could afford and then decided to take another detour. Brit, his niece, had recently graduated from high school. While her older brother, Isaiah, excelled in sports, Brit was one of the top students in her school. Her algebra grades were the highest amongst all the students in her class.

Brit had applied to Stanford, MIT, and Harvard. They would all go out and celebrate the moment she was accepted into one of her chosen schools. Holt had no doubt she would.

He regretted never spending much time with her. He was much closer with Isaiah. They had the same interests and hobbies. Holt played basketball in high school and Isaiah was a major star in college. There was a belief that he would have made it to the pros one day.

When it came to Brit, Holt found he could not keep up with her intellectually, but that did not mean he could not get to know her better. They found they both liked working on crossword puzzles. They raced each other to see who could finish one first. Holt was competitive by nature, and there were times he would make up solutions to beat her. She would catch him, of course, and they would argue for the longest time, but it was all in good fun. Holt and Brit's crossword battles were always the highlight of his visits to his sister's.

He searched the aisles of the department store. He knew Brit loved listening to music. He remembered she was complaining about her headphone wires tangling up. He knew what to get her for her graduation gift. He purchased the best wireless headphones he could buy. After that,
he drove straight home.

Nancy is waiting for me to pick her up, he thought.

FIFTY-EIGHT

Nina was already fast asleep when Patti came home. Callaway wanted to know all the details of her date, but he did not ask her. As Patti had said, who she dated was none of his business.

Throughout the evening, though, Callaway was irked that Dr. Michael Hayward was educated, good-looking, and far more accomplished than him.

As he left the house, he could not help but think about Patti.

He always had feelings for her, he just did not realize how strong they were until now. Knowing she was with another man ate away at him, but he had been with countless women after his marriage ended, so he had no right to point any fingers at her. Besides, he was not a hypocrite.

After what he had done, she deserved all the happiness in the world. He was surprised she had not gotten remarried sooner.

He knew the reason why.

Nina.

At the expense of her love life, Patti was devoted to their daughter. She knew how fragile this stage of her life was for her development as a person and, eventually, a woman. There were countless stories of children moving between divorced parents. There were just as many stories of children being affected by their parents' personal relationships. This did not mean that all children were not happy in second family units. On the contrary, if a person's first marriage was dysfunctional or abusive, the second marriage might provide the children the security and comfort they most needed.

Patti and Callaway's marriage was filled with love and understanding. They hardly ever fought, and never in front of Nina. Also, Callaway never cheated on her.

He was just bored and restless.

He wanted more out of life. Each day he spent not doing something exciting was draining his soul. There were times he could not even get out of bed. His joy was gone.

Patti saw how miserable he was becoming. She had let him go without any bickering.

He got the freedom he was searching for, but now he realized it was all an illusion. There was so much wisdom in the saying: *The grass is greener where you water it.*

Callaway had a steady job as a deputy sheriff. He had a beautiful wife who loved him, and he had a precious little girl who needed him the most.

Instead of working hard to make things work, he threw it all away.

When Callaway saw Patti get in the Ferrari with Dr. Hayward, he felt like a piece of his heart was cut out of him. The feeling was so intense, it was physical, something he had not experienced before.

His heart was broken.

You're a dumbass for letting her go, he scolded himself. *Don't be surprised if she ends up marrying him. He will be a far better husband and stepfather than you'll ever be. As a medical doctor, he'll give Patti the financial support she always deserved, and he'll be there for Nina like you never were. You had your chance, buddy, and you blew it.*

FIFTY-NINE

Callaway checked his watch. The time was now late. He could not very well go back to his empty hotel room. His emotions were all over the place. He needed to focus, get his mind preoccupied with something else.

He thought about going to a bar, but no good would come out of that. He would only get drunk by trying to drink his sorrows away, which would result in him arguing with the bartender and getting thrown out. Worse, he would get in an argument with another patron and get hit in the head with a bottle.

That had happened before. Callaway had to get eighteen stitches in the back of his head.

He could always go to his office, but it too was empty. He would end up ruminating about all the mistakes he had made in his life.

He decided to drive across the city. He parked in front of a gated house; it belonged to Isabel and Cary Gilford.

Whenever he was on a job—whether it was on a stakeout or gathering information—he felt alive.

Behind the property's walls, he could see lights on the second floor. His client and her husband were still awake.

He was not sure what he would find here, but he did not care.

If he had to spend the entire night in his car, he would.

Isabel Gilford had given him a substantial fee to dig up dirt on her husband, and Callaway would do just that.

He looked around. There were other cars parked on the street, so he was not worried about being spotted. Every once in a while, a car would drive by, its headlights almost blinding him. Whenever that happened, he would slide down in his seat.

He would hate for a neighbor to call the police on him.

How would he explain what he was doing here?

He tilted his seat back and decided to close his eyes.

Before he left Patti's house, she asked him if he could drop Nina off at school in the morning. She had an early shift and she had forgotten to remind her neighbor.

Since Callaway disliked said neighbor, he agreed without hesitation.

He did not know when, but he eventually fell asleep.

His eyes snapped open. He bolted up and looked around. He was still in the Charger.

He quickly realized what had awoken him.

It was the noise from the Gilford's front gate. He lowered himself even further into the seat. He watched as two headlights appeared behind the gate.

Cary Gilford's Audi emerged from the gate and drove away.

Callaway put the Charger in gear and followed after.

The clock on the dashboard showed it was well past midnight.

Where are you going this late at night? he thought. *Are you meeting your mistress?*

If that was it, then he had hit the jackpot. He would have the proof he was searching for.

The Audi moved through the empty streets and got onto a busy road. The Audi then pulled into a tavern's parking lot.

Callaway did the same.

He watched Cary Gilford get out and go inside.

Callaway debated whether to wait for him in the Charger, but he was here for a reason, and it would not be complete unless he got close to the action.

He left the Charger and entered the bar. He scanned the interior and caught Gilford in a booth in the far corner. He was wearing a baseball cap, jeans jacket, and khaki pants.

Callaway went to the other side of the bar and pulled up a stool.

So much for not going to a bar, he thought.

The bartender came over, and he ordered a drink. When the drink came, he took small sips.

Meanwhile, Gilford was flirting with a waitress who was young, blonde, and wore tight-fitting clothing.

Callaway's hands balled into fists. Gilford was the worst of the worst. He was cheating on his wife with his assistant, and on top of that, he was also physically violent toward his wife.

If Callaway had his way, he would teach the man a lesson right this minute. But if he did his job right, then Gilford's wife would teach him a lesson he would never forget.

Gilford drank from a tall glass and stared at his phone.

Almost forty-five minutes later, with his glass empty, he got up, paid his bill, and then left the tavern.

Callaway followed him back to his house. Afterwards, he decided to head home himself. He had given Patti his word that he would be at her house first thing in the morning.

If Patti's relationship with Dr. Hayward became serious, Callaway would need to be on her good side, or she might finally start limiting his access to Nina.

SIXTY

Fisher was at her local gym. Her feet pounded on the treadmill. She preferred running outside. Nothing compared to the feeling of fresh air in her lungs. But rain was falling when she woke up.

She liked going for an early morning jog each day, but this was not possible when she was deep in a new investigation. Last night, after Holt had left, she went through all the evidence they had on Big Bob's murder.

From photos from the crime scene to witness statements, it was a lot of material. She was up until two a.m. at the office when she finally decided to go home.

Sleep was fitful. She felt like she was missing a significant piece to this entire puzzle. She just was not sure what it was.

She ramped up the speed on the treadmill and went on a full sprint. Only when her legs were turning to pulp did she slow down and begin to jog again. Her heart felt like it was beating out of her chest. This gave her a good sweat. Fisher believed if she was not sweating hard, she was not running hard.

A man wearing a cut-off T-shirt, shorts, and runners was seated on a bench at the far end of the gym. He was curling his biceps with fifty-pound dumbbells. She had noticed him the moment she entered the gym. He watched her walk from the main doors to the treadmill. Even now he was staring in her direction.

The man was a regular. His muscles were bigger than his head. Fisher knew his type. They came to the gym to not only work out but also pick up girls. And if they saw a woman who had not been there before—Fisher was not a member, she had only purchased a day pass—he would make his move.

Fisher suddenly missed McConnell. They had both been working long hours, and they hardly saw each other lately. But neither complained. They knew the demands of the job before they became a couple. For this reason, Fisher believed this relationship might last longer than her others.

McConnell was also far more mature than other people she had gone out with. He was not needy. He did not call her every hour of every day. Sometimes she wished he did, but only because it made a girl feel like she was special. But when he did call, he rarely spoke about work, which was also refreshing.

She looked at the man on the bench again. The moment their eyes met, as she expected, he jumped on his feet and strolled over to her.

"Hey," he said with a grin. "I haven't seen you here before."

"It's my first time."

"You know if you need pointers on how to work out properly, I can help you." He leaned closer. His body spray was overwhelming. "My name is Zack."

Zack! Of course, she thought.

She smiled. "Oh, what a coincidence. My boyfriend's name is Zack as well."

Zack looked like he had been hit on the head. "It is?"

"Yes, and he's a police officer for the Milton PD."

Zack turned pale. "Police officer?"

"I will introduce him to you."

"Um… I should go finish my workout."

As he raced away, she yelled, "Nice to meet you."

She had a feeling Zack would no longer bother her for the remainder of her workout.

She glanced down at her watch.

She frowned.

I should get back to the station, she thought.

She walked over to her gym bag. She pulled out her cell phone and saw there were five missed calls, all from Holt.

She checked her voicemail.

Her eyes widened at what she heard.

She raced out of the gym.

SIXTY-ONE

On any other day, when the alarm clock would go off, Callaway would hit the snooze button and fall right back to sleep. Today was different. He could not be late to drop Nina off at school.

After washing his face and changing his clothes, he drove straight to Patti's house.

He knocked on the door. She answered. "You keep surprising me, Lee," she said.

"Why would you say that?"

"Last night you were there to watch Nina, and here you are first thing in the morning."

He shrugged. "People change, you know."

She stared at him. "I guess if Jimmy could change at his age, there is still hope for you."

Patti knew all about Jimmy Keith. Callaway told her all the details. Jimmy had taught Callaway a way of life that included being selfish and self-indulgent. Callaway had adhered to his teachings like they were gospel, something he now realized was foolish.

"Where's Nina?" he asked.

"She's having breakfast." Patti replied. "You had something to eat?"

"No, I came straight from bed."

"You look it. Come in. There's an extra cup of coffee in the pot. And you can make toast and jam. The jam's in the fridge." Patti grabbed her coat, purse, and said, "Nina's school doesn't open for another forty minutes, so don't drop her off too early."

"Don't worry, I won't leave her at the door and walk away," Callaway said.

Patti did not look like she believed him.

When she was gone, he went to the kitchen.

"Hi, Daddy," Nina said with a smile. She was having a bowl of oatmeal.

"Hey, sweetie," he said, kissing her on the forehead. He grabbed the pot and poured himself a cup. He then grabbed a bagel from the fridge and sat down across from Nina. He could not remember the last time he had breakfast with her.

Is this what I've missed all these years? he thought.

"You're excited about school?" he asked.

She beamed. "I am. I love my teachers. And Jamie and I are working on a project together."

His eyes narrowed. "Jamie's a girl, right?"

Nina laughed. "No, Dad, he's a boy."

They finished their meal. Nina jumped up from her chair. "I have to go change my clothes."

"Okay, dear, I'll be right here."

Callaway was still hungry. He rummaged through the fridge and grabbed a piece of lemon pie. The pie was leftover from several days ago, but he did not care. He ate the pie like it was the most delicious thing he had ever eaten.

Once Nina was ready, they walked the three blocks to her school. A boy ran up to them. He had curly hair, wore glasses, and he had braces on his teeth. He smiled and said, "Hi, Nina."

"Hi, Jamie."

So that's Jamie, he thought. *I saw him before.*

"I have so many ideas for our project," Jamie excitedly said.

"Me too," Nina replied.

The bell rang. Nina waved goodbye to Callaway.

Jamie was about to go with her when Callaway put a hand out to stop him. He said to Nina, "You go ahead, dear. I just want to speak to Jamie for a second."

Nina looked uncertain, but she walked away nonetheless.

Callaway turned to Jamie. "So, what're your intentions toward my daughter?"

Jamie looked confused.

Callaway said, "Do you love her?"

Jamie looked at his feet. "I dunno."

"Do you like her?"

"I guess so."

"You *guess* so?" Callaway repeated.

"I mean, she's nice and…"

"Do you plan on marrying her?"

Jamie's mouth dropped. "Marriage? I'm only nine."

"In some countries that's the legal age of marriage." Callaway was not sure if that was true, but he was not about to backtrack.

"Um… I should go."

Callaway got so close that he was inches away from Jamie's face. "I'm watching you, kid. If you break her heart, I will break you in half."

Callaway snapped his fingers. The sound made the boy jump.

Jamie raced up the steps and disappeared behind the main doors.

Callaway smiled. *I'm glad we had this talk.*

SIXTY-TWO

Fisher parked her SUV behind a strand of yellow police tape and got out. She was at a trailer park just an hour outside of Milton.

Holt approached her and said, "We found him."

"Chase Burley," she repeated as if to make sure.

He nodded.

"Who found him?" she asked.

"One of the trailer park's residents."

"Who's the owner of the trailer home?"

"It's registered to a woman named Debra Coleheim."

"Where is she?"

"Not sure. She wasn't here when we arrived."

"Okay, let's take a look."

They ducked underneath the tape and proceeded up a grassy hill. The trailer had aluminium siding and was slightly bigger than a pickup truck. She stepped onto a landing and then entered the crammed space.

The trailer's interior had a tiny kitchen in the middle, and a table and chairs were on the right with a TV next to the table. On the left, through a narrow door, was the bedroom.

She headed for the bedroom.

She found Chase Burley sprawled on the bed. Blood covered his chest.

"He was stabbed like his father," she said.

"That's the first thing that crossed my mind too," Holt said.

The bed took up the entire room. Fisher had to be careful maneuvering around the space. Fortunately, she was still dressed in her comfortable gym clothes. She pulled on latex gloves and then got on the bed. The sheets and pillows were soaked in red.

Fisher pulled out her penlight and flashed it across Chase's face. He had blond hair that was slicked back. He had a goatee and a diamond stud in the left ear. His eyes were open, but there were lacerations across his cheeks, nose, and temples.

"It looks like someone tortured him," she said.

"That would be my guess as well," Holt said.

She swept the light over Chase's hands. All his fingers were still intact.

Holt said, "I did a cursory look around the trailer, and I didn't find a safe of any kind."

"So why hurt him like this?" Fisher asked.

"It's simple," he replied.

She turned to him.

"The money from Robert Burley's safe," he said.

Fisher frowned. "I'm not so sure…"

"Think about it," Holt said. "Chase Burley was seen at his father's house prior to his murder. He was struggling for money and his father had refused to help him further. Robert Burley was known to keep a lot of cash on hand. He did not trust banks. His son would have known about the money in the safe."

"So, are you saying after the maid saw Chase leave, he returned later and killed his father and took the cash?"

"That's exactly what I'm saying. And," he added, pointing to the body, "someone must have found out what he'd done, and they tortured him to get the money."

Fisher pondered this scenario. "What about the drugs we found stashed in the house?"

"What about them?"

"I thought that was why he had gone to the house," Fisher said.

Holt shook his head. "Did you ever wonder why we found the drugs in the first place? Because Chase Burley had left them behind on *purpose*. He didn't need them. He had the money from the safe, which could have been a substantial amount."

Fisher turned to Chase's lifeless body. She could not help but wonder, *Is that why someone cut you up so badly?*

SIXTY-THREE

His name was Bull. Holt and Fisher were not sure if it was his real name, but that was what he told them. In size and girth, he was the polar opposite of his namesake. Bull stood less than five-feet in height, and he weighed less than a hundred pounds. From afar he looked more like a boy than a man. But up close, his wrinkled skin and graying hair gave his age away. Bull was also a heavy smoker. He reeked of cigarettes.

He took a drag on his current smoke and shook his head. "Man, I ain't never seen anything like that."

"Do you know Debra Coleheim? The woman who lives in the trailer?" Fisher asked.

"Yeah."

"Where can we find her?"

"I don't know where she is right now," Bull replied. "I would tell you if I did. After what I saw happen to that guy, I'm worried about her."

"You know her well?"

"Well enough." He shrugged. "I mean, whenever I saw her sitting out on her lawn chair with a beer in her hand, I'd join her. And it would be the same thing if she saw me outside my home, you know."

"What can you tell us about her?"

"Her parents are from Missouri. I think her dad was in prison for murder, so her mom raised her and her brothers and sister. Debra couldn't wait to get out, and she left the moment she turned eighteen."

"What does she do?"

Bull was silent.

"We want to find her," Fisher said. "We want to know that she is safe."

Bull sighed. "She's a lady of the night."

"She's a prostitute?"

He nodded. "But I know she wanted to stop doing it. She didn't like the kind of men who hired her."

"Is the guy in the trailer one of her clients?" Fisher asked.

"Yeah."

"You know who he is?"

"Kind of. Debra never mentioned names, but she said the guy's dad had won the lottery or something."

"So, Debra knew he had money?" Fisher prodded.

"She did. She was hoping he'd help her get out of here."

"When was the first time you saw him at Debra's place?" Fisher asked.

He searched his mind. "A month or so ago."

"And you didn't see him again until this morning, right?"

"No. I actually saw him a couple of nights ago."

Fisher glanced at Holt, who had been listening silently. Big Bob was murdered a couple of nights ago.

"What was he doing here?" Fisher asked.

"I dunno. I was looking forward to spending time with Debra when…"

"You're also one of her clients?"

Bull looked away. "A guy gets lonely, you know," he said.

"Sure, it's understandable," Fisher said. "So, what happened a couple of nights ago?"

"I knocked on her trailer, and *he* answered the door."

"The dead guy inside, you mean?"

"Yeah. I was surprised to see him. I asked where Debra was, and he said she'd stepped outside."

"How did this guy act? Was he nervous? Angry? Intimidating?"

"He wasn't intimidating, but I think he kind of looked nervous, like he was hiding from someone."

"What made you think that?"

"When I knocked, I saw someone move the curtain. I waited, but no one opened the door. I knocked again and that's when he asked who I was. I told him I was Debra's neighbor. Only then did he open the door."

Fisher pondered this. "After you spoke to him, then what happened?" she asked.

"I kept an eye on her trailer that night," Bull replied. "I had heard stories of guys hurting the girls they'd hired. I was concerned about her, but a few hours later, she came back carrying bags of groceries."

"Did you see the guy again?"

"Only once or twice."

"So, he never left her property?"

"As far as I can tell, no, he never did."

SIXTY-FOUR

Fisher walked around the trailer park with a frown on her face. She knew it was a bad area to look for evidence. There were no security cameras anywhere, there was hardly any traffic, and most of the residents kept to themselves.

There was a reason why some of them chose to live like this. They were running away from one problem or another. Bull spoke to them openly. Fisher got the sense that he had feelings for Debra. He must have been crushed to see Chase living at her home. He could have been jealous as well.

Holt and Fisher had examined Bull's trailer just in case. They saw nothing out of the ordinary. No bloody clothes or weapons of any kind.

Fisher doubted he was Chase's killer. Chase Burley was tortured and then stabbed in the chest. Bull was half Chase's size. She could not see him overpowering Chase.

And then there was the phone call. Why would Bull call 9-1-1 if he had brutally killed Chase?

Fisher's eyes narrowed when a thought occurred to her:

What if Debra killed Chase?

Maybe Chase had told her about the money. She wanted to stop being a prostitute, and what better opportunity to start a new life than with cash in her hand?

Debra could have stabbed Chase and run off with his money. Fisher thought it was odd that Chase's car was not at the trailer park. He had to have driven here. The obvious answer was Debra had used his car as the getaway vehicle.

That raised another question:

Was Bull protecting her? That possibility made sense, but at the same time, did not.

If Debra did kill Chase, then why did she torture him? Was it to find out where he kept the money? If so, then why did she not leave with Bull, who was supposedly her accomplice? Why did *he* stay behind?

Bull had nothing to do with Chase's death, she concluded. Debra might know something, but until they located her, she was only a person of interest.

There was another possibility, however. What if Debra was in hiding? What if she stumbled upon Chase's body, got scared, and ran away?

This made more sense. Whoever killed Big Bob also killed his son. The *modus operandi* was the same.

What if this was never about Big Bob but about Chase all along?

What if the same people who shot up his house in Westport were the same people who murdered him?

Chase was involved in a turf war with a local gang. Chase had gone to his father's house to get his stash of drugs. The gang followed him to the house, and he somehow managed to escape, leaving his father behind. Cornered, Big Bob must have told them about the money in his safe. They killed him nonetheless. And to tie up loose ends, they tracked down Chase and killed him too.

But then how did the maid fit into all of this? She never mentioned seeing anyone at the house other than Big Bob and Chase. And she had clearly heard them arguing inside the house.

And why sever Big Bob's thumb when he supposedly told his killers where he kept the safe?

Fisher felt a migraine coming on.

Instead of finding answers, she was faced with even more questions.

SIXTY-FIVE

Callaway was once again parked across from the office tower. This was his fifth trip in several days, and apart from his very first visit, he rarely saw Gilford come out for lunch.

Maybe this time I really did spook him, he thought. *Maybe he now has his guard up.*

Nevertheless, Callaway had to find a way to fulfil his duties or else Isabel Gilford might ask for her money back. He did not have a refund policy, but there was a mutual understanding that funds would be returned if Callaway was unable to accomplish his task. There was a reason why clients paid half up front and the remainder upon completion.

Callaway stared at the glass building and squinted. He still did not know the name of the assistant. She was not listed on the website for Gilford's firm, and Isabel Gilford did not know her real name either.

He found this last part very odd.

If Callaway knew his spouse was cheating on him, the first thing he would do is find out more about this other person. What if Cary Gilford did not like talking about business at home? Isabel Gilford came across as a woman who had lived a sheltered life.

Callaway's research on Isabel revealed that she was the only child of a prominent businessman and his philanthropic wife. She grew up riding horses and skiing in Aspen. She met Cary Gilford at a horse show and they dated for two years before getting married in a medieval castle in Spain.

Callaway had attained all this information from a profile piece on Cary Gilford by a well-respected business magazine. Cary had just opened his firm and he was looking to attract investors. He had graduated *summa cum laude* from Columbia Business School and promptly gotten a job on Wall Street. He quit after getting married, and with generous help from his father-in-law, Gilford started his own investment firm. The piece on him was positive overall, and it also delved into Gilford's hobbies. He played polo and he ran in marathons around the world.

Regardless of Isabel Gilford's background, and her lack of knowledge about her husband's firm's employees, she was still Callaway's employer. As such, he had to work with whatever information she gave him.

He would have to find the assistant's name on his own.

He just did not know how.

SIXTY-SIX

An hour had gone by, and still there was no sign of Cary Gilford. Callaway normally did not get anxious on a case, but right now he felt like he needed to do something.

The longer he waited, the more he felt like the job was slipping away from him. He was no closer to getting that perfect shot of Gilford with his assistant. And sooner or later, Gilford would realize something was up.

This was inevitable.

A person would have to wear blinders not to see they were being watched. Even if Callaway was careful and avoided being caught, Isabel Gilford could do something that could expose him. That had happened before, and there was no reason why it could not happen now.

He once had a client who wanted Callaway to follow her cheating husband. Callaway did so for days, which ended up turning into weeks. During this time, the client blurted out to her best friend that she had hired a private investigator. She did not know at the time that it was her best friend the husband was having the affair with. Needless to say, Callaway's investigation came to an abrupt halt and he eventually had to abandon it all together. Only much later did the truth finally come out.

He saw a delivery truck pull into a plaza across from the office tower. A man in a uniform got out and walked to a fast-food restaurant.

Callaway suddenly had an idea. He removed his coat and got out of the Charger. He raced up to the delivery truck, stopped, and surveyed his surroundings. When he was certain no one was looking, he pulled the handle of the driver's side door. As he expected, it opened without much effort. Most drivers did not lock their doors. They were only gone from their trucks for a few minutes, and anyway, stealing mail was a federal offense.

Callaway had no intention of touching any of the mail. He was looking for something else. He searched the truck's interior until he spotted what he was looking for. A cap with the delivery company's logo on it was lying on the passenger seat. He grabbed the cap. He then searched again and found a clipboard with a pen attached to it. The clipboard held a list of all the deliveries for the day. He left the list, but he took the clipboard.

He hurried away from the truck. He returned to the Charger and took a deep breath. He waited to see if he had raised any alarms.

The delivery truck driver was not running after him or making a commotion. In fact, he was not even back yet.

Callaway moved toward the office tower.

He reached the entrance, went through a set of glass doors, and took the elevator up to the nineteenth floor. Getting off the elevator, he consulted a directory on the wall of a carpeted hallway. The directory indicated he had to go right in order to get to his destination. He moved past other businesses and slowed in front of a glass wall. The sign on the door read: Gilford Investments.

He saw a young woman behind the desk. She was not the assistant. He placed the cap on his head, and with the clipboard in hand, he entered.

The young woman immediately smiled at him. "Welcome to Gilford Investments," she said.

"Hi there," he said. "I'm here to pick up a package."

The woman looked around. "Oh, I don't see anything here for you."

"Are you sure?" Callaway asked in mock surprise.

"Yes. Brooke usually leaves it underneath the desk."

"Brooke?" Callaway asked.

"Mr. Gilford's assistant."

Callaway pretended to scan the clipboard. "What's her full name?"

"Brooke O'Shea."

"Can you spell that for me?" He wanted to make sure he got it right. Some people used an apostrophe and others did not.

The woman spelled the name and he made a mental note of it. He frowned. "I don't see her name here."

The woman reached for the phone. "Brooke's not in, but I can call and ask her."

"Found it," Callaway said. "I'm actually supposed to pick it up tomorrow. How foolish of me."

He apologized and then quickly extricated himself from the situation. He did not want Gilford coming out of his office and seeing him.

As Callaway took the elevator down, he could not help but smile.

SIXTY-SEVEN

Before returning to the Charger, Callaway discarded his impromptu disguise and then walked around the office tower's parking lot. To his shock, Cary Gilford's Audi was not there.

How could I've not seen it leave? he thought. *I followed him in this morning, and I was here the entire time.*

He frowned.

Wait. What if he left while I was procuring my disguise?

That would make sense as to why Callaway did not see Gilford inside his office. Gilford Investments occupied a small space, so anyone could have heard his conversation with the woman at the desk. Cary would have surely come out at the sound of his mistress's name.

Brooke O'Shea was not in the office either. Did she and Cary leave together?

Callaway cursed himself.

I've just lost another opportunity. They could be anywhere.

Instead of scolding himself further, he decided to utilize his time. He got behind the wheel of his Charger and drove to a building he had seen on his way over. The place was an impressive structure, made of concrete with white columns in the front and a dozen steps leading up to a massive oak door.

The Milton Public Library housed original manuscripts from some of the twentieth century's most respected writers. Works by F. Scott Fitzgerald, Joseph Conrad, Virginia Woolf, Graham Greene, and by many others could be found there. Callaway rarely read, so he was not here to peruse any of the masterpieces on display. He was here to do some research. He spoke to a librarian who had him fill out a form because he did not have a library card, and then she led him to a computer terminal in the corner.

Once he was online, Callaway entered the name "Brooke O'Shea" in the search field. There were dozens of people with that name. He then typed in "Gilford Investments" next to the name. Several links came up and he clicked on the first one, which was for a career networking site. The profile photo showed a woman with blonde hair, bright red lipstick, and wearing a striped suit jacket. Brooke O'Shea looked professional, and, Callaway would not hesitate to admit, also looked stunning. As a man, he could see why Cary Gilford would be attracted to her.

Callaway scrolled further through her profile. She graduated from an acting school in New York. After small parts in TV shows and B-movies, she started to work as a secretary for a law firm. She then joined Gilford Investments, and in her spare time she was working toward becoming a paralegal. At the bottom of her profile was a quote from her: "*Although I have had to take on various positions to pay the bills, my passion is and will always be acting. Nothing gets me excited more than to get inside the skin of a stranger. If I can make a viewer believe I am this other person, then I have done my job as an actress.*"

He clicked on other sites. Most had the same basic information on the projects she had starred in. One of the sites was for a talent agency. Callaway assumed they represented her. There was a telephone number listed at the bottom.

He decided to give them a call.

SIXTY-EIGHT

Callaway waited as the phone rang. A moment later, a female voice said,
"Tanner Creative Agency."

Callaway spoke in a southern drawl. "Hi there. My name is Gator Peckerwood, and before you ask me if that's my real name, unfortunately, it is. My parents were from Louisiana. Anyway, I am calling from DBC Studios and I was supposed to deliver a script to one of your actresses, Ms. Brooke O'Shea."

"Oh yes," came the chirpy reply. "We represent Brooke."

"I was wondering if you could give me her home address."

There was a pause on the other end. "Which studio are you calling from again?" the woman asked.

"DBC Studios. We're based out of Vancouver, Canada."

"You can mail the script to us at Tanner Creative Agency and we'll make sure she gets it."

It was Callaway's turn to pause. He wanted to let the silence hang so the woman on the other end would feel uncomfortable.

"Sir, are you still there?" the woman asked with a trace of anxiety.

"I am. I have specific instructions to hand deliver the script to Ms. O'Shea and Ms. O'Shea only. I am to fly to Milton, wait until Ms. O'Shea has read the script, and then return to Vancouver with the script in my possession. If this is not possible, then we will look at other actresses on our list." Callaway knew secrecy was paramount in productions with large budgets. With the advent of the internet, studio executives worried about scripts being leaked online.

"No, that won't be necessary," the woman said. "I know Brooke would be perfect for the role. Do you have a pen on hand?"

"I do."

She relayed the address to him.

"Thank you. You have been most helpful," he said, and hung up.

He got in the Charger and drove twenty-five minutes to a condominium complex. Three high-rises circled a children's playground.

Callaway wanted to drive into the complex, but there was a security guard stationed at the entrance. All unknown drivers had to check in at his booth before they could proceed further. Callaway did not know anyone in the complex, so he could not bluff his way in by claiming he was here to visit someone. And there was no way he wanted Brooke O'Shea to know he was even here.

So, what am I doing here anyway? he thought.

He knew the answer. He wanted to see where she lived and how she lived. The condo complex looked upscale. If he had to guess, each unit cost over three-hundred thousand dollars. How could a washed-up actress, on the salary of an assistant, afford such a place? The answer was she could not, but her employer, Cary Gilford, could.

Callaway felt a tingling sensation in the back of his head which came whenever he was excited. If his hunch turned out right, then his client, Isabel Gilford, would be pleased to know her husband was paying for his mistress's accommodation. This would give her more ammunition to seize control of her husband's business during the divorce.

To confirm this, Callaway would have to go back to his office and run the address through the government's property tax records. As a license private investigator, Callaway had access to dozens of databases. A necessity in his line of work. If the results came back as he hoped, he would drive straight to his client and deliver the news to her. This might even satisfy her, and he could be done with the case.

Afterwards, he could finally decide what to do with the remaining money from the twenty-five thousand she had given him.

SIXTY-NINE

Callaway was about to leave the condo complex when something caught his attention. A car was coming down the road toward him. He squinted and realized it was Gilford's Audi.

Jackpot! he thought.

Gilford drove past him and entered the complex. He pulled up to the security guard's booth, the barrier came up, and he drove in.

Callaway smiled. *This keeps getting better and better.*

The Charger was on the other side of the road, across from the condo buildings. Callaway scanned his surroundings. He saw a coffee shop one traffic light away from the complex.

He drove to the coffee shop and parked in the visitor's lot. He removed a bag from the trunk and then jogged back to the complex.

Gilford was there to see his assistant, which meant this was his chance to get the photos his client so desperately coveted. He was not sure how he would accomplish this task, but he had a plan.

There was no security if someone *walked* into the complex. Callaway had seen residents of the three buildings do just that without anyone questioning them. The security guard was more preoccupied with parking. Most buildings had limited space, and as such, building management did not want residents parking in visitor spots or vice versa.

Callaway walked down a concrete sidewalk and then cut through the children's playground. He spotted a few parents with little ones in the area. They did not pay any attention to him. They were too busy watching their kids run around the slides, play in the dirt, or ride the swings.

Condo building number one was adjacent to number two. Condo building number two was adjacent to number three. Building one was across from building three, with the children's park in between them.

Brooke O'Shea was in number three. If Callaway wanted a view of her unit, he would have to go to number one.

He made a beeline for number one's entrance.

As he approached the main doors, he saw a couple exiting. The man smiled and held the door for him out of courtesy.

He thinks I live in the building, Callaway thought.

Callaway thanked him and went inside. He took the elevator all the way to the top. He got off, went down a hall and entered the roof of the building. The developers had converted that space into an outdoor patio. Lounge chairs, benches, and barbecues were laid out for residents to use. Fortunately, the patio was empty at the moment.

He raced to the other side of the roof and looked over. He could see building number three across from him. He counted the floors from bottom to top. He stopped at eighteen. He then counted across and stopped at eight.

1808. Brooke O'Shea's unit number.

He looked around to see if the coast was clear.

He pulled out his digital camera from the backpack, attached an external lens, and then zoomed in on 1808.

Luckily, the drapes in the condo were not drawn. He moved the camera from one room window to another.

He stopped at the living room.

Bingo.

O'Shea and Gilford were seated on the sofa with a glass of wine in their hands. He focused the camera. He could see that Gilford was talking and O'Shea was smiling. Callaway snapped a few photos of them together.

He hoped after the wine they would move to the bedroom. He did not like this part of his job—he felt like a voyeur—but over the years he had learned how to capture shots that were not fully explicit. No matter how much a client wanted to confirm the affair with their own eyes, they were never prepared to see someone they loved in compromising positions. Callaway's technique cushioned the blow.

O'Shea leaned closer to kiss Gilford. Suddenly, she stopped, stood up, and said something to him in anger, her arms flailing as she did so. Gilford stood up and pointed a finger at her. He too was now angry.

They exchanged a few more words.

Gilford hit her across the face.

Callaway blinked. He was not expecting this.

O'Shea retaliated by balling her fists and swinging at him. Gilford was bigger, and he quickly restrained her by grabbing her wrists. She pulled away and then ran into the bathroom and slammed the door shut.

Gilford went after her. He yelled something at the closed door. He then grabbed his suit jacket and left the apartment.

Callaway had captured the entire incident on his camera.

SEVENTY

Callaway walked back to his car. He was disturbed by what he saw. Gilford had not only been violent toward his wife but also his mistress.

What kind of a man would do that? he thought.

A monster. And one who deserves what will happen next.

Callaway drove straight to his office. He raced up the metal stairs, and once he was inside, he turned on his laptop. While the computer booted up, he scrolled through the photos he had taken.

They showed Gilford with his mistress. They also showed him striking her across the face. Callaway would love to forward these to the authorities, but then they would ask how he had gotten them. He could not tell them he had gone on private property and then intruded on a personal situation from a distance. The courts would deem the photos inadmissible and therefore the authorities would not even bother looking at them.

He could mail them to the authorities anonymously. This would force them to at least look into the matter. But then Gilford would know someone was watching him.

But then again, the photos were not his property. They were his client's. He had taken them for her, and as such it was not up to him what happened to them. His client could choose not to take them to the police. Perhaps that might even work more to her advantage. Gilford's reputation and career would be in tatters if the photos ever got out to the public. He would do anything for that not to happen, even if that meant handing over his namesake firm to his soon to be ex-wife.

Callaway felt giddy at that last thought. He never imagined his visit to the condo complex would turn out to be so fruitful.

He turned his attention to the laptop. He punched in Brooke O'Shea's address in one of the online databases. To his dismay, the property was registered under her name. Gilford was not paying for it, at least on record, so that could not be used against him.

No worries, he thought. *I still have damning evidence to destroy both Gilford and his mistress.*

His cell phone rang. He answered.

He raced out of the office.

Fifteen minutes later, he was ringing Patti's doorbell.

Patti answered. Before he could utter a word, she asked, "What did *you* do?"

"I didn't do anything," he replied. "At least, I don't remember doing anything."

"Nina's been crying for twenty minutes."

His heart sank. "Why?"

"She said you said something to her friend."

"What friend?"

"Jamie."

Callaway opened his mouth but then shut it.

Patti glared at him. "Did you ask him if he wanted to marry Nina?"

"Um... I just wanted to know his intentions toward my daughter."

"Marriage? Really? They're both only nine years old."

"In some countries..."

She put her hand up to stop him. "Don't even go there."

Nina stuck her head out. Her eyes were red and filled with anger.

He broke into a smile. "Hey, baby."

"I hate you, Daddy!" she shouted.

Nina stormed upstairs to her room.

Callaway felt like someone had seared his heart with a hot poker.

"She doesn't mean it," Patti said in a calm voice. "Kids can get overly dramatic."

"Are they always like this?" he asked.

"Oh yeah, for sure. If you were more involved, you'd know."

He suddenly felt physically ill.

SEVENTY-ONE

Callaway took a sip from his glass. His head was bowed as he stared at the bar's countertop. He could not believe he had screwed things up even when he was not trying to. Nina was mad at him. She had been cross before, but never to the extent she was now.

I hate you, Daddy.

Those words stung worse than anything he had felt before, and Callaway had been through his share of pain. Mostly physical, though. When he failed to return payment to a loan shark, they would send someone to recover their money. Callaway had found himself at the other end of a fist, foot, and elbow. He had his nose broken twice, had been left with several black eyes and even a missing tooth. This was on top of the bruised ribs and ego.

But all that did not compare to the pain he was feeling right now. Nina was his life. He never realized it when she was younger, but things were different now. He wanted to be there for her when she needed him.

He sighed. He was only trying to protect her. He did not want to see her get hurt. Instead, *he* had somehow hurt her.

He felt movement beside him.

"You okay, Lee?" a voice asked.

He turned and saw it was Fisher.

"Dana," he said. "What're you doing here?"

"I could ask you the same thing," she replied.

He took another sip. "Trying to clear my head."

"What did you do *now*?"

"How do you know I did anything?"

"It's written all over your face." She pulled up a stool next to his. "I heard you had quit PI work. Is that right?"

"I did for a short while, but then I got a new case."

"Let me guess," she said. "Your client wants you to follow her cheating husband."

His jaw dropped. "How'd you know?"

She laughed, knowing he was joking. "Let's just say, I'm psychic,"

"It pays well," he said. "So, drinks on me."

Fisher gave him a look. "You know I can't drink while on duty."

"Then I go back to my initial question: what are you doing here?"

She sighed. "Trying to clear my head."

"Hey, don't steal my lines."

The bartender came over. Fisher ordered a soda.

"Put it on my tab," Callaway said.

The bartender nodded and then returned with her drink.

She took a sip and said, "So what's *really* bothering you?"

"You really wanna know?"

"I do."

He told her.

When he was done, she said, "I wouldn't worry too much about it. Kids can be overly dramatic."

"Those were the exact words Patti used," he said, genuinely surprised. "You *are* psychic."

Fisher laughed again. "I have four nieces and nephews, so I'm familiar with how kids think at that age."

Callaway turned back to his drink.

Fisher said, "I'm proud that you are making an effort. The old Lee Callaway wouldn't have even known his daughter had a friend named Jamie."

"True," he said. After a brief pause, he asked, "So, what're you working on right now?"

"You know I can't discuss cases with you."

Callaway smirked. "Did it have something to do with the dead lottery winner?"

"How'd you know?"

"I'm also psychic."

Fisher sighed and rolled her eyes. "Okay, enough with the psychic jokes."

"I heard he left behind a ton of money."

"And a ton of problems."

"Are you saying money doesn't solve all your problems? Money sure solves my problems.'"

"Most of your problems revolve around money, or lack of it." Her cell phone buzzed. She answered and then hung up. "I have to go," she said.

"Work?"

"It always is."

"Take it easy," he said with a wave.

She moved away, but then she stopped and turned to him. "You managed to mess things up with Nina, but that doesn't mean you can't fix them. Kids can be very forgiving. Trust me."

He smiled. "Thanks, Dana."

SEVENTY-TWO

Debra Coleheim lay in the back of a Chevy Tahoe which was registered to Chase Burley.

Her face was purple and bruised, her eyes were swollen and shut, and her lips were cut and puffy.

I was only half correct, Fisher thought as she stared at the lifeless body. *Debra had left the trailer park in Chase's vehicle, but she had not driven it. Someone else had.*

Holt stood next to her. He had called her the moment he had arrived on the scene.

There were marks across Coleheim's neck which indicated she had been strangled. Fisher could not tell if it was with a rope or by bare hands. An autopsy would confirm the exact cause of death.

The Tahoe was parked in a ditch next to a rural road. The ditch was so deep that it was near impossible to see the Tahoe from the road.

As if reading her mind, Holt pointed to a sedan parked on the side of the road, "The guy had a flat tire, so he pulled over. When he got out to change it, he saw the back of the Tahoe. He went to check to see if someone might have had an accident and saw her body in the back."

"Did you notify the ME?" Fisher asked.

"She's on her way."

Fisher felt a headache coming on. She kind of wished she had sipped a *real* drink at the bar when Callaway had offered one to her. Now they were up to *three* murders.

A thought occurred to her. "Why not kill her back at the trailer park?"

Holt frowned. "What do you mean?"

"Whoever killed Chase Burley also killed Debra Coleheim."

"That would be my conclusion as well."

"So why leave Chase's body in the trailer home and hers all the way out here?"

Holt's brow furrowed. "Maybe the killer wanted something from her."

"Yes, and I think I know what."

Holt looked confused.

She leaned down into the trunk and lifted up the side of Debra Coleheim's dress.

The dress was torn.

"You think she was… *raped*?" Holt asked.

"Yes, or she let her killer do whatever he wanted with her in the hope that he would let her go. She was a prostitute, after all."

Holt's face darkened. He took sexual assault very seriously. Such crimes had everything to do with power, specifically male over female. In some countries, sexual assault was used as a weapon against the female population in order to keep them subdued. Even the threat of such violence would silence a woman against her oppressors, which in most cases were their husbands or relatives.

Fisher said, "It would explain why we didn't find Chase's vehicle at the trailer park. The killer had taken it. It also explains why we didn't find Debra Coleheim at the trailer park either. The killer had taken her too."

Holt looked away, clearly troubled.

Fisher suddenly felt bad for Bull, Debra's neighbor. He was worried for her and rightly so. He would be crushed to know what had happened to her.

Holt looked back at Fisher. "I don't think this has anything to do with Chase's drug problem."

Fisher saw what he was getting at. They had formulated a theory that the people who had shot up Chase's house in Westport had traced him to his father's house, killed his father for the money in the safe, and then, to tie up loose ends, they found Chase in the trailer home and killed him. But there were not too many cases of drug dealers murdering a rival dealer and raping their wives or girlfriends for revenge. Fisher had heard of such stories in Mexico or Colombia, but not in the United States. And even in those instances, the murder and rape by gang members was only done to send a message so that no one messed with them.

Debra Coleheim was neither Chase's wife nor girlfriend. She was someone he hired for the night whenever he was in Milton.

Maybe the killer or killers did not know that. Chase was found hiding in her home, so she could have been collateral damage, or someone who was at the wrong place at the wrong time.

Regardless, Fisher knew they were no closer to solving who had murdered Big Bob, Chase Burley, and now Debra Coleheim.

She shook her head and walked over to the motorist who had spotted the Tahoe. She hoped he had seen something that might help in their investigation. But she could not help shake off the feeling it would be another dead end.

SEVENTY-THREE

When Callaway called Isabel Gilford, he was surprised by her response. He expected her to tell him to wait by the side of the road for her. Instead, she gave him an address and told him she would be waiting for him there.

The house was located thirty miles outside of Milton. A winding road led to the property's entrance, and Callaway had to drive another quarter of a mile on a gravel path until he was in front of a house which had a white exterior and a black roof. There were flower pots in the front, and clay statues of various animals were scattered about the property.

He parked next to a bird feeder and got out. He looked around. He did not see another vehicle. He was certain the black limousine would be here. Isabel Gilford never went anywhere without it.

Maybe I'm early, he thought.

Prior to driving over, he did a quick search on the address and found that the house was listed under Isabel Gilford.

He walked up to the front door and knocked. While he waited, he looked around again. There was not another house as far as his eyes could see. The property was next to a lake and it was surrounded by a lush forest.

There were no noises of any kind to break the tranquility. Callaway felt a wave of serenity wash over him. He shut his eyes and let the silence take hold of him.

His eyes snapped open when he heard a noise.

He turned and saw Isabel Gilford standing next to the house. She was wearing a long white dress that went down to her ankles. Her silver hair was covered by a sun hat. She was not wearing dark sunglasses like before. Instead, her gray eyes were staring at him.

"I didn't mean to disturb you," she said.

"Um... I... I..." he stammered, searching for the right words.

She smiled. "It's okay. It's so beautiful here that I too find myself savoring each moment I'm here."

"I knocked on the door several times," he said.

"I apologize. I was in the backyard and I didn't hear you. I knew you'd be coming soon, so I came out to check, and that's when I saw your car parked out in front. Please follow me."

She took him through the side of the house. Callaway said, "I noticed that your driver is not here."

"I sent him away," she replied. "This is *my* retreat. I don't invite a lot of people here. Cary's only been here a handful of times. Remember I told you I had sold an expensive brooch Cary had given me? Well, I used the money from the sale to purchase this place. I bought it without even visiting it. I saw the real estate listing when it came up and I knew I had to have it." Her smile widened. "I think I made the right decision, don't you think?"

"It's amazing here," he said.

The dark bruise under her eye was still noticeable, but this time she was trying not to hide it.

"Wait till I show you the backyard," she said with a gleam in her eyes.

They entered through a gate. Callaway's mouth dropped. The garden looked like it had been pulled out of a magazine. Flowers of all colors imaginable covered the space, and a wide variety of plants were carefully arranged on the ground. In between the horticulture was a pebbled walkway, and manicured green grass lay beyond the garden.

They headed down the walkway. Callaway saw the path led directly to a gazebo.

"I have a confession to make, Mr. Callaway," she said.

"Um… sure, and please, call me Lee," he said."

"Okay, Lee," she said with a smile. "I'm afraid I don't have a green thumb. What you see around you has nothing to do with me. I have a professional gardener who comes once a week to make sure everything is taken care of."

"How many times do you come here?" he asked.

"I never used to come here often, but lately, with things being... complicated with Cary, I've been coming regularly."

"If I had a place like this, I'd come here often too."

They stopped before the gazebo. She said, "In your telephone call, you said you had something urgent to show me."

Callaway reached into his coat pocket and pulled out an envelope.

Her eyes widened. "Are they what I think they are?"

"They are not exactly what you had requested, but I think you'll find them very useful."

She paused and then slowly said, "Perhaps we should go inside. I could use a drink. Do you drink, Lee?"

"I sometimes drink more than I should," he joked.

SEVENTY-FOUR

Isabel Gilford laughed and then giggled.

Callaway and Isabel Gilford were seated in the living room. They each had a glass of wine in their hand.

Earlier, after they had gone inside the house, Callaway had shown the photos he had taken of Cary Gilford and Brooke O'Shea. Isabel Gilford went through each photo slowly and carefully, as if she was trying to burn the images in her mind. When she reached the last set of photos, she put her hand over her mouth. She then reached for the nearest chair and sat down. She looked at him as if to confirm what she was seeing.

"Yes, your husband struck his mistress," Callaway had said.

Her initial reaction was anger. She could not believe she had married a monster. But then her mood changed to excitement. She could use these photos in her divorce. But then, just as quickly, her emotions turned to sadness. She covered her face and began to cry. She knew her marriage was over, but it was the years she wasted with Cary that she most regretted.

She confessed to Callaway that her husband had been unfaithful twice before in their marriage. Each time she vowed to leave him, but he somehow managed to win her back. He was always contrite, and he would turn into the most devoted husband imaginable. He would take her on amazing trips around the world. As a child she had travelled to exotic locations. Her father was a successful businessman, after all, but with Cary it was different. He doted on her and made her feel special. For a moment she always believed everything would be okay. But then time would pass, and he would go back to his philandering ways.

Cary, she admitted, could be so caring, but also so cruel.

Isabel Gilford snorted out another laugh. She turned beet red. "I'm so sorry. I haven't laughed this hard in a long time."

Callaway grinned. "Don't worry. I blame the wine."

She smiled. "Okay, Lee, your turn."

His brow furrowed. "My turn?"

"You know a lot about me, but I know very little about you."

"What would you like to know?"

"Everything."

He took another sip. "Alright, I was married once."

Her eyebrows shot up. "I never saw you as the married type."

"I'm not, or at least, I wasn't when I got married."

"And what happened?"

He paused.

Well, why not? he thought.

He told her an abbreviated version of his life's story.

When he was done, she said, "If you ask me, you still harbor feelings for your ex-wife."

"That's exactly what someone else said too." He was thinking of Fisher. She and Callaway had dated once, and she quickly ended the relationship because she believed there was a chance Patti and Callaway could get back together.

Isabel Gilford grabbed his glass. "Let me get you some more."

"Um… I don't know…. I have to drive back."

"Don't worry. If you're too drunk, my driver will take you home."

He watched her leave the room. A moment later, she returned with his glass; it was filled to the brim.

"Isn't that a lot?" he asked.

She smiled and winked. "We have all night to finish it."

SEVENTY-FIVE

Callaway tried to lift his head up, but when he did, everything swirled around him. He shut his eyes and waited until the spinning went away. He blinked and then looked around. He was in a room, and by the looks of it, it was someone's bedroom.

The sun shined through the open windows. He squinted as the light hit his eyes.

How long have I been asleep? he thought.

He slowly lifted his head again and this time he managed to sit upright. He spotted a photo frame on the dresser. He blinked to clear the fog from his eyes. He saw the photo was of Cary and Isabel Gilford, and it was taken on their wedding day. They were both younger, although, when he stared at the picture carefully, Isabel Gilford looked... *different.*

That must've been taken twenty years ago, he thought. *The years have not been kind to her.*

He grimaced as a wave of dizziness struck him. He covered his face and tried to remember what happened last night.

When he had arrived at the house, the sun had started to set. He remembered sitting in the living room with Isabel Gilford, sharing a bottle of wine. He remembered they talked about her marriage and his. He remembered feeling guilty about not asking Patti out again. He remembered feeling worse when he thought of Dr. Michael Hayward. Patti had found someone that was in every way better than him.

He then remembered Isabel Gilford kissing him. He could tell she was a little drunk and so was he. He did not stop her. They were both heartbroken, and they needed someone to make them feel wanted.

But... but he could not recall what happened next. It was as if he had blacked out.

He looked down and realized he was only wearing his boxers.

He frantically searched the room and found his pants, shoes, and coat on the floor, but not his shirt. He got dressed, sans shirt, and hurried downstairs. The lights were off. He thought about calling out her name.

Maybe she's in the garden, he thought.

192

He winced as another sharp pain ripped through his head. He leaned against the wall for support. When he got his bearings, he left the house.

He saw his beloved Charger parked where he had left it. He looked around and saw no sign of the limousine.

She must have gone back to her house in Milton.

He got behind the wheel and started the engine. He pressed the accelerator and revved it a few times, waiting to see if Isabel heard the noise and came out. She did not.

He drove away from the house. He was racing down the gravel road when he slammed on the brakes. In front of him, not two feet away, was a man with a Basset Hound. They had emerged from the forest and were crossing the road.

The man glared at Callaway. The dog barked at the Charger and its errant driver.

Callaway rolled down the window. "I'm really sorry," he said.

The man did not reply. He shook his head and dragged the barking dog away. They finished crossing the road and disappeared into the forest.

Callaway took a deep breath to steady his nerves.

He carefully drove away at a slow speed.

SEVENTY-SIX

Callaway pulled up to the hotel's underground parking lot. He realized he was missing his room key and parking access card. He double-checked his coat pockets, but the cards were not there.

I must have dropped them back at Isabel's house, he thought.

He was not about to drive sixty miles both ways to retrieve them. He drove around and parked in the hotel's visitor parking lot.

He approached the desk clerk.

"A rough night?" the clerk asked with a wry smile.

I must look like crap, Callaway thought.

"Yeah, you can say that," he replied to the clerk. "Um… I seem to have lost my room key and parking card. Can I get another?"

"Of course. We get that a lot. But we do charge for replacement keys and cards."

"Sure." He reached into his coat pocket and pulled out a small bundle of cash. He dropped a bill.

The clerk took the bill and said, "Give me a minute."

While Callaway waited, a thought occurred to him:

Where's my camera?

He left the front desk and hurried back to the Charger. He scanned the interior. The camera was not there. He opened the trunk. The camera was not there either.

He frowned. He had gone to an instant-print shop, printed out the photos he had taken of Cary Gilford and Brooke O'Shea, and then driven straight to Isabel's private property. He did not stop at the hotel or his office.

So where could it be? Did I leave the camera behind at the instant-print shop?

He felt another headache coming on. He could not believe the day had started off so badly. Today was supposed to have been celebratory. After delivering the photos to his client, his job was complete.

Luckily, his digital camera required a password to access it. He had little concern someone might see the camera's files.

Regardless, the camera had cost a substantial sum, and he would have to fork over more money to buy a replacement.

He returned to the front desk.

The clerk said, "You know what?"

"What?"

"I found your key."

He blinked. "Found it?"

"Apparently, someone—likely a cleaning staff member—had left it in our lost and found bin." He held the key up for him.

Callaway grabbed the key.

The clerk smiled. "You may have been in a hurry and it might have slipped out of your pocket. It happens more than people realize."

Callaway stared at him. "Um… yeah, sure. But what about the access card? I do need to park my car in the underground garage."

"Here you go," the clerk said, handing him a white card.

"Thanks for your help," Callaway said.

He took the elevator up to his room. He could have taken the stairs, but his headache had turned into a full-blown migraine. The pain was sharp and unrelenting.

He entered his room and headed straight for the bathroom. He opened the top cabinet, found the bottle, and downed two painkillers with a glass of water.

He pulled off his coat, dropped it on the floor, and then fell on the bed. He rested his head on the pillow and shut his eyes.

Within minutes he was passed out.

SEVENTY-SEVEN

Callaway rubbed his eyes. He checked the clock on the wall.

I can't believe I slept for three hours straight, he thought.

He slowly got up. He felt much better than before, but not by a whole lot. At least the throbbing pain in his head was gone.

He thought about Isabel Gilford. He knew he had spent the night with her, but why could he not remember any of it? Maybe he should call her. But what would he say? "Hey, I know something happened between us last night, but can you tell me exactly what?"

He shook his head.

You dumbass. No woman wants to hear that. They want to feel loved and special.

If Callaway could not recollect what happened, that meant he was drunk out of his mind.

There had been a few occasions in the past where he was too wasted to remember who he had been with, but at least he did not have to see them again.

He hoped that was the case with Isabel Gilford. He could see no positive outcome to them being together. She was a married woman. She was also his employer. A rival divorce lawyer would chew him up on the stand about his relationship with a client.

He had his money and she had her evidence. Case closed.

He got up and decided to take a cold shower. He then dressed in some comfortable clothes and left. He took the stairs down and walked to his Charger.

He still could not believe he had lost his camera. He decided to head for the instant-print shop. Once he was there, he spoke to all the associates and the manager. No one had seen a digital camera.

Someone must have taken it, he grumbled. *Likely another customer. I can't track it down. Guess I'll have to shell out for a new one.*

But that would be another day. Right now, he was famished.

His stomach grumbled as he drove to Joely's restaurant.

He found a table by the windows and waited for her to finish serving a customer.

When she came over, she had a smile on her face. "Is it a late breakfast or an early lunch?"

"I would say a late breakfast," he replied.

"No freebies. You know the rules."

He pulled out a bill and placed it on the table. "I can pay for my own meal, thank you."

"Great, so what would you like?"

"What do you recommend?"

"We have the best waffles in the city."

"Don't they all say that?"

"They do, but you won't know if ours is the best unless you try them for yourself."

"Sure, waffles it is, and a cup of your fresh brewed coffee."

"Coming right up."

Joely left.

He turned his attention to the window. The sun was shining bright, and for a moment he felt complete and utter peace.

He smiled.

With the case over, it was time to think about what he should do with all that money. He debated whether to go on a long overseas trip or maybe even buy nice furniture for his new apartment.

Speaking of which, he thought. *I still have to hand over the first and last month's rent to the new landlord.*

Callaway wanted to do so the moment Nina and Patti had approved of the apartment, but the landlord had requested a certified check instead of cash, which required him to go to a bank nearby and get one prepared.

He would get the check right after breakfast.

Joely brought his plate and cup. "Enjoy," she said.

He grabbed a knife and fork and dug into his meal. The waffle was warm, and the coffee was hot. Just the way he liked them.

He was cutting a piece of the waffle when he felt someone next to him.

He looked up and smiled. "Dana, what're you doing here?"

Fisher had a grim look on her face, and her hand was on her holster.

"Lee Callaway, you are under arrest for the murder of… *Isabel Gilford.*"

Callaway dropped his knife and fork.

SEVENTY-EIGHT

When Fisher received the call early in the morning, she never imagined the case would end up in Callaway's arrest. The call was simple, one she had heard dozens of times before. A body had been found in a house some thirty miles outside of Milton. The body had suffered trauma which led the police to believe it could be murder. Until she or some other detective confirmed otherwise, the death was going to be treated as suspicious.

She had debated whether to pass the case to someone else. She already had three unsolved deaths on her desk: Big Bob, Chase Burley, and Debra Coleheim. She had a strong feeling they were all linked. A break in one case would solve the others.

Reluctantly, she agreed to take on the new case.

After notifying Holt, she made the long drive to the house where the body had been found. She was surprised to find Holt waiting for her. Next to him was another man. He identified himself as the husband of the deceased.

His name was Cary Gilford. He told them the house was registered under his wife's name; she was known to stay there for days on end, but she was supposed to be home last night. They had planned to meet with a group of her friends. He called her several times, but he figured she was not answering because she was still upset with him. He confessed that they had been going through a rough patch and he may have said some horrible things to her in the process. When she did not return home by morning, he decided to drive over to check on her.

Fisher's gaze was focused on Cary Gilford as he led them inside the house. She wanted to study his behavior. In her experience, one spouse often was to blame for the other's death.

There was a body on the floor in the living room. The victim was female with silver hair and wearing a white dress.

She had a knife stuck in her chest.

Fisher's first instinct was the same person who had killed Big Bob and his son had done the deed, but there was a big, glaring difference. In their case, the killer had not left a knife behind.

The Milton PD had upgraded their evidence gathering technology. Previously, fingerprints that were lifted from the scene used to be taken back to the station and run through the police databases, which could take hours. Now, all the detectives had to do was lift the fingerprints using a special strip, photograph the results on their cell phones, and upload the file to a server online. The server would then run the print through the various databases the department was linked with. The entire process from start to finish took less than twenty minutes.

Holt proceeded to do just that.

While they waited for the results, Fisher decided to survey the scene. She walked around the living room, examining every inch. The beige carpet was now stained with red. She spotted two wine glasses on the coffee table. One still had some wine left in it. She lifted the empty one up with a gloved hand and held it up in the light. She could clearly see smudges on the glass. She decided to grab prints from both the glasses, uploaded them, and headed straight for the kitchen.

She needed only a second to see that a knife was missing from the wooden block.

If she had to guess, it was the same knife in the victim's chest.

She returned to the living room. Holt was staring at his cell phone. He held the phone up for her and said, "I think you better take a look at this."

She was shocked.

Lee Callaway?!

Several years back, Callaway had been arrested for drunk driving. The Milton PD had his prints in the system.

"This isn't right," she told Holt.

Holt, to his credit, ran the prints again. While they waited, her cell phone buzzed. The results from the wine glasses were back. For one of the glasses there was no match found in the system, but this only meant whoever drank from the glass was never fingerprinted.

The fingerprints on the second glass were matched 99% to a Lee Callaway. His mugshot popped up on her cell phone along with all the details of his DUI arrest.

Fisher's knees buckled. She almost fell onto the sofa, but she was able to regain her composure and hold onto the armrest for support.

They proceeded to gather further evidence. After that, they had no choice but to bring the suspect in for questioning.

She was grateful Holt let her conduct the arrest, but it was no secret she was friends with Callaway.

For that very reason, she was now behind a glass wall, staring at Holt and Callaway in the interview room.

She prayed Callaway had an explanation for what they had found at the house.

SEVENTY-NINE

Once Fisher had cuffed Callaway at the restaurant, she had taken him outside. He was confused, and he kept asking her why she was doing this. She told him that it was his right to remain silent and that anything he said can and will be used against him in a court of law. But he was not listening. He wanted answers and she would not give them to him. At one point he got angry with her and he said something which he now regretted. Never once did she retaliate. Her eyes were moist, and it looked like she was on the verge of breaking down. Holt appeared out of nowhere and had taken possession of him. His grip was strong as he pushed him into the backseat of a waiting car. Holt had then driven Callaway to the station, and after getting booked, he was placed in the interview room.

"This is a mistake," Callaway said.

Holt was seated across from him. His arms were crossed over his chest and he had a stern look on his face.

"I'm afraid it's no mistake," Holt said.

"Where's Dana?"

"She's not here."

"I want to speak to her."

"That won't be possible."

Callaway tried to cover his face with his hands, but the cuffs on his wrists were attached to the table.

Callaway held up the cuffs. "Is this necessary?"

"Standard procedure," Holt replied.

Callaway stared at him. "You're enjoying this, aren't you?"

"I enjoy my work, if that's what you mean," Holt shot back.

Callaway did not look like he believed him.

He and Holt had a history. Callaway thought Holt was like a Rottweiler who, when he had a suspect in his grasp, would not let go until he had a conviction. Sometimes it did not matter to him what evidence he had, only that he got the suspect in the end.

Holt, on the other hand, thought very little of private investigators. To him they were unnecessary to society, and they impeded *real* police work.

"Let's go back to last night," Holt said.

"What do you want to know?"

"Whatever you can tell me."

"Like what?"

"Did you go to *Mrs.* Isabel Gilford's house?" Holt asked, emphasizing the "Mrs." on purpose. He was fully aware of Callaway's tendency to sleep with married women. Another thing he despised about him.

"I did go to her house, yes," Callaway conceded. "But I didn't go there to spend the night."

"Then why did you go?"

"She asked me to come."

Holt raised an eyebrow. "Why?"

"She hired me to follow her husband."

"Why would she do that?"

"She believed he was cheating on her."

"And?"

"I had proof that he was."

"What kind of proof?"

"I had photos."

"Where are these photos?"

"I don't have them. I gave prints of them to her."

Holt studied him. "We found no such photos anywhere in the house. And believe me, in a murder investigation, we go through the crime scene with a fine-tooth comb."

Callaway's eyes darted around the room as if he was searching for an explanation. "Who found her body?"

"Her husband."

"Then *he* must have taken them."

"Why would he do that?"

"Why wouldn't he?" Callaway spat. "He was in those photos."

Holt fell silent. "Do you have a backup of these photos?" he asked.

Callaway opened his mouth but then shut it. He looked away and said, "They were on my camera. I can't find it."

Holt snickered. "How convenient."

Callaway's head began to spin. He had to shut his eyes to make the dizziness stop.

Holt slid a glossy 8x10 across the table. Callaway opened his eyes and saw that it was an enlarged photo of a bloody knife.

Holt said, "We found a knife at the crime scene. It was lodged in the victim's chest. This knife had *your* fingerprints on it. Why is that?"

Callaway felt like throwing up. "That's not possible," he slowly replied.

"Just to be certain, we ran the prints several times through our database, and each time it came back with a match. They are yours."

Callaway's eyes began to tear up. "I've never seen that knife before."

"It came from the victim's kitchen."

Callaway's shoulders slumped. "I didn't kill her."

Holt leaned closer. "You agree that you were with the victim last night?"

Callaway nodded.

"Do you also agree that you and the victim were having wine last night?"

He nodded again. "We had several glasses, and I think by the end, we were both drunk. Maybe that's why I passed out."

"We found prints on the wine glasses. One set belongs to you, and we assume the other belongs to the victim. She's not in our system, so we couldn't get a match, but I am certain a toxicology report would show her consuming alcohol prior to her death."

Callaway shook his head. "She was alive when I... I..."

"You what?"

Callaway looked at him. "I... I don't remember what happened at the house. I only remember waking up this morning. It was as if I had blacked out the entire night."

Holt almost chuckled. "You can't use the same excuse that your client Paul Gardener used."

"Paul was innocent," Callaway said.

"Yes, thanks to you. But this time you're charged for murder and not someone else."

Callaway swallowed.

"I want my lawyer."

EIGHTY

Forty minutes later, the door to the interview room opened. A man wearing a striped suit, leather shoes, and a gold watch entered. The watch's dial was encrusted in diamonds. The watch likely cost the man more than Callaway made in a year. He was clean shaven, and his hair was slicked back, making him look like a 1940s gangster.

The moment Holt had uttered the name Paul Gardener, Callaway knew what attorney he was going to call.

Evan Roth had been Paul's lawyer at the time of his arrest. Callaway hoped Roth remembered what he did for his client.

Roth smiled and extended his hand. "Mr. Callaway, I was surprised to receive your call."

"Thanks for coming," Callaway said.

Roth placed his expensive briefcase on the table, unbuttoned his suit coat, and sat across from Callaway. Roth was one of the most sought-after defense lawyers in the city. He was the best, and he did not come cheap.

"I didn't know who else to call," Callaway said.

"You made the right call."

"I have some money. I can…"

Roth held up his hand to stop him. "We'll discuss fees later. Right now, tell me what happened last night *and* this morning."

Callaway laid out his story in detail. When he was done, Roth said, "Okay, so I've heard your version. Now, based on the evidence against you, they—I mean, the prosecution—will create their own version of events. I've been through these kinds of situations too many times, so I know how they think. They will say that you and Mrs. Gilford were involved in a passionate affair…"

"That's a lie," Callaway interjected.

The smile on Roth's face never dropped. "They will say that. But we will refute it. They do have your fingerprints on the murder weapon, however…

"I don't know how they got there."

"And you were seen fleeing the scene."

"I didn't see anyone at the house," Callaway said.

"Yes, but a neighbor saw you leave."

Callaway's face creased. "When?"

"According to a statement, a neighbor was walking his dog in the morning when you nearly ran them over in a hurry."

Callaway remembered.

"The neighbor gave the detectives your license plate number."

Callaway sighed and shook his head in disbelief. He looked up at Roth. "What motive do I have for killing Mrs. Gilford? She was my client."

"I agree. I don't think they have a motive yet, but I wouldn't be surprised if they come up with something when they go before a judge."

"Cary Gilford had a motive," Callaway said.

"The dead woman's husband?"

"Yes. He was having an affair with his assistant, and I had seen Isabel Gilford with bruising around her face."

Roth's eyes narrowed. "That's interesting. Did she report it to the police?"

"I told her to, but I don't know if she did."

"Don't worry, we can always pull up records to see if he had a history of violence."

Callaway liked the sound of that.

Roth said, "You said you don't remember anything from last night."

"I don't."

"Do you think you were drugged?" Roth suggested. Paul Gardener could not remember anything either when he was charged with murdering his daughter.

"I may have. I mean, I drank a couple glasses of wine."

"Was Isabel Gilford drinking too?"

"Yes. She was the one who kept refilling my glass."

Roth nodded. "It might be best to conduct a drug test on you. But first things first. I'll try to schedule a court date for your bail. Do you know anyone who can put up the money?"

EIGHTY-ONE

Holt and Fisher approached the front desk and rang a bell. They were at the address Callaway had provided them upon his arrest. Holt had frowned when he found out the man was living at a hotel.

How can he afford it? his initial thought had been. But now that he was here, he saw the place was more akin to a motel than a hotel.

The clerk appeared from the backroom. Holt and Fisher flashed their badges and told him they needed a key to Callaway's room.

"That's funny," the clerk said.

"What is?" Holt asked, not smiling.

"Mr. Callaway was here this morning asking for a key, too."

"Why would he do that?" Fisher asked.

"I don't know."

"And did you give him one?"

"I didn't have to. Someone had dropped off the key in our lost and found box. Probably one of the cleaning staff found it."

Fisher's face turned hard. Holt had seen that look before when she was faced with something that troubled her.

"Are you sure about that?" she asked.

The clerk gave a non-committal shrug.

"Can you get us a key to the room?" Holt asked the clerk.

"One moment," the clerk replied.

He disappeared into the backroom.

Holt turned to Fisher. "What's bothering you?"

"Everything about this case is bothering me."

"I know you had a relationship with him once…"

"We are friends," she corrected him.

"Okay, right, so it is understandable that you have feelings in this case. I just hope it doesn't conflict with your judgement."

"It won't. Just like it didn't with you when we were investigating Isaiah's case," she shot back.

Ouch, he thought. *She has me there.*

The clerk returned just in time to break the tension. He handed them a key. "It's on the third floor. If you want, you can take the stairs like Mr. Callaway does."

"We'll take the elevator," Holt said.

As they waited for one to arrive, Fisher said, "I know you have strong opinions about Callaway. I just hope they don't conflict with *your* judgement on this case."

Holt grimaced. "I am going to follow the evidence wherever it leads me."

"I hope so," Fisher said.

The elevator arrived.

Holt got the feeling this was going to be a long investigation.

They took the elevator up and got off on the third floor. They pulled on latex gloves and unlocked the front door.

Holt sensed that this was the first time Fisher had been here. She looked around the cramped space with disappointment, as if she expected more from Callaway.

I don't, he thought. *He's nothing but a skirt chaser who finally took things too far.*

Holt was devoted to his wife, and he abhorred men who slept with married women. In his mind, Callaway was the worst kind. Even so, Holt would view the facts with an unbiased gaze, even if it resulted in setting Callaway free.

Callaway had retained Evan Roth as his lawyer, which meant they had to be careful with any evidence found at the defendant's place of residence. Everything of relevance would be documented and photographed, and a copy would be provided to the defense.

Holt believed they already had sufficient evidence against Callaway. All they were doing here was trying to build a stronger case.

There was not much to go through anyway. Callaway hardly lived at the hotel. He only used the place for sleep. He had three pieces of luggage with all his belongings and a few articles of clothing hanging in the closet.

Holt knelt to look underneath the bed. He saw something. He reached in and pulled out a duffel bag. He unzipped the bag when Fisher came over.

"What did you find?" she asked.

He did not even have to answer. She knew exactly what it was.

Inside the bag was a shirt stained with red.

"Why would he be so careless to leave evidence in his apartment?" she wondered out loud.

"Just like he left a knife with his prints at the scene," Holt said. "He never thought we'd link him to the victim."

Fisher fell silent.

Checkmate, Holt thought.

EIGHTY-TWO

Callaway nervously paced in the eight-by-ten cell. There was a metal bed and a metal toilet and sink. The security camera near the ceiling that captured his every move unnerved him the most about his confinement. He felt exposed. He knew prisoners had no right to privacy, but he was not a criminal.

I shouldn't be here, he kept thinking. *I didn't kill anyone.*

He balled his fists whenever he came up empty at what happened the night before. He felt anger blaze inside him, but he knew he had to keep his fury contained. The prosecution needed ammunition to deny him bail, and if the camera recorded him having a fit, they would argue he was violent, prone to sudden outbursts, and a threat to both the public and himself.

Callaway did not want to spend even an extra minute locked up. He feared if his bail was denied, he would be hauled from the Milton PD straight to the state penitentiary. Who knew which murderous inmate would become his bunk buddy?

He shuddered at the thought of a big, hulking cell mate having his way with him.

I must get out of here.

The only way for that to happen was if someone posted bail and the judge accepted it.   As if on cue, the cell door was unlocked, and the guard held it open.

When he saw her, a smile crossed his face.

Patti rushed in and hugged him. He could not believe how good it felt to touch her and hold her.

He looked at her. She had tears in her eyes. "Is it true?" she asked.

He tried to say something, but no words came out.

He broke down and cried. She held onto him.

He wiped away the tears and said, "I didn't kill anyone, Patti. I swear."

They sat down on the hard mattress. She did not let go of his hand. "When your lawyer called me, I thought it was a sick joke, but what he told me made me physically ill," Patti said.

"I'm so sorry," Callaway said. "I never wanted to get you involved, but I don't know who else to turn to."

"What were you doing at that woman's house?" she asked.

He turned to the camera. Their conversation did not fall under attorney-client privileges. Every word recorded would be used against him.

"If I get out, I'll tell you everything," he said. "I promise."

Patti said, "You know I don't have the money for the bail. My salary as a nurse barely covers the bills."

"I know, but Roth thinks he can work out a deal if you put up the house as collateral."

Patti stood up and turned away from him.

After he walked away from their marriage, he left her the house. He was always behind on alimony and child support, but the down payment on the house made her feel like she had something of value.

And now he even wanted that from her.

He said, "If you think I'll run away and won't show up in court to face the charges…"

"You did run away from Nina and me," she said, not looking at him.

After a brief pause, he said, "You're right. I don't deserve your trust. If you walk out now, I won't hold it against you. I've been a selfish jerk all my life, I know that, but I'm *not* a murderer."

For a minute she stood still, and he thought she would leave. But then her shoulders slumped, and she sighed. "I'll do it," Patti said. "I'll put up the house as collateral." She turned and faced him. "But remember one thing, Lee. I'm not doing this for you. I'm doing this for Nina. If she ever found out I let her father rot in prison when I had the power to do something, she would never forgive me."

Patti had every right to be angry with him. He had abandoned them, and she spent all her time and energy focused on Nina. She had built a stable and secure life for their daughter.

He was now putting all that at risk.

EIGHTY-THREE

Fisher waited in the back of the soup and noodle shop. She still could not wrap her head around Callaway being a murderer. In her line of work, she had dealt with psychopaths, con artists, serial killers, and people far worse. They were all able to hide behind a veil of normality. Some were average folks with families who turned out to have committed evil crimes.

Callaway was not one of those people. He never hid behind a mask. With him you got what you saw. And he was always one of the first people to admit his faults. He never denied that he was a lousy father, that he was terrible with money, and sometimes even reckless and irresponsible. But he lived by a code that went: *Always do the right thing even if it goes against your interests.*

Callaway had taken on cases where the pay was minuscule compared to the work involved. He did them because he wanted to right a wrong. Paul Gardener had been wronged and Callaway had poured his heart and soul into the case, even when all odds were against him.

Fisher believed in her heart that Callaway genuinely did not remember what had transpired the night before. If he did, he would tell her. At least, she hoped he would.

But then again, when it came to people's freedom, they did and said anything for it not to be taken away.

She shook her head. *I can't believe it has come to this*, she thought.

Holt appeared around the corner, accompanied by a small Asian woman. She was holding a key, and judging by the look on her face, she was not happy at what she was about to do. But Holt, Fisher knew, had given her no choice.

Callaway was charged with a crime, and as the detectives on his case, they could interview anyone closely related to him, and search properties he was known to frequent or use.

They followed the woman up the flight of metal stairs. They stopped at the landing, and the woman unlocked the door.

"Thank you," Holt said to her. "We'll lock it once we leave."

Without uttering a word, the woman hurried away.

Holt and Fisher pulled on latex gloves and entered.

Holt looked around and quipped, "He won't have any trouble getting used to living in a cell."

His joke was crass, but Fisher saw his point. Callaway's office was no bigger than two cells combined. There was a sofa, a TV, and a desk.

"We should take his laptop," Holt said.

"You think he's got an electronic diary of all the people he's killed?" she asked.

"I'm just saying it might contain pertinent information, that's all," he replied.

She knew he was right. What if Callaway had stored on his laptop the photos he had taken that night? What if he had photos of other crimes he had committed? Of other murders, perhaps?

Fisher would not allow herself to believe that.

"It's your call," Fisher said.

Holt thought about it but then he pulled open the desk drawer and lifted out a gun with two fingers. "Look what I found," he said with a smile as he held the gun for her to see.

"He's got a license for it," Fisher said. "I've seen it."

"Even then, he's got a weapon."

"Sure, but then that means it wasn't premeditated."

Holt frowned. "What makes you say that?"

"If he went to the victim's house with the intention to kill her, then why not take the gun with him? It would have been far easier than stabbing her."

Holt did not like the sound of that.

She moved her hand between the sofa cushions. When she lifted one cushion, she saw an envelope stuck inside a slit in the sofa frame's fabric. She peeked inside the envelope and saw a stack of hundred-dollar bills.

"Where do you suppose he got all the money?" Holt asked

"I don't know, and I don't care," Fisher replied. "Unless you want to seize it as evidence."

Holt shook his head.

She placed the money back where she found it.

Holt picked up a small framed photo sitting next to the laptop. The picture showed Callaway and Jimmy Keith standing next to each other.

Fisher had the unfortunate luck of also arresting Jimmy, but in Jimmy's case, he turned himself in.

Holt asked, "Do you recognize the watch Callaway is wearing in the photo?"

She did.

It was the same watch they had found next to the bed in Isabel Gilford's house.

EIGHTY-FOUR

Callaway was surprised at how fast Roth was able to schedule the bail hearing. Normally it could take days or even a week in some cases, but Roth had a certain clout in the legal community. He also had powerful connections.

Callaway was glad he used those connections to quickly get him before a judge.

Callaway was dressed in a dark blue suit provided to him by Roth, who sat next to him at the defense table. Patti sat a few rows behind them, wearing a black dress. Callaway was grateful Nina was not here to see this. His heart would break if he saw his daughter's face when she heard what he was accused of.

Seated at the prosecutor's table was a fresh-faced lawyer who looked like he had just passed the bar exam.

Roth leaned over to Callaway and whispered, "You're lucky Barrows isn't here."

District Attorney Judy Barrows was a legend in the court system. She rarely lost a case, and she especially hated losing one to Roth. No one would have been surprised if she had shown up at the bail hearing, but there was a reason why she chose not to.

Barrows was recently diagnosed with lung cancer. She had been a chain smoker for decades, and her habit had shown its ugly side.

There was another reason why she did not come. Callaway's case was not a front-page story, at least not yet, and if it did turn into one, Roth would bet his career that Barrows would appear in court even with an IV stuck to her arm.

Roth had already explained to Callaway the factors that influenced bail. The seriousness of the crime, the defendant's past criminal history, the defendant's employment status, and the defendant's ties to the community.

The murder of Isabel Gilford could lead to a life sentence. Callaway had been booked for misdemeanor offenses, but nothing that would raise a red flag. His employment record was sketchy, and he did not have a permanent address. But he did have a daughter and an ex-wife in the city.

The prosecution, naturally, wanted bail denied and put their case before the judge. Roth countered with his own reasons as to why bail should be allowed. In the end, the judge ruled in the defense's favor and set the bail for one-hundred thousand dollars. The main reasoning for his decision was the property put up by Patti as collateral. But the bail came with conditions. Callaway had to hand over his passport, he could not carry any firearms, and he could not leave Milton without advising the courts first.

Callaway agreed to all the conditions. He would not survive another minute inside a cell.

EIGHTY-FIVE

Wakefield stood next to the gurney that held Isabel Gilford's body. "Death was definitely caused by the knife penetrating the heart," she said. "She died upon being struck."

"Was there alcohol in her system?" Fisher asked.

"Yes, but not enough to get her drunk."

Holt said, "But the accused stated he was drinking heavily with the deceased on the night she was killed."

Fisher knew where Holt was going with this. According to Callaway, he had several drinks with Isabel Gilford before he passed out.

Wakefield shook her head. "I wouldn't call it *heavily*."

"A few glasses, let's say," Holt said.

"The amount of alcohol in her bloodstream could have come from, perhaps, half a glass of wine. But then again, some people can drink six beers and not even feel a buzz, while others can get tipsy after just one bottle. It depends on each individual."

"To confirm, was she inebriated or not?" Holt asked.

"You want my personal opinion, or do you want a stated fact?" Wakefield asked in reply.

"Your opinion would be fine."

"I don't think she consumed enough wine to lose her faculties."

Holt was trying to make a point that if Isabel Gilford was not drunk, then neither was Callaway. Which meant he likely did not black out like he wanted them to believe.

"Did you find anything else of interest?" Fisher asked, trying to move the discussion along.

"There was a bruise around her eye," Wakefield said.

"I was going to ask you about that," Fisher said. "How old do you think it is?"

"I would have to say it's quite fresh."

Fisher blinked. "How fresh?"

"If I had to take a guess, I'd say not even a day old."

Fisher fell silent.

"So, it's very recent?" Holt asked.

"Yes."

Callaway had stated that he had seen Isabel Gilford with a bruise under the eye, which he said was inflicted by her husband. If the bruise was less than a day old, that could only mean Callaway had hit her before he stabbed her.

Lee's lying, Fisher thought. *Or is he?*

Holt's phone buzzed. He excused himself to answer the call.

Fisher turned to Wakefield. "Is there a possibility the victim could have fallen and hit her face on the side of… perhaps, the coffee table or something?"

Wakefield smiled. "I'm aware of your relationship with the accused, Detective Fisher, and I applaud you for your loyalty toward him, but I can state without any hesitation that the mark on the victim's face could only have come from the end of a fist."

Holt returned and said, "The judge has granted Callaway bail. I hope that made your day."

It didn't, Fisher thought. *If the evidence keeps piling up against Lee, he's as good as locked up for life.*

EIGHTY-SIX

Callaway sat in Patti's living room. She was in the kitchen making a cup of tea.

When the judge was considering his decision, Callaway felt like the weight of the moment was crushing his chest. Only when the judge allowed bail could he breathe again.

He could not imagine what he would go through while the jury deliberated to decide his fate. The wait would almost surely kill him.

He covered his face with his hands. *When will I wake up from this nightmare?* he thought.

The answer came back: *Never.*

What was happening to him was real and not a figment of his imagination. He would have to stand before the judge again, and when he did, he would have to face the consequences of what he had done.

But what have I done?

Each time he tried to remember what happened, he was faced with a blank screen.

Patti returned with two cups in her hand. "Would you like something to eat?"

He shook his head. Before the bail hearing, Callaway had thrown up in a toilet in the men's bathroom. Even after being freed, his appetite had not returned. He knew his freedom was only temporary. He would be back in court to fight for his future, one that could involve being locked up twenty-three hours of the day inside a cell.

He shuddered at the thought.

"Everything will be alright," Patti said, trying to reassure him. She always saw the bright side of everything. Even when he ran away from her and Nina, she put a positive spin on it. She would say his desertion gave her an opportunity to get closer to her only child. They went grocery shopping together, watched TV together, and went for walks together. But the truth was it was hard raising a child on her own.

He took a sip from the cup. "Thank you," he said.

"You've said it a dozen times already."

"It's still not enough."

She gave him a rueful smile. "Wish you said that more often when we were married."

"I wish I had."

They were silent a moment.

"Things are different now, Lee. We don't need you like we needed you before."

"I know." He stared at his cup. "I didn't kill that woman. And I didn't sleep with her."

"Okay, sure," Patti said. He could tell she did not believe him.

"She was my client and I went to her house to give her what she'd asked me to get."

"You don't owe me an explanation, Lee."

He felt like he did. She had always been there for him, but he was hardly there for her.

"Are you and Dr. Hayward together?" he asked.

Her eyes narrowed. "Like I told you before, it's none of your business."

"I know, but if you are, I'm happy that Nina will finally have a positive influence in her life. I mean… I might not be around to see her grow older." His eyes welled up at the thought of not being there to see his daughter go to college or walk her down the aisle when she got married.

Patti sighed. "It was only one date."

"He seemed like a nice guy."

"I didn't know this until recently, but Michael has a reputation of sleeping with nurses. So, to answer your question, we're not together. I didn't want to become another notch in his belt, so to speak."

"I'm sorry it didn't work out." A part of him was elated that it did not, but another part of him worried what would happen to Nina and Patti after he was gone.

Why am I suddenly so interested in their wellbeing? I never cared how they managed before.

He sighed.

You know why, Lee. You always thought you had time to make things up to Patti and Nina. Damn it, I wish I had done a lot of things, because now I might never get the chance to.

EIGHTY-SEVEN

Fisher could see the evidence mounting against Callaway As a friend she was devastated and appalled. Devastated because she could see his life would never be the same. Appalled because he could be involved in something as heinous as murder.

Holt said very little when they returned to the Milton PD, but Fisher knew he was quietly gloating. She could not hold that against her partner. Callaway had made Holt look like a fool on several occasions and now it was his turn to show who was the bigger fool.

"You okay?" Holt asked, coming over to her desk.

"Why do you care?" she replied, not looking at him.

"Listen," he said, "if you want me to get off this case, I'll talk to the sergeant myself."

She gave him a skeptical look.

"I'm serious. I value our friendship more than any case."

She was silent. She was not expecting that response. Holt lived for detective work. He would not hand over a case so lightly.

She sighed. "I'm sorry."

"For what?"

"For griping at you. I know you're doing your job."

"I won't deny that I don't get some pleasure…"

"I knew it!" she said, pointing at him.

He put his hands up in defense. "But more than putting Callaway away in prison, I feel I have an obligation to Isabel Gilford's family. I want you to know, if *I* had committed a terrible offense, I would hope you would not let our relationship get in the way of justice."

She could tell he meant every word. Holt valued the law above everything else.

"I hope I never have to put handcuffs on you," she said with a smile.

"I hope so too," he replied. "You still have not mastered the art of cuffing."

She raised an eyebrow. "Excuse me?"

"I've seen the way you do it. The suspects are left with bruised wrists."

"It's because they try to squirm when I cuff them."

"I'm just saying, that's all."

A uniformed officer approached them. "Sorry to interrupt, but there is a lady downstairs to see you."

"Who?" Fisher asked.

"She said her name was Caroline Leary."

Fisher knew why she was here. She wanted an update on her father's and brother's murders.

Holt moved toward the elevator.

Fisher said, "Wait. Stop!"

He turned around. "Shouldn't we go speak to her?"

"Only I should."

He looked confused.

She said, "I think *you* should continue with Callaway's investigation, and I should work on finding who murdered Caroline Leary's father and brother and Debra Coleheim."

Holt stared at her. "Are you sure?"

"Yes, I am," she replied. "And also, I don't think I can live with myself knowing I put a friend away for life."

EIGHTY-EIGHT

Roth showed up at Patti's house. He wanted to discuss some things with Callaway. Patti moved to the kitchen to give them privacy.

Roth and Callaway sat across from each other in the living room. Callaway said, "Thanks for getting me out so fast. You wouldn't believe what a relief it is to be outside a cell."

Roth smiled. "That's what all my clients say as well. They tell me they didn't realize how precious freedom is until it is taken away."

"I know the feeling. It's given me a new perspective."

Roth loosened his suit coat. "I'm glad to hear that. Now, I'm sure you know why I'm here."

Callaway knew. He had been mulling the matter ever since Roth took his phone call.

"My firm has the best legal team in the city," Roth continued. "That's my opinion, of course. But I'm proud to say we win more cases than we lose. A lot more. But that success comes with a price."

"I have slightly over twenty thousand in cash," Callaway quickly said. He saw the irony in his offer. He was going to use Isabel's money to defend himself against the charge of killing her.

"I can obviously take it as a retainer," Roth said, "but I must warn you, it won't nearly be enough if we go to trial."

Callaway sat up straight. "If?"

Roth paused to give Callaway a moment to brace himself for what he was about to say next. "There is always a plea deal."

Callaway jumped up. "You don't believe I'm innocent?"

"It's not whether I believe it, it's whether the jury will believe it," Roth calmly replied.

"But I didn't kill her!" Callaway yelled.

Patti stuck her head through the kitchen door. "Is everything okay?"

"Yes, everything is fine," Callaway quickly replied.

He sat down and covered his face with his hands.

Roth leaned closer. "I know this is tough for you to hear. Believe me, I do. But I wouldn't be doing my duty as a lawyer if I didn't give you all the options available to you. Right now, the prosecution is building a case against you. They have likely gone through your home, your office, and wherever else you go on a regular basis. They have a witness who saw you run away from the crime scene. Your fingerprints are on the murder weapon. Your prints are also on a wine glass that you drank from while at the house. I wouldn't be surprised that when I get back to my office, there'll be a message waiting for me from the District Attorney's office. It'll be to inform me of additional evidence linking you to the murder."

Callaway listened to what Roth was saying, but at the same time he was not listening. His mind was all over the place. He looked up at Roth. "What motive do I have for killing my client?"

"I don't know, but in my experience with these kinds of cases, the longer you take to decide whether you would like to plead guilty or not, the more time you give the detectives to formulate a motive."

Callaway felt like someone had wrapped their hands around his neck and was squeezing his throat tight.

"What about taking on my case pro bono?" he asked.

"I would, but my firm is already involved in several wrongful conviction cases, which has stretched our resources to the limit. We are not able to take on another case without severely putting financial stress on the firm. I don't want to do that and jeopardize all those people we are currently representing."

Roth paused and then said in a low voice, "Think about what I just said. But don't think too long. It might mean being in prison for ten years with a chance of parole after seven or spending the rest of your life locked up with no chance of parole."

EIGHTY-NINE

After her conversation with Caroline Leary, Fisher was mentally and emotionally exhausted.

Caroline had wept as she spoke of losing her father and brother. She genuinely believed the lottery winnings had destroyed her family. Her father was a devoted husband and all-around family man, but the moment the check was in his hand, a different side of him came out. He became consumed with the money and what he could do with it. He also became more suspicious of others. He used to try to help people whenever he could, but now he avoided them whenever possible. He grew tired of getting constant requests for money, and he became isolated and depressed.

Her brother did not fare well either after the financial windfall. He used to be a good student and dreamed of one day becoming a sportscaster. But when he realized he did not have to work to pay for his needs, his motivation fell away. Instead of being focused on getting into a career, he spent his time partying and doing drugs.

Caroline remembered her brother as loving, kind, and responsible. The man he became later in life was the polar opposite of who he was when he was growing up. He would have done anything for her. And she felt helpless she could not do anything for him.

Fisher tried to reassure her they were making progress in their investigation, but her words felt hollow. They had hit a wall in the investigation, and if they did not get a break soon, both cases would be pushed aside.

Detectives took pride in the number of convictions they got in the course of their career. They also took pride in how long it took to seek out a suspect. They loved being assigned cases that were so-called "quick-hits," ones where all the puzzle pieces were available and all they had to do was put them together.

The fastest case Fisher ever solved was in three hours. The murder occurred at nine a.m., and by noon they had a suspect in custody. The fact the victim miraculously survived a near-death attack and pointed out her assailant was a major break, but those cases were rare.

Fisher had some of the pieces to Big Bob's and Chase Burley's murders, but she did not know how they fit together, or if they fit at all. What if Big Bob's death had nothing to do with the money in his safe? Or with the drugs Chase was involved in? What if Fisher was looking at the whole situation from the wrong angle?

There were a dozen scenarios, and none of them led her to finding who the killer was.

And if that was not draining enough, Callaway's murder charges had blindsided her. She still could not fathom if he was capable of such a crime. She was grateful she no longer had to build a case against him. That was up to Holt.

For all his faults, Holt was a damn good detective and he would follow proper procedures and protocols to get a conviction. If the evidence led to Callaway, there was nothing she could do to help him.

NINETY

Holt rang the doorbell and waited. A moment later, Cary Gilford answered.

"Detective Holt," he said. "Please come inside."

Holt followed him into the living room. When they were seated, Holt said, "On the phone you said it was urgent."

"It is," Gilford replied. "I know you have a person in custody for my wife's death."

"He's no longer in custody," Holt corrected him. "He's out on bail, but he's charged with the crime."

"Oh right, sure," Gilford said. "I should have mentioned this to you when we first met at my wife's house, but as you can imagine, I was not in the right state of mind. I had just discovered my wife's dead body."

Holt put his hand up. "No need to explain. It's understandable."

Holt could not imagine how he would react if something terrible were to happen to Nancy. He would rather slit his wrists than live the rest of his life without her.

Gilford said, "I will admit that I have not been a very faithful husband. I have cheated in our marriage, but that does not mean I didn't love my wife. What I'm trying to say is, while my wife had hired a private investigator to follow me, I too had hired a private investigator to follow her."

Holt sat up straight. *This is interesting*, he thought.

"If a wife can sense her husband may be involved with another woman, so too can a husband sense his wife may be involved with another man."

Gilford walked over to a side table, returned with an envelope, and held it out for Holt.

Holt took the envelope and opened it. There was a dozen black-and-white photos. They were taken from a distance, but Holt could easily see that the man was Callaway and the woman, even though she had on dark glasses and a long coat, was Isabel Gilford. Her silver hair was clearly visible.

"My private investigator caught them together."

"Of course they were together," Holt said dismissively. "She was his client."

"And, I'm afraid, also his lover."

Holt was taken aback. "I'm sorry?"

"At first, I didn't believe it either. Until I received a call from my insurance company. My wife had tried to change her life insurance policy. In fact, an amended policy was faxed to the insurance company."

Gilford walked over to the side table and returned with another envelope for Holt.

Holt snatched the envelope from Gilford's hand and pulled out a set of documents.

Gilford said, "On page four you will see the name of the beneficiary."

Holt quickly flipped to the page. "Lee Callaway," he read.

"Yes. And on the last page you'll see my wife's signature and also the date it was signed."

"It was yesterday," Holt said.

Gilford nodded. "Naturally, I am going to fight it. I don't believe it is valid."

Holt stared at the wall. His mind was elsewhere.

It was always about the money, he thought.

Callaway was always broke, and so, killing Isabel was his chance to get rich.

Holt now had a motive.

"There is something else," Gilford said.

"And what is that?"

"Yesterday morning, my wife had asked me to come to the house by the lake."

"Why?"

"I don't know. I was surprised too. It was her place to get away from everything, including me sometimes. Whenever we got into a fight, she would go there. Anyway, I didn't go, and I now regret it tremendously."

Holt's eyes narrowed. "Why didn't you?"

Gilford looked away. "I was with another woman that night."

"Who?"

"My assistant."

Holt was not sure if this was relevant.

"Do you suppose my wife wanted me dead?" Gilford asked.

Holt frowned. "Why do you believe that?"

"Only a month before, my wife asked me to increase *my* life insurance policy. Naturally, I did, because I want her taken care of after I'm gone."

Holt mulled this over. "And you think your wife and Mr. Callaway wanted to kill you once you arrived at the house?"

"I don't know, but the thought did occur to me. And if I had gone, and my wife was there with her lover, what do you think could have happened?"

Holt's eyes narrowed again. "I'm not sure," he said, "but it was a good thing you didn't go."

NINETY-ONE

Once Roth had left, Callaway decided to go for a walk. He needed to clear his mind.

Roth had made it very clear that he was not going to take Callaway on as a client. He was aware of Callaway's financial situation, Callaway knew there was another reason, one Roth would not admit to him face-to-face. The evidence was stacked against him, and Roth did not want a loss on his resume.

Roth's career hung on his impeccable winning percentage. Wealthy or prominent clients relied on him to get them out of trouble. Callaway had heard that politicians, businessmen, and even sports stars had him on retainer. He was available to them twenty-four-seven.

Callaway, on the other hand, would not get past the preliminary hearing with the money he had.

Roth's visit to Callaway was a way to pay back Callaway for what he had done for Roth's more affluent client, Paul Gardener. Roth did not seem like the type of guy who liked to owe anything to anyone. But Callaway knew that was as far as Roth would go for him. He had gotten him out of a cell for now, but he would not keep him out of a cell permanently.

Callaway had debated contacting Paul. He did not give up on him when everyone else had, including even Paul's family. But then again, Paul had paid Callaway handsomely for his services. Callaway had used that money to help Patti and Nina at a time when they needed it most. Patti's roof was in dire shape. Water had started to leak whenever rain came. And there were other repairs that required immediate attention. And now that house was collateral on his bail.

Going to Paul's house for help was out of the question. There was no telling how much the lawyer fees would add up. Paul was not family. He was a former client.

Disheartened, Callaway decided to go to a bar. He needed something in his system to numb the pain he was feeling right now.

I can't spend the rest of my life in prison, he thought.

He considered going to Joely's restaurant. She was in shock when he was led away in handcuffs. She must have a ton of questions for him.

He was not ready to answer them.

He wanted to hide from the world, and himself.

What if I had killed that woman?

He tried to shake the thought away, but it always came back like a boomerang.

He entered the bar and put a fifty-dollar bill on the counter. "Keep bringing 'em until it's all gone," he told the bartender.

The bartender looked at him, shrugged, and brought him his first glass.

Callaway drank the booze in one gulp.

Half an hour later, Callaway had consumed four glasses. He could feel the buzz already. A couple more drinks, and he would be fully drunk.

"I'm not pleading guilty," he mumbled to himself. "I'm *not* guilty, okay?"

He lifted the glass up to finish it and order another.

His eyes caught something on the TV behind the bar.

He squinted, and then he got on top of the counter to take a closer look.

"Hey!" the bartender yelled.

Callaway was inches away from the screen when his eyes widened in disbelief.

The bartender rushed over and pulled him off the bar.

"You need to leave now, mister," he said, "or else I'm calling the cops."

Callaway was not listening to him. He was already rushing out of the bar.

NINETY-TWO

Fisher's investigation was leading nowhere, so she decided to start from the beginning. She went back to Big Bob's house. Unlike the previous times, the house was no longer an active crime scene. Fisher would have to seek permission first before taking another look around.

She pulled up to the mansion. There was a black GMC Terrain parked in front. Fisher parked next to the GMC and got out. She went up to the house and rang the doorbell. She waited a moment before the door swung open.

A man wearing a white T-shirt, blue jeans, and black boots stood at the door. He had long hair that was pulled back in a ponytail. His muscular arms were covered in tattoos and he was a good foot taller than Fisher.

"Can I help you?" he said.

"Suzanne Burley?" Fisher asked.

"She's not in," the man replied.

"You are?"

The man's face turned hard. "Who wants to know?"

Fisher held up her badge.

He relaxed and said, "I'm Suzanne's boyfriend."

Fisher paused and then asked, "Mrs. Burley was seeing you while she was still married?"

"She was separated."

"And you two live together?"

"Yeah, I live at her other place, but after what happened to her... um, husband, we've been staying here."

Right, Fisher thought.

"Do you know when Mrs. Burley will be back?"

"She's at her yoga class, so maybe in an hour or so."

Before Fisher left, she asked, "Is that your car parked in the front?"

"It is."

"It's nice."

She got behind the wheel of her SUV. She drove a couple blocks away from the house, found a spot by the side of the road, and parked.

She pulled out her laptop and punched in the GMC's licence plate number.

The plate was registered to a Rick Castroni.

She punched his name into the police database and found that Castroni had been in and out of prison for armed robbery, assault with a deadly weapon, and for tampering with evidence.

Why didn't I see this before? she thought.

She knew the answer. Suzanne Burley was never a suspect to begin with. She had nothing to gain financially from her husband's death. Big Bob was smart not to have a life insurance policy, especially one where his younger wife was the beneficiary. Anything Suzanne Burley received would come from the pre-nup, which was iron-clad as far as Fisher was concerned.

But that did not mean someone else could not have committed the crime.

Fisher began to see a scenario that started to make sense.

When Fisher had first arrived at the scene, she did not see another vehicle outside the house apart from Holt's car, McConnell's cruiser, and Big Bob's Rolls Royce. This meant someone had driven Suzanne to the house, and it could have only been Castroni.

Was Castroni the reason for Big Bob and Suzanne's impending divorce?

If so, this would explain why Castroni was never at the scene. If he was, Fisher and Holt would have looked into him. They would have realized he was an ex-con.

There was nothing to indicate that Big Bob had changed the alarm code after Mrs. Burley had moved out. She could have disabled the code to let Castroni in. Castroni could have killed Big Bob for the money in his safe. Big Bob was a large man, but it would not be hard for Castroni to subdue someone much older than him. After the crime was committed, Suzanne showed up at the house the next morning and called 9-1-1.

It was a perfect plan because no one pointed a finger in her direction.

Until now.

NINETY-THREE

Holt knocked on the door and waited. After speaking to Cary Gilford, he had driven straight to his assistant's condo. According to Gilford, on the night of his wife's death, he was with Brooke O'Shea.

O'Shea answered the door with a smile on her face. "You must be Detective Holt," she said. "Cary told me you'd be coming."

"I would like to ask you a few questions, if you don't mind."

"Of course, please come in."

She held the door for him.

The interior was brightly colored. Holt saw Brooke owned designer furniture and new appliances. Once they were seated on a leather sofa, Holt asked, "What happened to your face?"

O'Shea instantly put her hand over her eye. "It was an accident," she replied. "I can be clumsy sometimes."

Even with the makeup concealer, Holt could tell someone had struck her face. "Did Mr. Gilford hurt you?" he asked.

"Cary is a very caring man…"

Holt cut her off. "We have reason to believe he has struck his wife before."

In his statement to the police, Callaway had made similar assertions. But Wakefield believed the mark on Isabel Burley's face was recent, which meant it could have likely come from Callaway's hands.

But two different individuals with similar wounds cannot be a coincidence. Can it?

O'Shea sighed. "We had a heated argument and Cary lost control."

"Where did this happen?"

"In my condo."

"When?"

"Yesterday."

"And you still decided to spend the night with him?"

"I know how this looks," she said. "Cary is not a violent person. I wouldn't stay with him if he was."

"But he still hit you."

"I said some horrible things to him. I don't think any man would appreciate their manhood being attacked."

Holt gave O'Shea a hard look. "No one deserves to be subjected to abuse, no matter what was said."

"Cary felt terrible about what happened, and later that night he came back to make it up to me. He bought me a diamond necklace." The smile returned to her face. "Would you like to see it?"

"No, thank you," Holt replied. "And when Mr. Gilford came to apologize, he ended up spending the night with you?"

O'Shea looked away in embarrassment. "Yes, he was here the entire night. But I can tell you, Cary and I are not proud of what happened."

"What do you mean?"

"I'm not sure what Cary told you, but he was supposed to see Isabel. But one thing led to another and he didn't leave until the next morning." Brooke O'Shea shook her head, tears brimming in her eyes. She choked up and said, "I never thought something like that would happen to her."

"But you were sleeping with her husband," Holt said. "I would assume you would be happy to see her go."

She looked horrified. "I didn't hate her. I had never even met or spoken to her." She wiped her eyes. "Yes, I love Cary, but that doesn't mean I wanted her gone."

Holt stared at her.

"Plus, Cary was going to leave her anyway," O'Shea added.

NINETY-FOUR

Callaway hung up the phone in frustration. He had spoken to Fisher, but she told him she was no longer working his case. Holt was.

She advised him to go through a lawyer if he wanted to discuss anything with the police.

Callaway was not sure if Roth would be willing to look at his case from a different angle. As far as he was concerned, Callaway should look at securing other legal counsel.

I don't have time for that, Callaway thought.

Begrudgingly, he drove straight to the Milton PD. At the front desk he asked for Holt. As he waited in the lobby, Holt appeared from the elevators. He had a look of disdain on his face.

"I hope you've come to confess," he said.

"I'm here to tell you that I've been set up," Callaway replied.

Holt gave him a hard stare. "Sure, that's what they all say."

"No, I'm serious."

Callaway held up the day's newspaper. On the third page there was a photo of Isabel Gilford. She was standing on the deck of a boat, wearing a patterned shirt and khaki pants, and she had a smile on her face. "The woman who hired me to follow her husband was *not* Isabel Gilford."

Holt scoffed. "So, who was it?"

"I don't know, but it wasn't this woman."

"How can you be so sure?"

Callaway pointed at the photo. "The hair is the same, maybe the nose too, but the eyes and the smile are different."

"You shouldn't be talking to me without your lawyer."

"That's what Fisher said too."

"And she's right."

Holt turned to leave.

Callaway reached out and grabbed his arm.

Holt's eyes lit up with fury.

Callaway quickly pulled his hand away.

"I'm sorry, I shouldn't have done that," Callaway slowly said. "But I don't know who else to turn to."

"Call legal aid. They'll help you."

"You have to believe me. The woman who was with me last night was not the woman who was found dead this morning."

"So, who was with you then?"

Callaway's shoulders sank. "I don't know."

Callaway was certain without a shadow of a doubt he was right. The photo of Isabel he saw on TV back at the bar clearly showed he had been meeting with an imposter.

He now realized the meetings inside the dark limousine were not to hide what they were up to. The meetings were to hide... *her*.

She did not want her true self known. She wore hats, large sunglasses, and even oversized clothing. She was playing a character, and that character was Isabel Gilford.

But why? What was the charade all about?

And how could Callaway prove what he knew to be true?

He had been thrown into a deep, dark hole he did not know how to get out of.

Holt's voice broke his reverie. "You wasted your time coming here, Callaway."

"Listen," Callaway said to him. "I know you don't like me or what I do as a private investigator, but it is your sworn duty as a police detective to catch the real murderer. You may believe that I'm that person, and that's fine for you. It's not fine for me. I'm not guilty, and I will keep saying so until I reach my grave."

NINETY-FIVE

The more Fisher thought about Rick Castroni, the more she was convinced he was Big Bob's killer. He fit the profile. He was big and strong. He was dating Big Bob's wife, Suzanne. And he had a rap sheet that included armed robbery and assault with a deadly weapon.

Fisher now wished she had caught on to Castroni earlier. Perhaps Chase Burley and Debra Coleheim would have been saved.

But one thing troubled her.

Debra Coleheim was also raped. Castroni's record did not include sexual assault.

This, however, did not mean he could not have committed the heinous crime. Debra Coleheim worked as a prostitute, which Castroni could have taken as his right to attack her.

Fisher was parked across from Big Bob's house when she saw Castroni come out. He walked over to the GMC Terrain, got behind the wheel, and drove away.

Fisher followed him.

She did not have a plan per se. She just wanted to see where he was going, what he was doing, and who he was meeting. This would give her a better understanding who she was up against.

Castroni was a dangerous man, but was he also a killer and a rapist? She wanted to find out. She also hoped he would commit some infraction that would give her the opening she needed to arrest him. This way she would get him inside a room to interrogate him. She believed in her abilities to get a confession out of him.

The GMC weaved through traffic, sometimes at speeds slightly over the limit, but still not enough for her to pull him over. The arrest should be such that a defense lawyer could not tear it apart in front of a judge and jury.

Everything she did from now until later had to be done by the book. If Castroni *was* involved in any illegal activity, then she had a duty to act.   Ten minutes later, the GMC pulled into the back of a church.

Fisher was suddenly confused.

She watched as Castroni got out and entered the church.

She thought about driving away, but she did not want Castroni out of her sight. This was the first big break she had on the case and she was not about to lose it.

She got out of the SUV, walked up the flight of stairs, and entered through a set of wooden doors. The nave of the church was empty.

She moved further in and spotted a door on the right. She went through the door and down a narrow corridor. She saw a light coming through another set of doors. She stopped and peeked inside.

The room was well lit. There were a dozen chairs placed in a circle in the middle of the room. All the chairs were occupied.

Castroni was sitting in one. He looked calm and collected.

Fisher decided to head back to her SUV.

NINETY-SIX

The rain pounded on the Charger's windshield. Callaway sat behind the wheel with a somber look on his face. He did not know what to do next. His visit to Holt had been a waste of time.

What was I expecting anyway? he thought. *"Okay, Lee, I will take a look"? The guy hates my guts, and he's got no reason to listen to me if I've got nothing concrete.*

He drummed his fingers on the steering wheel.

He considered going back to the house where her body was discovered. But he talked himself out of it. The house was still an active crime scene. A police cruiser was most likely stationed on the property.

If Callaway was caught snooping around, there would be additional charges on top of the murder charge. But he could not sit idle while Holt and the District Attorney's office nailed him in a coffin. If he was smart, he would get himself a lawyer from legal aid and hope and pray he or she was competent enough to defend him, or at the very least make sure he did not get the death penalty.

There was also the plea deal Roth had mentioned. If Callaway picked up the phone right now and told Roth he was ready to agree to one, Roth would make sure to hammer out a deal that was beneficial to him.

Callaway was not going to plead guilty, no matter how dire the situation was. He was not a murderer. He knew himself better than anyone. He was not capable of committing such a terrible act.

Then there was Nina.

What would she think knowing her father was a convicted murderer?

Patti had so far told her nothing. She was going to wait until after the trial to break the news to her. Callaway hoped the news of his arrest had not made it to her school yet.

If the news has, she's in for some hazing, Callaway thought. *Kids can be cruel.*

He sighed.

I'd rather jump in front of a truck than see my little girl suffer like that.

The rain had turned into a light drizzle.

Callaway was parked across from Cary and Isabel Gilford's house.

Gilford's Audi was parked in front.

Callaway was building the courage to go up and ring the bell. After speaking to Holt, he decided to do some more research on Cary and Isabel. As he sifted through the information once more, something stuck out.

A week ago, Callaway had followed Gilford from his work to his house. When Gilford was getting out of the Audi, he was carrying flowers and chocolates. The next day, the fake Isabel Gilford had told him the flowers and chocolates were for their wedding anniversary.

Callaway had discovered that their actual wedding anniversary was not for another four months.

So what kind of charade was Gilford playing with the flowers and chocolates? And why was he and this fake Isabel Gilford working together?

Callaway wanted to confront Gilford and ask him.

He saw a black Subaru pull up to the house and park next to the Audi.

A woman emerged from the driver's side. Her hair was damp—likely from the rain—and as she walked up to the front door, Callaway's eyes widened in disbelief.

She's Brooke O'Shea. Aka, Isabel Gilford!

The silver hair was now blonde, and the long coat was gone, but her walk gave her away.

A person could use makeup as a disguise, or speak with a different accent, but it was near impossible to fake a walk for a long time.

Brooke O'Shea rang the doorbell. A moment later, Cary Gilford answered the door with a smile on his face.

They embraced and kissed before disappearing behind the door.

Callaway tightened his grip on the steering wheel.

He gritted his teeth.

Callaway started the Charger and then drove off.

NINETY-SEVEN

An hour had gone by and Castroni still had not left the church. Fisher still was not sure why he was here. There was nothing posted anywhere in the church to indicate what the meeting was about.

The church doors opened, and men began to stroll out one by one. A couple of them stopped and gathered around another man. He was tall and balding, and he wore a clerical collar.

Fisher saw none of the men was Castroni.

Where did you go? she wondered.

Castroni exited the church.

He headed straight for his vehicle, got in, and drove off.

Fisher debated following him, but she wanted to know what he was doing here.

She watched as the men slowly began to clear out. She then got out of her SUV and walked to the front of the church.

The priest was speaking to another man. He was short, with shaggy hair, and he had a nervous air about him.

"The pain will never fully go away," the priest said to him. "But time will make it more bearable."

The man nodded, and then left.

The priest saw her standing by the steps. He smiled and said, "You're here to make a prayer?"

Fisher approached him. "I'm actually here to ask a few questions, Father."

"I don't know if I have all the answers you seek, but I'll do my best."

"I was inside the church earlier, and I saw all these men gathered in a room. I'm assuming it's some sort of AA meeting?"

The smile never left the priest's face. "Not quite. Can I ask why you're so interested?"

She flashed her badge.

The smile faded. "Is someone in trouble?" he asked, concerned.

"It'll depend on what you tell me."

The priest fell silent. He studied her and said, "The men in that room have all suffered some form of pain. Sexual abuse, physical abuse, substance abuse, depression, alcohol dependency— you name it, they've gone through it. The meetings are a way for them to vent their frustrations. We offer a sympathetic ear, and if they are interested, we also offer programs to guide them so that they can lead a somewhat normal life."

"And why is Rick Castroni here?" Fisher asked.

The smile came back to the priest's face. "I see what this is about."

"I'm sorry?" she said.

"The other men in the group don't know, but Rick told me in private that he is seeing someone whose husband was recently murdered. You are here because of that, is it not?"

"I am."

"Rick went through a difficult childhood. His father was, to say it lightly, *very* harsh with him. He dropped out of school at a young age. He got in trouble, and he was in and out of prison, but I can assure you, he is a changed man now."

I'll be the judge of that, Fisher thought.

"How regularly do you meet?" she asked.

"Three times a week."

"Okay, and can you remember if you held a meeting on…" She gave him the date of the night Big Bob was murdered.

The smile widened on the priest's face. Fisher did not like that. "Follow me," he said. They went inside the church, back through the narrow corridor, and into the room where she saw Castroni with the other men.

The priest walked over to a table in the corner, picked up a piece of paper, and handed it to her. It was an advertisement for an event held at the church. "The fundraiser was from eight to ten p.m., and because of the turnout we ended up going very late. Rick and a couple of other guys stayed to help clean up. I think he was still here after eleven. I can give you the other men's names who can vouch for him."

Fisher stared at the advertisement. "How many people were at the fundraiser?"

"If I had to take a guess, I'd say close to fifty."

Fisher frowned. That was way too many people to interview. She hated to admit it, but she was now back to square one.

NINETY-EIGHT

When Callaway returned to his office, the first thing he did was turn on his laptop. While the computer booted up, he counted the money he had stashed in his sofa. He knew Holt and Fisher had already combed through his office, so he wanted to make sure everything was where it should be. Not that he thought the detectives—especially Fisher—would take the cash, but everything was now vital to him.

He wished he still had his gun, but of course, he had to leave the gun where it was as part of his bail condition.

On the laptop he typed in "Jackie Wolfe," the name Brooke O'Shea had fed him when he asked if she knew the assistant's name. O'Shea likely did not want to reveal her real name to him, so she gave another one.

The results of his search filled his screen. Jackie Wolfe was a character Brooke O'Shea had played in an independent movie that was shown in a handful of theatres. Jackie Wolfe was a housewife who believed her husband was cheating on her. In order to catch him red-handed, she struck up an online conversation with him, posing as someone else. After weeks of intense conversation, they agreed to meet at a hotel. The next day, the husband's dead body was found in the hotel room. The detectives were stumped because the person he was chatting with online did not exist.

Callaway could guess the ending. Jackie Wolfe had lured her husband to the hotel, killed him, and then somehow gotten away with the murder. His death was justifiable because he had wronged her.

Brooke O'Shea had played Jackie Wolfe when she lured Callaway to Isabel Gilford's house. Instead of murdering Callaway, she had killed the real Isabel Gilford and framed him for the murder. And she must have done so with the help of her lover, Cary Gilford.

Where was the real Isabel Gilford during this time? he thought. *And how can I find that out?*

He had an idea. He searched online and found what he was looking for.

The real Isabel Gilford was an only child of Melvin and Irene Worsley. Their current address and phone number was in Florida.

He dialed the number and waited

A moment later, a male voice answered. "Mel Worsley."

"Sorry to bother you, sir," Callaway said, "but I'm calling from the Milton Equestrian Club." Callaway was not sure such a club existed, but in his earlier research, he had found that Isabel Gilford loved horses.

"Okay," Worsley replied.

"I was wondering if you knew how we could get in touch with Mrs. Isabel Gilford. She had a riding session booked at the club, but she hasn't arrived. We tried contacting her husband, but he is not answering his phone."

There was a sigh on the other end. "I'm afraid Isabel has passed away," Worsley said, his voice breaking.

"Oh my God," Callaway said, feigning shock. "I'm so sorry to hear that. My condolences to you."

"Thank you."

"If you don't mind me asking, when did it happen?"

"Last night. We were scheduled to fly over to Milton this morning, but my wife's heart condition got worse at hearing the news, so we'll be flying over later today."

"That's understandable," Callaway said. "The only reason I asked was because she missed her previous two sessions as well.'"

"Isabel was visiting family in England," Worsley said. "She only returned just yesterday."

"My condolences again, and I'm so sorry for your loss," Callaway said, and hung up.

He leaned back in his chair and stared at the ceiling. That explained why he never once saw the real Isabel Gilford while he was being conned by Brooke O'Shea and Cary Gilford.

They had planned everything out in detail.

Brooke O'Shea kept asking for more evidence even when he thought he had finished his job. She was prolonging his case. Only when the real Isabel Gilford was back in Milton did they put the final touches to their plan.

Callaway grimaced.

I fell right into their trap.

NINETY-NINE

Holt shook his head as he hung up the phone. Callaway had called to tell him how he had been setup.

Callaway had concocted a farfetched scenario where Isabel Gilford's husband and his assistant had conspired to implicate him in murder. Callaway rambled on about Brooke O'Shea being an actress and how she had used makeup and prosthetics to play a character. He mentioned some movie Holt had never heard of, nor did he care to look up.

Callaway was a desperate man who was blindly throwing darts, hoping one would hit the target.

But there was something Callaway said that caught Holt's attention.

He debated whether to look in to it or ignore it completely. He checked his watch. He still had some time before he headed home. Plus, Nancy was visiting her mother's, so she would not be back until later anyway.

Prior to getting behind the wheel, he made a call to confirm certain details.

He then drove to the property where Isabel Gilford was found dead. Instead of pulling up at the house, he passed it and pulled into the neighbor's property. He parked next to a 4x4 truck and got out.

He rang the doorbell and waited.

When he did not get an answer, he peeked through the window. The lights were on inside, but it looked like no one was home.

He frowned.

This was a waste of time, he thought. *I should have never come all this way.*

He heard a noise in the distance. He listened. It was a dog barking. He walked in the direction the barking was coming from.

He cut through a path and entered a forest. He weaved his way through several trees and bushes in the darkening woods. As he got closer, the noise became more distinct.

"Bad Bessie, bad dog," a male voice yelled.

Holt spotted a man pulling the leash of an overly excited Basset Hound. The dog was barking at something on the ground a few feet away. Holt squinted and realized the object was a dead rabbit.

The man spotted Holt and said, "Their instincts take over and they can't help themselves."

Holt flashed his badge when the man said, "Do you mind taking Bessie back to the house? I have to bury the rabbit deep underground or else Bessie will keep coming back for it. Her breed has got a keen sense of smell, you know?"

Holt grabbed the leash and tugged Bessie away.

He waited by the house steps for the man to return. His name was Rob Bushman, and he was the one who had seen Callaway race away in his car.

Bushman returned and said, "Thanks for looking after Bessie."

Holt scratched Bessie under her ears and patted her neck. "She was a good girl."

"You're Detective Holt, right?" Bushman asked.

"I am."

"I recognized you. You're investigating the murder next door?"

"Yes. I tried calling you, but it wasn't going through," Holt said.

"Sometimes I lose signal when I am deep in the forest," Bushman explained. "It's only after I come out that I realize I have missed calls or messages. So, what can I do for you?"

"Were you here all day yesterday?"

"I was."

"Did you by any chance see your neighbor, Isabel Gilford, at her house?"

Bushman thought a moment. "I believe I did when I took Bessie out for a walk. I do it at least three times a day, twice for sure. I suffer from depression and anxiety, and I find the walks help put my mind to ease."

"What time did you see Mrs. Gilford?"

"I think it was in the afternoon."

Holt's eyes narrowed. "Are you sure?"

"Maybe late in the afternoon, but definitely during sunlight."

"Did you see the man in the Dodge Charger yesterday?"

Bushman smiled. "He's the one who's charged with murdering her?"

Holt did not reply.

"I saw it on the news," Bushman said. "And to answer your question, I didn't see him yesterday."

"How about last night?"

"I don't go out for walks at night. It's easy to get lost in the dark. So, I can't say if he was there or not. But I did see him in the morning. Even Bessie saw him. Didn't you, Bessie?" Bessie stared at the ground.

"And you are certain Mrs. Gilford was here during the day?"

"Absolutely. I even waved to her as I walked past her property."

"And you're sure it was her?"

Bushman blinked. "Why do you ask?"

"Never mind," Holt said. "Thank you for your time."

As Holt walked back to his car, he had a nagging feeling that something was not right. On his drive over, Holt had spoken to someone in U.S. Customs and Border Protection. They were able to find out that Isabel Gilford had indeed flown back from England yesterday, and that her flight did not land until later that evening.

How could Bushman have seen Isabel Gilford at the same time she was on a plane flying over the Atlantic? Holt thought. *He couldn't, unless…*

Holt's eyes widened.

…unless Callaway is telling the truth.

Someone was indeed playing a dangerous game.

ONE-HUNDRED

Callaway received a text from Holt.

YOU WERE RIGHT, BUT I HAVE TO FOLLOW THE EVIDENCE. AND RIGHT NOW, IT POINTS TO YOU.

Even though the reply was not promising, and Callaway was not expecting a reply to begin with, the message did give him some solace.

Still, his hands are tied, Callaway thought.

Callaway put the phone away. There was some unfinished business he had to deal with before he made his next move.

He left his office and drove to Joely's restaurant. The moment Joely saw him enter, she dropped everything and rushed over. She hugged him with tears in her eyes.

"Is it true?" she asked.

"Of course it isn't," he replied. "I didn't do it."

"I knew it," she said with full conviction. "You're a cad, Lee Callaway, but you're no killer."

"That's what I keep saying."

"Do you want something to eat?" she asked. "It's on the house."

He was not very hungry, but he did not want to turn down her offer.

Who knows when I might see a good meal again?

"I'll have whatever you can give me," he said.

She smiled and walked away.

He took a seat at a corner table. He then saw a familiar face enter the restaurant. He was not sure if he should smile or frown.

Fisher came over. "I knew I'd find you here."

"You've come to arrest me *again*?" he asked.

"If it wasn't me, it would have been Holt."

He stared at her and then nodded.

"Mind if I sit with you?" Fisher said.

"Won't you get in trouble for talking to me?" he asked. "I mean, you are the arresting officer in my case."

"I'm no longer in charge of your investigation. And if anyone asks, I was hoping to get you to confess and save the taxpayers the cost of a lengthy trial."

"Funny."

"So?"

"What?"

"Can I join you?"

"It's a free country."

She sat down.

Joely returned with a plate and placed it before Callaway. "You have some nerve coming back here," Joely said to Fisher with a scowl.

Callaway smiled. "It's all right. Dana is a friend."

"Some friend," Joely said, and walked away.

Fisher leaned over. "Do you think I should order something? I am kind of hungry."

"I wouldn't if I were you. There's no telling what Joely might put in your meal."

Fisher's eyes widened. "Are you serious?"

Callaway laughed. "Of course not, but she is upset, so I'd play it safe if I were you."

"I'll grab some drive-thru on my way back to the station."

Callaway saw that Joely had brought steak, mashed potatoes, and corn. His favourite. He cut into the steak and said, "How's your case coming along?"

"Which one?"

"The one with the lottery winner."

"I've hit a brick wall, I'm afraid."

"Thanks to you I'll be staring *at* a brick wall while I'm in prison."

"Ouch," she said, wincing.

"Sorry, I couldn't help it."

"I spoke to Holt," she said.

"And?"

"He doesn't like what he sees in your investigation."

"Like what?" Callaway asked, curious.

"The murder weapon with your prints. The bloody shirt in your hotel room. It all seems like it was staged."

"Exactly!" Callaway said. "I was setup, and no one is listening to me."

Fisher gave him an imploring look. "Lee, if you didn't commit this crime, then do whatever you have to in order to prove your innocence."

"How can I?" he asked.

"Do you know *why* Holt doesn't like you?" she asked instead.

"Yeah, because I'm young and good looking and he's old and ugly."

"I'm being serious."

"Okay, sorry."

"He doesn't like you because you don't have to follow the rules like he does. You can skirt around the law. You somehow found a way to help Paul Gardener. And now, you will have to find a way to help yourself."

Callaway pondered her words. He knew how hard it was for her to come here and face him, but she came because she believed him.

"Thanks, Dana," he finally said.

ONE-HUNDRED ONE

Callaway knew Fisher was right. If he wanted to save his skin, he would have to resort to doing things he otherwise would not do, which meant he would have to ask for help from certain people he preferred to stay away from.

He banged his fist on the steel door and waited. A minute later, a small window slid open and two eyes appeared.

The eyes went wide when they saw who it was.

The door opened, and Baxter came out. "Mr. Callaway," he said.

Mister? Callaway thought.

"How can I help you, sir?" Baxter asked.

Sir? Did Baxter go take a crash course in Manners 101 or something?

"I need to speak to Mason," Callaway replied.

Baxter stared at him. He looked unnerved and even a little scared.

"Um… Mason is busy at the moment," he said.

"He's never too busy to see me," Callaway said. He took a step forward, expecting Baxter to block his path. Instead, Baxter recoiled as if Callaway was carrying the Ebola virus.

What's going on?

Callaway moved past him and headed up the stairs. At the top, he waited for Baxter to open the door to Mason's office like he always did. But this time, Baxter did not even follow him up the steps.

Callaway was confused. He shook his head and entered Mason's office.

Mason was on the phone, but the moment he saw Callaway, he dropped the receiver and jumped out of his chair.

"Lee, buddy, pal, bro," he nervously said. "What're you doing here?"

"I need to speak to you, Mason," Callaway said.

"Yeah, sure, alright, but you could have just called me. You didn't have to drive all the way here."

Baxter came up the stairs. He and Mason exchanged looks.

Callaway crossed his arms over his chest. "Okay, what's going on?"

Mason sheepishly shrugged. "Nothing is going on."

Callaway caught sight of a newspaper on Mason's desk. The paper was opened to a page with an article on Isabel Gilford's murder.

So that's why they're acting so weird.

"I didn't kill her," Callaway said.

"Of course you didn't. We never believe anything they write in the newspapers. Isn't that right, Baxter?"

Baxter was pale. He swallowed. "Yes, Boss."

"I was setup," Callaway said.

"Of course you were."

Callaway grabbed the closest chair and, for the first time ever on a visit to Mason, sat down. Right now, Mason and Baxter were more afraid of him than he was of them.

Callaway shut his eyes and sighed. *Why did I even bother coming here?*

A few minutes went by before Mason said, "Lee, you okay?"

"No, I'm not okay!" Callaway snapped.

Mason and Baxter jumped back.

"I'm angry and I'm pissed," Callaway continued. "Yesterday I was a free man, and today I could be facing life behind bars. And the people responsible for my predicament are laughing it up. At least that's what I think they are doing. I don't know why they chose me. I have a lot of questions but no answers. I am here to ask for your help."

"Um... sure, Lee. We are more than happy to help you, *but* we can't help you get away with murder," Mason said. "I've got a business to worry about, and Baxter wouldn't survive a day in prison."

I highly doubt your last claim, Callaway thought. *Baxter could take down half a cell block.*

"I don't need your help to get away with murder," Callaway said. "I need your help to prove my innocence."

Mason's brow furrowed. "How're we going to do that?"

"I have an idea."

Mason paused and then said, "Lee, we like you a lot. We've done business together many times, but we don't do you favors. You should know that by now."

Callaway smiled. "I do."

He reached into his pocket.

Mason and Baxter took a step back.

Callaway pulled out an envelope and dropped it on Mason's desk.

"What's that?" Mason asked, eyeing the envelope suspiciously.

"Ten grand."

Mason reached out and pulled the envelope closer. He looked inside, and his eyes sparkled.

"Okay, so what do you have in mind?" he asked.

ONE-HUNDRED TWO

Fisher stared at the blue evidence folder on her desk. This one was for Big Bob's murder. Next to the folder were two others, slightly thinner than the first, but they contained information on Chase Burley and Debra Coleheim's deaths.

Fisher knew the cases were linked, but now that she had hit yet another dead end, she began to feel all three would end up as cold cases, cases that would haunt her into her retirement.

She saw McConnell exit the elevator. He made a beeline straight for her desk. "I've been calling you nonstop for the past hour," he said.

She had been avoiding answering his calls. She was in such a dour mood that she did not want to say something she might regret later, even though McConnell was the one person who would truly understand what she was going through.

She smiled. "I'm sorry. I know I've been too wrapped up in my work. I should have called you back."

"It's not about that," he said.

Her heart sank. *Is he going to break up with me?* she thought. Her mouth went dry. "It's not?"

"Come with me. I want to show you something."

"What?"

"Just come."

She followed him to a room with a two-way mirror. In the adjacent room a man was seated at a metal table. He looked pale and visibly shaken. He had jet-black hair which was parted down the middle and he was wearing a dress shirt with the collar buttoned up.

"Who is he?" Fisher asked.

"I pulled him over for a routine stop," McConnell replied. "I searched his vehicle, and I found a bag of cocaine in the glove compartment."

"He looks scared."

"He should be," McConnell said. "He's nineteen. No priors, not even a speeding ticket, and he is a student at Baker Polytechnic Institute."

"From what I've heard," Fisher said, "you have to be super smart to get into one of their programs."

"I applied to it right after high school and got rejected."

"You did?" Fisher asked, surprised.

"Yeah, I guess I wasn't smart enough," McConnell replied, "but then I got into the academy. Go figure."

"So, what's a bright kid like him doing with a bag of cocaine?" Fisher asked.

"That's what I asked him."

"And?"

"He said it's not his but his cousin's."

Fisher frowned. "So why did you bring me here to see him?"

"I haven't booked him yet, but I figured you would like to speak to him first."

"Why would I?"

"He said he has some information he'd like to share with us."

"What kind of information?"

"The murder of Robert Burley, aka, Big Bob."

The moment Fisher heard the name, she raced into the adjacent room. She took a seat across from the youth. "I'm Detective Dana Fisher," she said. "Is it true you have information on a murder?"

The youth swallowed and then nodded.

"What's your name?" Fisher asked.

"Juan."

"Full name?"

"Juan Herrera."

Fisher's eyes narrowed. "Do you know someone by the name of Manuela Herrera?"

He stared at her, bit his lip, and said, "She's my sister."

Fisher's heart skipped a beat.

ONE-HUNDRED THREE

"What do you know about Robert Burley's murder?" Fisher sternly asked.

Juan looked at her. "The drugs are not mine."

"It was in your car."

He fell silent, but then he said, "If I give you something, will you help me."

Juan was smart, she knew, and he was willing to cut a deal. "Okay, sure," Fisher said. "If I like what I hear, I'll talk to the officer who brought you here and see what we can do about letting you go." McConnell had not booked him, which meant no charges had been laid yet. If he had been booked, then it would be up to the prosecution and then ultimately a judge to decide whether to drop the charges. Right now, Fisher had some control over the situation.

"Tell me what happened the night Robert Burley was murdered."

Juan took a deep breath. "I never saw anything happen with my own eyes, okay? But I was there that night."

"At his house?"

"Sort of."

"Okay."

"I had an evening class that day, and when I was driving home, I saw that there were several missed calls from my sister."

"Manuela?"

He nodded. "I tried calling her back, but they would go straight to voicemail. When I got home, I saw my cousin…"

"The one the cocaine belongs to?"

"Yes. He was sitting on the porch smoking a joint."

"What's his name?"

Juan hesitated.

"You have to be truthful or else I can't help you," Fisher said.

"Diego Murcia."

"Then what happened?"

"He told me we were going for a ride. I thought maybe he wanted me to drop him somewhere, but when I saw that we were near Mr. Burley's house, I thought we were there to pick up Manuela. Diego told me to wait in the car. I saw him walk up to the door and then go inside."

"The front door wasn't locked?" Fisher asked.

Juan shook his head. "I don't think so. I waited for twenty minutes or maybe longer, I don't know, when Diego came running out of the house. He had blood on his hands and shirt. He was also carrying a plastic bag."

"Did you see what was in the bag?"

"Yes. Money. Lots of it."

That was the cash from Big Bob's safe, she thought.

"Okay, keep going," Fisher said.

"I asked Diego what happened," Juan said. "He told me to drive fast. I was scared. I did exactly what he wanted. We drove to a remote spot where Diego took off his shirt and washed his hands and face with a bottle of water. He took the money out of the plastic bag and he stuffed it in my school bag. He then put the shirt and another item inside the plastic bag."

"What was this other item?"

"I don't know."

"Could it have been a knife?"

He thought a moment. "It could have, but I didn't see it. We then drove to an industrial area where Diego dumped the plastic bag behind a building. We spent the next couple of hours driving around the city. We went to a couple of bars. Diego drank. I didn't. And at the end of the night, Diego took my school bag. He told me he would return it the next day. He handed me a bundle of hundred-dollar bills and told me to keep my mouth shut or else I'd be in serious trouble. I took the money. I'm a student. I barely make minimum wage. I then drove home. Manuela asked where I was. I didn't tell her any details. Next morning, we both saw the news that Mr. Burley was murdered."

"And you knew who had done it? Your cousin?" Fisher asked.

Juan lowered his head. "I never actually saw him do it, but yes."

Fisher pondered her next question. "Did Diego ask you to drive him other times?"

He looked confused.

"I mean, did he ask you to drive him to a trailer park, perhaps?"

His eyes widened in surprise. "How did you know?"

That was where Chase Burley was found dead, she wanted to say, but did not. Instead she said, "So did you drive him to a trailer park?"

"I did. He told me it was a short ride, but it was actually longer. I didn't ask him any questions. He can lose his temper in a split second. I dropped him off and drove straight home."

"And then a few hours later, he asked you to pick him up next to a rural road, isn't that right?" Fisher said.

Juan's eyes again widened in surprise.

Fisher knew Diego had gone to the trailer park to torture and kill Chase Burley. Maybe he thought Chase knew something. Diego then took Debra Coleheim in Chase's Chevy Tahoe to a rural area, had his way with her, strangled her, and then left her dead body in the trunk.

"Where can we find Diego?" Fisher asked.

"He likes to go to a club on Devon Street," Juan replied.

Fisher had her killer, but before she went after Diego Murcia, there was one more place she wanted to visit first.

ONE-HUNDRED FOUR

Callaway sat in his Charger across from an empty parking lot. He checked his watch for the umpteenth time. He took a deep breath to calm his nerves. What he was about to attempt was dangerous, not to mention illegal. The ploy could even backfire on him. But Cary Gilford and Brooke O'Shea had pushed him into a corner.

He was not going down without a fight.

He saw a black Escalade pull into the parking lot and stop in the middle. A moment later, Callaway's cell phone buzzed.

He pressed "answer."

"Who are you guys? What do you want from me?" Cary Gilford demanded.

Mason's voice came on. "You need to calm down, man."

"Can you take off my blindfold?" Gilford said. "I'm claustrophobic."

"If we did that, you'd see who we are, and that means we'd have to kill you. Is that what you want?"

"No, no, no. I don't want to die. Please. I have a wife and children."

Callaway scoffed.

"Speaking of your wife," Mason said, "we heard she was worth a lot of money."

"She is, and her family will pay whatever you ask in ransom."

"We also heard that she is dead."

There was silence on the other line.

Gilford said, "She was murdered."

"By who?" Mason asked.

"Some private investigator she had hired."

"What's his name?"

"Lee Callaway."

Callaway gritted his teeth at the sound of his name.

Mason asked, "Why would he kill your wife?"

"I don't know, maybe for money," Gilford replied.

"Well, that's not what I heard."

Silence.

"What are you talking about?" Gilford asked.

"What I heard is that you framed this private investigator for your wife's murder."

"That's a lie!" Gilford snapped

A punch sounded, followed by an audible groan and whimper. Baxter had likely used force on Gilford.

"I warned you not to get too excited," Mason said.

There was heavy breathing.

Mason said, "Listen, I don't have all day. Someone's paid us to get rid of you, okay?"

"Who? Who was it?"

Mason paused, and then, as if reading from a script, he said, "Some lady. She showed up at our door in a limousine. She didn't give her name, only that she wanted you gone."

"Did the woman have silver hair?"

"Yes."

"And was she wearing a long coat and dark sunglasses?"

"Yeah, she actually was. Do you know her?"

"Of course I do. Her name is Brooke O'Shea, and she was the one who planned the entire thing."

Callaway was shaken to his core.

"Planned what?" Mason asked.

"My wife's murder."

"Well, she said *you* planned it."

"That's a…" Gilford suddenly stopped. He did not want to be on the end of another one of Baxter's punches.

"I have proof she is not telling you the truth," Gilford said.

"What kind of proof?"

There was a long pause.

"She has a safe deposit box at a bank near her condo building," Gilford replied. "Inside, you'll find all the evidence about how she planned the murder."

"What kind of evidence?"

"The list of drugs to knock someone out with…"

So, I was *drugged*, Callaway thought. *I knew it.*

"…and the disguise she used to fool the private investigator."

"Speaking of this private investigator, why did you choose to frame *him*?"

Callaway had demanded Mason ask that question.

"He was an easy target," Gilford replied. "He had a history of sleeping with his clients. Plus, he was always desperate for money, so he became the perfect patsy."

Callaway's blood boiled.

They sure did their homework on me, he thought. *I never thought I'd see the day my past would come back and bite me so bad.*

"Why would she keep this evidence?" Mason asked.

"After my wife's funeral, Brooke and I were going to take a long trip on my boat. We were going to dump the evidence in the ocean."

"What if she's already gotten rid of this evidence?" Mason asked.

Callaway could not help but smile. Mason was earning every penny he had given him for the job.

"Even if she did," Gilford said, "I will go before a judge and testify against her."

There was silence on the line. Callaway could tell Mason was debating what to do next. The plan was simple. Get Gilford to confess and then let him go. How Mason was going to do this was up to him.

Mason asked, "You got money?"

"Yes, I do." There was optimism in Gilford's voice. "If you let me go, I'll pay you double what she paid you."

"Double, huh?"

Callaway hung up the phone. Mason was a businessman. He was always looking for a way to make money.

Callaway was not interested in what they did next.

He had what he was looking for. It was now time to see if the evidence was worth the ten thousand he had spent to get it.

ONE-HUNDRED FIVE

Manuela Herrera covered her face and wept.

Even though Fisher had Juan's sworn statement, she wanted to verify certain details. Juan was scared and desperate. He could say just about anything to escape prison time. He could also retract his statements. He could tell a judge the cocaine was planted in order to get a confession out of him.

Juan had a clean record, and he was a model citizen. This could sway a judge's decision in his favor.

Fisher was not going to take any chances. She was too close.

"You're going to have to be truthful with me, Manuela," Fisher said. "Lying to a police officer is a crime."

Manuela looked up with moist eyes. "I didn't lie, ma'am. Big Bob gave me the money that night and I went home."

"But something else *happened* that night, which you did not disclose to us when we last spoke."

Manuela lowered her eyes.

Fisher paused and then said, "When we interviewed you at your house, were you alone?"

Manuela shook her head.

Fisher always had a feeling someone else was in the house that day. She had searched the interior but found no one. But that did not mean someone could not have escaped through the back.

"Was your cousin, Diego, with you that day?"

She nodded.

"Your brother is right now at the Milton PD," Fisher said. "We are holding him because we found drugs in his vehicle."

"Juan doesn't do drugs," Manuela said. "He's never done drugs in his life."

"We know they belong to Diego. We have Juan's side of the story. Now, I want to know yours. What happened that day when you went to Big Bob's house?"

Manuela swallowed. "Big Bob pays me every two weeks for cleaning his house. I called to ask him if I can get my money. He told me to come later that day. When I went to his house, I heard him arguing with his son."

"Chase Burley?"

"Yes. I thought about leaving because they were loud."

"What were they arguing about?"

"Money, I think. And I also heard Big Bob say something about drugs."

Fisher was right. After Chase's house in Westport was shot up by rival drug dealers, he was desperate for cash. He had stashed some of his drugs in his father's house for safekeeping. Big Bob likely was not aware of this, and when Chase went back to retrieve his goods, Big Bob was irate, leading to their heated argument.

"After you saw Chase leave the house, then what happened?" Fisher asked.

"I knocked on the door," Manuela replied. "Big Bob came outside and then he invited me in. He went into his office, and he came back with my money. He gave it to me and then asked me if I wanted a drink. I told him no and that I wanted to go home. He kept saying it was only one drink. He was lonely, and he needed company. I work for him, so I didn't want to hurt his feelings. We sat down in the living room and we drank. He then asked if I would go to bed with him." Manuela's body shook at the memory. "I was horrified. I told him I didn't do that with strangers. He said he wasn't a stranger and that we were friends. He then offered me money to sleep with him. I refused, and then he got angry. He was big, and he tried to…" She fell silent. Fisher gave her a moment to compose herself. "He tried to force himself on me. I hit him across the face. I think I hurt him."

Fisher noticed a ring on Manuela's finger.

So that is what caused the gash across Big Bob's cheek, she thought.

"I tried to run out of the house, but he blocked my path to the front door. I then ran up the stairs and locked myself in a room. He came up after me. He was yelling and screaming for me to come out. I then heard him go downstairs. I thought he was going to calm down, but then I heard a noise. I had to cover my ears because it was so loud. He was shooting at the door. I had to hide in the corner. I cried." Manuela's eyes were wide with fright as she remembered the ordeal. "I called my brother, but he didn't answer his phone. An hour later, when I didn't hear any noise from outside, I quietly left the room and went downstairs. I saw Big Bob sleeping in the armchair. He had a gun in one hand and a glass in the other. I rushed out of the house."

"Was the door locked when you left?" Fisher asked.

Manuela looked at her like she was crazy. "I didn't check. I wanted to get as far away from that house as possible."

That explains how Diego was able to get inside the house without Big Bob knowing it, Fisher thought.

"And when did you see Diego?" Fisher asked.

"I took the bus home. I saw him sitting on our front porch. He saw my face and asked what happened. Diego is hotheaded. He's gotten in trouble with the law before. But he's still family, and he makes sure nothing happens to me and my brother. I was so scared, and I told him everything. Maybe I shouldn't have. But I told him not to do anything, and he promised he wouldn't. I didn't know later that night he got Juan to drive him to Big Bob's house. It was the next morning when Juan and I found out something bad had happened at the house."

Fisher now had the missing pieces to the puzzle. It was time to bring Diego Murcia in for the murders of Big Bob, Chase Burley, and Debra Coleheim.

ONE-HUNDRED SIX

Holt walked out of the bank with the contents of the safety deposit box in his hands. He then drove straight to an address he was familiar with.

Prior to going to the bank, he had a visitor at the Milton PD. Callaway had shown up holding a USB.

"What is it?" Holt had asked.

"It's Cary Gilford confessing to the murder of his wife, Isabel Gilford."

"How'd you get it?"

"It's not important."

Holt gave Callaway a hard stare. "If Gilford was coerced to confess, then it won't hold up in court."

Callaway smiled. "I don't expect it to hold up in court."

"Then what good is it to me?"

"You'll know what to do with it when you hear it."

Holt did listen, and what he heard made him take quick action.

He knocked on the door and waited.

A moment later, Brooke O'Shea answered.

"Detective," she said with a smile. "What a surprise."

"Can I come in?" he asked.

She looked unsure, but then she obliged.

He walked in and took a seat on the sofa. He unbuttoned his suit jacket.

"What is this about?" she asked.

"We've stumbled upon some new evidence."

"What kind of evidence?"

"Let me play it for you." Holt had copied the audio file Callaway had given him onto his cell phone. What he did not know was that Callaway had altered the contents to fit a narrative. Holt pressed a button.

Cary Gilford's voice boomed out. "Brooke O'Shea was the one who planned my wife's murder. Lee Callaway was always desperate for money, so he became the perfect patsy. Brooke has a safe deposit box at a bank near her condo building. Inside, you'll find all the evidence of how she planned to do it. Brooke was going to dump the evidence in the ocean."

Holt stopped the recording. "We have seized the deposit box's contents as evidence."

O'Shea's face turned pale. "How'd you get into *my* box?"

Holt held up a piece of paper. "We got a warrant for it. It's signed by a judge."

She paused and then broke down in tears. "I had no choice," she said. "Cary made me do it."

"And you agreed to go along with it?" Holt asked.

"If I didn't, he would have hurt me." She pointed to the bruise on her face. "He did this to me. He has a violent temper. *He* is the real murderer. I was helpless to stop him."

Holt stared at her and then clapped his hands. "You're a very good actress, Ms. O'Shea. But I have to say, your charade won't work with me. We have Mr. Gilford on tape pointing to you as the killer. If I were you, I would tell your side of the story."

O'Shea stared at Holt and then sat down across from him. "Cary was in financial trouble. His investment firm wasn't as successful as he'd led people to believe. In fact, it was a Ponzi scheme. His biggest investor was his wife's parents. His wife was naïve and sheltered, but she wasn't stupid. She could tell something was up when Cary was constantly trying to raise more funds. She demanded he come clean or else she'd go to the FBI. By this time, I had started a relationship with Cary. He was older, but he had money. I know this sounds so 1950s, but I wanted someone to take care of me. All women crave some form of security, whether it's from their marriage or with money. When his wife gave him an ultimatum, he came to me and told me the truth. I loved him. So, I told him about a character I had played in a movie. And *together* we came up with a plan."

"How would getting rid of Isabel Gilford solve your financial woes?" Holt asked.

"Isabel had a trust fund valued at over two-point-eight million dollars. If the beneficiary was deceased, the money in the fund would go to the surviving spouse. It was not enough to pay back all the investors Cary owed money to, but it was enough for us to take his boat and sail to some Caribbean island and start a new life together."

"So, walk me through that night," Holt said.

O'Shea paused, sighed, and said, "I asked Lee Callaway to come see me at the other house—the one under Isabel's name. I then drugged his wine glass. During this time Cary picked up Isabel from the airport and drove her straight to the house. Cary offered her wine…"

"You needed her fingerprints on the wine glass to show that she and Callaway were actually together that night," Holt said. "And you also wanted to show she had alcohol in her system, just like Callaway."

"Yes."

"Did you drug her, too?"

"No. We knew during the autopsy they would check her blood for foreign substances."

"So, who stabbed Isabel Gilford?" Holt asked.

O'Shea was silent for a moment.

"Cary plunged the knife into her chest and I merely pushed it in further," she replied. She let out a nervous laugh. "We were a team, and we wanted both of us to be equally involved."

"How did Isabel Gilford get the bruise on her face?" Holt asked.

"Once she was dead, Cary hit her across the face. We had to make sure her injuries and my injuries were the same."

"What did you do with Callaway?"

"He was still sedated, so we placed his fingerprints on the knife. We then took his digital camera, his dress shirt, and his hotel key. We planted the shirt in his hotel and destroyed the camera."

"Why destroy the camera?"

"We were afraid it might have something incriminating against us."

"Did it?"

"We didn't have time to check."

Holt let silence hang in the air for a moment before he stood up and cuffed O'Shea's wrists. After reading O'Shea her rights, he escorted her down to a waiting police cruiser.

ONE-HUNDRED SEVEN

Diego Murcia was a dangerous man.

Fisher never went into a situation like this without backup. She would have preferred Holt next to her when she made the arrest, but he was preoccupied with Callaway's investigation.

Instead, she went with the second-best option:

Officer Lance McConnell.

She had gotten to know him well enough to trust him. He was not going to take her safety lightly.

She could request a SWAT team or additional officers, but that would attract too much attention. She wanted Diego alive.

Fisher was parked across from the club. There was already a long line of clubbers snaking around the building. A bouncer was selectively allowing the patrons in. Whenever the club's doors were opened, Fisher heard loud music coming from inside.

McConnell sat behind the building in an unmarked vehicle. If Diego exited via the back, McConnell would be on him.

Fisher chose not to go into the club because there was no telling how Diego would react if he was cornered. With so many people in such a confined space, there was bound to be casualties if Diego put up a fight. Fisher would not allow innocent bystanders to get hurt.

It was better they waited for Diego to come out.

She was certain they would catch him. If Diego eluded them here and fled Milton, they would issue a nationwide warrant for his arrest.

Right now, she hoped it would not come to that.

She wanted to be the one to bring him in.

Twenty-five minutes later, Diego walked out of the club.

His hair was pulled back into a ponytail, and the sides of his head were shaved. He had a pencil-thin moustache, and whiskers covered his chin. His arms were adorned with a variety of tattoos, and he wore a gold chain around his neck.

Fisher got out of the SUV and crossed the road. Diego casually strolled away from the club. He shoved his hand in one of his pants pockets. Fisher's hand instinctively moved to her holster. To her relief, he pulled out a pack of cigarettes and lit one up.

She was twenty feet away from him.

Diego blew out a plume of thick smoke, looking like he did not have a care in the world. The pack slipped out of his hands and fell to the ground. He turned and reached down to pick it up.

His eyes met hers.

She froze.

Their stares locked for a good second or two, and then Diego bolted.

"Shit," Fisher cursed, and ran after him.

Diego was fast, and, in no time, there was a half a block gap between them. He had not reckoned with Fisher being as good a runner, though.

Seeing she was still following, he sprinted across the road, narrowly getting hit by an oncoming car.

The driver honked and yelled, but Diego paid him no heed.

Fisher gritted her teeth and followed.

There were more honks, punctuated by the sound of screeching brakes, but she also managed to get across without being run over.

Up ahead, Diego was barrelling through pedestrians. He knocked an elderly man to the ground and shoved a woman with a stroller. Two men almost went after him for what he had done. They stopped when they saw Fisher running toward them with a gun in her hand.

"Police!" she yelled.

The men got out of her way.

Diego was a good fifty feet away from her when she heard the sound of an approaching train.

There was a bridge that went over a set of tracks. Fisher stopped and looked to her right. A commuter train was approaching the overpass.

She looked up and saw that Diego had stopped too.

She had a bad feeling in the pit of her stomach.

Her fear turned out to be correct. He ran to the middle of the bridge and hauled himself on top of the metal railing.

He's going to jump on the train! she thought.

270

It was a dangerous move, but the train's speed might work in Diego's favor. If he jumped at the right moment, he might just make it.

Fisher was not going to take any chances

Seeing there was no one else on the bridge, she knelt, aimed her weapon, and fired a shot at the precise moment Diego was about to leap.

She heard an audible scream and saw him disappear over the bridge.

Shit. I hope I did not send him under the train, Fisher thought.

She raced up and looked over.

The train was already gone, but Diego was hanging onto the edge of the bridge with one hand.

"You shot my leg," he cried.

A car pulled up next to her.

McConnell jumped out.

"Are you okay?" he asked.

"I'm fine," she replied. "But he could use some help."

McConnell glanced over. Diego looked like he was in excruciating pain.

"You sure we shouldn't leave him like that?" McConnell asked.

Fisher sighed. "It's not a bad idea, but I have a lot of questions I want to ask him, and I can't do that if he's dead."

"But you've solved the case," McConnell said with a smile. "You know he killed all those people."

"Yes, but I still want to know what he did with the money he took from Big Bob's safe."

"You're the boss."

McConnell reached down and pulled Diego up.

ONE-HUNDRED EIGHT

Callaway was in his office when he heard footsteps coming up the metal stairs.

He got up from his desk and saw Holt was standing outside his door.

"Detective Holt," he said. "I'm surprised to see you here."

"I didn't want to do this over the phone."

Callaway's back arched. "Do what?"

"Tell you that we have Cary Gilford and Brooke O'Shea in custody. They are both willing to testify against each other. I feel we have enough to charge them for the death of Isabel Gilford."

"You should also charge them with conspiracy to frame an innocent man."

"We can look at other charges, of course, such as providing false statements to the police or obstruction of justice. However, I think murder is sufficient enough to put them away for a very long time. You are free to file a civil suit against them if you like."

Callaway's eyes narrowed. "I might just do that."

Holt held up a hand. "But I must warn you that Cary Gilford was running a Ponzi scheme. You might not get anything once his investors get their share."

Callaway frowned. "If I remember correctly, you said there was an insurance policy with my name on it," he said.

"It's invalid. The victim's signature was forged."

"So, I'm not rich?" Callaway asked.

"No, but you are free."

Callaway smiled. "I can live with that."

After a minute of silence passed, Holt said, "You're okay for a private investigator."

"And you're okay for a detective."

Holt smiled and then left.

Callaway smiled too.

If Holt can *smile. There is hope for humanity yet.*

ONE-HUNDRED NINE

The commuter train Diego nearly jumped on top of turned out to be a good omen. After interviewing him at the hospital, Fisher drove to the Cupperton Train Station, which was located ten miles from where she had caught Diego.

With a key in her hand, Fisher approached a set of blue lockers. She searched for locker number 1228, found it, unlocked it, and pulled out a gray school backpack. Inside were bundles of hundred-dollar bills wrapped in elastic bands.

Diego confessed he had gone to Big Bob's house to teach him a lesson for what he had done to Manuela. Big Bob and Diego got into an argument, and Diego stabbed him to death. He then decided to rob him as well. Chase had seen Manuela on the night his father had died. Diego worried that when the police caught up to him, Chase might reveal something that could lead back to Manuela and to him, so Diego found him and killed him. He also killed and raped Debra Coleheim because she was a witness to Chase's murder.

Fisher was about to zip up the backpack when something caught her attention. An object was lying between the stacks of money. She reached in and pulled out a wallet. It was gold plated with the letters "R.B." encrusted in diamonds. Fisher knew the initials stood for Robert Burley.

She could see why Diego took the wallet. Such a fancy item would fetch a nice sum on the black market.

She noticed a piece of paper folded inside the wallet.

She pulled the paper out and found a letter written in blue ink:

Dear Mr. Burley,

My name is Irma Randall. I am writing to you because I know you claimed my lottery ticket. On the day you won the big prize, I had sold my Ford station wagon to you at your dealership. I had lost my job and I needed the money to pay my rent. I have two young children, and I am raising them without their father, who died in a terrible car accident.

I know the ticket was mine because I play the same numbers each week: 9, 32, 11, 3, 29.

9 is the date of my daughter's birthday.

32 was how old my husband was at the time of his death.

11 is the date of my son's birthday.

3 is my lucky number.

29 was the day when my husband and I got married.

I always kept my lottery tickets stuck to the Ford's visor, and I forgot to remove my ticket when I handed over the vehicle to you. When I realized my mistake, I went back to your dealership that very day, but by then it was closed.

I have tried contacting you, but you have refused to speak to me. I have also gone to several lawyers, but unless I pay them a retainer, they won't even look into my case.

I know I can't prove this in court, but I hope you would do the right thing. I am not greedy. I don't want the entire lottery winnings. I just need enough to take care of my children and to provide a roof over our heads.

Signed,
Irma Randall

Fisher knew it was not uncommon for strangers to show up claiming a piece of the lottery winnings. It was also not uncommon for strangers to beg, lie, and tell their sob stories to the winners with the hope that they would receive a share of the money.

So maybe this Irma Randall was laying a guilt trip on Big Bob, Fisher thought. *But then, why did Big Bob keep her note in his expensive wallet for all these years?*

Also, Big Bob was stabbed in his living room, but he crawled across the house and died on his way to his office.

Fisher always thought he was concerned about the money in the safe. What if he was more concerned about the letter inside the safe and what it would mean if it got out into the world?

Fisher was not sure if that was the case, but there was one thing she was sure of. No one knew the exact amount Diego had taken from Big Bob's safe. By Fisher's estimate, there was a substantial sum still in the backpack.

Fisher knew if Irma Randall lived in Milton, it would not be hard to track her down. It might be a little too late, but something was better than nothing.

ONE-HUNDRED TEN

Callaway found Nina sitting on a swing at a playground near Patti's house. His daughter had her head down, and she looked gloomy.

She was still upset with him for what he had said to Jamie. Callaway could live with Nina being upset with him. He was just glad she was not aware of what he had gone through the last couple of days.

He took a seat on the swing next to hers.

"Hey, kiddo," he said.

She did not reply.

"You come here often?" he asked.

Still no reply.

He shoved his hand in his pocket and pulled out a basic mobile phone. "I got this for you."

She looked at the phone. "It's ugly."

"It's not much to look at, but from what I've been told, it's got an amazing battery that can last for days without a single charge."

"Can I take photos with it?" she asked.

"I'm afraid not, but you can text," he replied.

"Yeah, but it'll take forever on that keypad."

"I know it's not one of those fancy smartphones you wanted, but it was the only way I could convince your mom to let you have a cell phone."

Nina did not look happy.

"You can call Jamie on it," he said.

"I don't have his number."

Callaway pulled out a piece of paper. "I spoke to him today, and I apologized for the way I acted. He seems like a nice kid. I think he likes you."

"I don't like him," she said, but the smile on her face told Callaway that was not true.

"Sure, sure, but you can be friends, right?" he said.

After a pause, Nina took the phone from him. "Thanks, Daddy," she said.

"You're welcome, darling."

She got off the swing and hugged him.

Callaway's heart swelled with emotion. Nina was everything to him, and he could not bear her being cross with him.

They walked back to Patti's house.

Patti was waiting for them at the door.

Waving her new phone, Nina raced inside the house.

"How did it go?" Patti asked.

"We're friends again," Callaway replied.

"Kids can be very forgiving."

"What about adults?"

Her brow furrowed. "What do you mean?"

"I mean…" He paused to collect his thoughts. "I've been meaning to ask you for a while now. Would you like to go out with me?"

She was surprised. "You mean like a date?"

He shrugged. "Yeah, maybe for dinner or something."

"I don't know."

"One date. That's all I'm asking. I promise it'll be better than your date with Dr. Hayward."

Patti stared at Callaway and then smiled. "Alright, one date, but you better wine and dine me like royalty."

He grinned and bowed. "As you wish, Your Highness."

Visit the author's website:
www.finchambooks.com

Contact:
finchambooks@gmail.com

LEE CALLAWAY

The Dead Daughter (Lee Callaway #1)
The Gone Sister (Lee Callaway #2)
The Falling Girl (Lee Callaway #3)

HYDER ALI

The Silent Reporter (Hyder Ali #1)
The Rogue Reporter (Hyder Ali #2)
The Runaway Reporter (Hyder Ali #3)
The Serial Reporter (Hyder Ali #4)
The Street Reporter (Hyder Ali #5)
The Student Reporter (Hyder Ali #0)

MARTIN RHODES

Close Your Eyes (Martin Rhodes #1)
Cross Your Heart (Martin Rhodes #2)
Say Your Prayers (Martin Rhodes #3)
Fear Your Enemy (Martin Rhodes #0)

ECHO ROSE

The Rose Garden (Echo Rose #1)
The Rose Tattoo (Echo Rose #2)
The Rose Thorn (Echo Rose #3)
The Rose Water (Echo Rose #4)

STANDALONE

The Blue Hornet
The October Five
The Paperboys Club
Killing Them Gently
The Solaire Trilogy

THOMAS FINCHAM holds a graduate degree in Economics. His travels throughout the world have given him an appreciation for other cultures and beliefs. He has lived in Africa, Asia, and North America. An avid reader of mysteries and thrillers, he decided to give writing a try. Several novels later, he can honestly say he has found his calling. He is married and lives in a hundred-year-old house. He is the author of THE PAPERBOYS CLUB, THE OCTOBER FIVE, THE BLUE HORNET, KILLING THEM GENTLY, and the HYDER ALI SERIES.

Made in the USA
Coppell, TX
07 December 2020